PRAISE FOR

'There is something special about Karly Lane's novels. She inspires, uplifts, encourages, advises and even provides a heavenly escape through her fictional worlds where characters come alive and become friends we never want to say goodbye to . . . *For Once in My Life* is no exception.' —Cindy L. Spear

'Lane's engaging storytelling instantly draws us into Jenny's world . . . a compelling, fast-paced and engaging read with heart and substance, perfect for summer reading.' —Better Reading

'If you are looking for a good holiday read, then definitely choose *For Once In My Life* . . . sit back and relax and enjoy the characters.' —Blue Wolf Reviews

PRAISE FOR *Time After Time*

'*Time After Time* moves from a small country town in Australia to the red carpet of London and Karly Lane has woven a story of dreams, fashion, fame and second chances.' —The Burgeoning Bookshelf

'With a stunning second chance love story, a picturesque country backdrop, pressing rural community themes and characters that grow on you, *Time After Time* is another warmly-told read from one of my favourite writers.' —Mrs B's Book Reviews

'Proving herself once again top of the game in this genre, Karly Lane brings us a tale that juxtaposes the high-end London fashion industry and a small-town community.' —Living Arts Canberra

'Heart-warming . . . an enjoyable read that will be warmly welcomed by fans of Australian romance writing.' —*Canberra Weekly*

'Karly Lane has a way of dragging you in and making you feel like you are a part of the story . . . It is a wonderful read.' —Beauty and Lace

'Lane vividly evokes Australian rural communities, and gives due recognition to its challenges, especially for farmers. Written with the warmth, humour and heart for which Lane's rural romances are known, *Time After Time* is an engaging read.' —Book'd Out

PRAISE FOR *Wish You Were Here*

'A comely rural romance that encapsulates the heart and emotions of Australian country life . . . You can't go wrong with a Karly Lane novel and this latest one was no exception. —Mrs B's Book Reviews

'It's always a great day when a new Karly Lane book is released . . . *Wish You Were Here* has all the small town country vibes you could want in a closed door romance with a whole lot of heart.' —Noveltea Corner

'. . . a fabulous rural romance, the perfect book to snuggle up with on the recliner! Loved it.' —Mrs G's Bookshelf

'With the magic of country atmosphere, a cast of incredible characters . . . true community spirit and a relatable romance, it has all the contents of an engaging read. You can smell the way of life, feel the weather and breathe in the fresh air as Karly's inviting storytelling comes to life from the pages.' —HappyValley BooksRead

PRAISE FOR *A Stone's Throw Away*

'Fans will not be disappointed and new readers are likely to be converted . . . those looking for romance, suspense or contemporary novels will all find something to enjoy.' —Beauty and Lace

'With its appealing characters, well-crafted setting and layered storyline, *A Stone's Throw Away* is an entertaining read.' —Book'd Out

'Karly Lane has delivered a wonderfully immersive novel with a highly engaging plot, gripping suspense and compelling twists. *A Stone's Throw Away* is a story of courage, resilience and a passion for the truth.' —The Burgeoning Bookshelf

'I'm always highly impressed by Lane's ability to write compelling, entertaining and emotional storylines and weave some of Australia's history through her stories . . . an absolute treat.' — Noveltea Corner

PRAISE FOR *Once Burnt, Twice Shy*

'Well written, and bravely done . . . *Once Burnt, Twice Shy* is Karly Lane's best yet, celebrating the power of community working to support one another in terrible calamity.' —Blue Wolf Reviews

'Karly Lane gives it her all in *Once Burnt, Twice Shy* . . . a story of faith, courage, strength and future prospects, Lane's eighteenth novel is a sizzling summer read.' —Mrs B's Book Reviews

'This book has a huge amount of hope after loss, a wonderful read.' —Noveltea Corner

'Heart in mouth stuff, readers. You won't be able to put the book down till you know what happens to Jack and Sam.' —Australian Romance Readers

PRAISE FOR *Take Me Home*

'Full of romance, humour and a touch of the supernatural, this is another engaging tale by the reliable Karly Lane.' —*Canberra Weekly Magazine*

'Such a fun read . . . Karly has smashed the contemporary fiction genre with *Take Me Home*.' —Beauty and Lace

'*Take Me Home* is a delight to read. I loved the change of scenery while still enjoying Karly Lane's wonderful, familiar storytelling.' —Book'd Out

PRAISE FOR *Something Like This*

'Another unmissable rural romance story of pain, loss, suffering and the power of love . . . Karly Lane is firmly on my must-read list.' —Beauty and Lace

'There is more to this narrative than rural romance; this is a multi-faceted exploration of loss, grief, families, second chances and courage . . . I loved this!' —Reading, Writing and Riesling

'An engaging story, set at a gentle pace, told with genuine warmth for her characters and setting, *Something Like This* is a lovely and eminently satisfying read.' —Book'd Out

Karly Lane lives on the beautiful mid-North Coast of New South Wales, and she is the proud mum of four children and an assortment of four-legged animals.

Before becoming an author, Karly worked as a pathology collector. Now, after surviving three teenage children and with one more to go, she's confident she can add referee, hostage negotiator, law enforcer, peacekeeper, ruiner-of-social-lives, driving instructor and expert-at-silently-counting-to-ten to her resume.

When she isn't at her keyboard, Karly can be found hanging out with her beloved horses and dogs, happily ignoring the housework.

Karly writes Rural and Women's Fiction set in small country towns, blending contemporary stories with historical heritage. She is a passionate advocate for rural Australia, with a focus on rural communities and current issues. She has published over twenty books with Allen & Unwin.

The One That Got Away

KARLY LANE

The One That Got Away

ALLEN&UNWIN

SYDNEY·MELBOURNE·AUCKLAND·LONDON

Allen & Unwin
Cammeraygal Country
83 Alexander Street
Crows Nest NSW 2065
Australia
Phone: (61 2) 8425 0100
Email: info@allenandunwin.com
Web: www.allenandunwin.com

*Allen & Unwin acknowledges the Traditional Owners of the Country
on which we live and work. We pay our respects to all Aboriginal and
Torres Strait Islander Elders, past and present.*

 A catalogue record for this
book is available from the
National Library of Australia

ISBN 978 1 76106 613 9

Set in 12.5/18.25 pt Simoncini Garamond Std by Bookhouse, Sydney
Printed and bound in Australia by the Opus Group

10 9 8 7 6 5 4 3 2 1

 The paper in this book is FSC® certified.
FSC® promotes environmentally responsible,
socially beneficial and economically viable
management of the world's forests.

Glenda Gray,
18/7/1959–16/9/2023

A beautiful friend to many—deeply missed by all.

I was so grateful to have had you as my trusted advisor on all things rural and cattle related over the years. You have been such a wonderful advocate for farming and rural Australia, as well as a role model to not only myself but so many others. The world has lost one of its true angels, my lovely friend.

Gone, but never forgotten.

One

Alex Kelly drove over the last rise into town and caught her breath at the sight before her. The bluest of oceans, its shades blending in a wide arc framed by a strip of sand, row upon row of white caps curling as waves broke onto the shore in an endless, soothing rhythm as old as time. She hadn't been back in Rockne Heads—or Rocky, as locals referred to it—in years, but the view was always the same: beautiful.

A small stab of pain went through Alex as a bout of home-sickness flooded her. *Home.* The word echoed in the silence of her car almost as though it had been spoken out loud. But Rockne Heads wasn't home—and hadn't been for a long time.

As she continued along the road, her gaze fell on a large handwritten sign stuck to someone's front fence: *No! to Ermon Nicholades!* Across the road was another one saying, *Save our Village!* She'd passed larger ones with similar messages

1

along the road leading in from the highway and wondered what was going on. Something had clearly gotten up the locals' noses.

She turned into her old street and drove along the familiar, narrow road to the lookout at the end of the small cul-de-sac. There were no cars parked there today, so she had plenty of room to turn into her driveway. In a few weeks' time, tourists would be parked all along the little street as they stopped to take photographs or check out the surf. She hoped that wouldn't be her problem—she wasn't planning on being here that long. If everything went according to plan, she'd go through her father's belongings and throw most of them out before giving the place a good clean and putting it on the market. It should only take four days—five, max, she decided. She planned on spending the rest of her three-week holiday somewhere restful, maybe a resort further north, before returning to the UK. She hadn't had a proper relaxing holiday in years. She wasn't even sure she *remembered* how to relax, to be honest, but it was high time she did.

The car air conditioner had lulled her into a false sense of security and the humid air raced in to slap her across the face as she opened the door. This was bullcrap. If there was one thing she'd never been able to handle, it was humidity. She'd become acclimatised to the UK weather during the six years she'd been working for the Department of Foreign Affairs in London, and she preferred it. Alex had moved around a lot over the last eighteen years, never really settling down; there were too many adventures yet to have to stay in one place too long, too many things to see and explore. But now she'd found a place where she wanted to settle and the only thing standing between her and buying the little cottage of her dreams was this place.

Four Winds had been in her father's family for five generations. Her great-grandfather had been given the piece of land on the top of the headland by *his* father and it was passed down to her grandfather then her father before coming to her. Not that she'd wanted it. She wasn't ungrateful, not really. It was . . . complicated.

She stood in the overgrown front yard of the white-clad house and sighed deeply. The front of the house hadn't changed in the last eighty-odd years apart from her father installing the cladding over the original weatherboards. Built in the early nineteen forties, the cottage had replaced an older tin shed. Her grandfather had added on the back section of the house, sunken slightly so it formed a down-stairs area with large, curved windows to take in the endless blue ocean below. The weight of all that family history was a heavy burden. Alex had always been proud of her heritage. She had roots here—she was connected to the land and to the ocean. Her ancestors were buried in the small, white picket–fenced cemetery situated on the next headland over. She belonged here and yet . . . she didn't. Not anymore. She hadn't in a very long time.

Alex inserted the key into the front door and pushed it open, breathing in the familiar scent of the house and feeling as though she had been thrown back in time. She could almost be stepping through the front door after coming home from school. The only thing missing was the smell of her mother's baking or dinner cooking on the stove. She swallowed past an unexpectedly tightening throat and blinked rapidly. She hadn't expected those memories to hit quite so hard.

Her parents had divorced when she was eighteen and she and her mother had moved to Sydney. A few years after Alex had moved overseas, her mother had decided to come on an extended holiday and it had been nice having her mum with her in London. But then, her mother had met a man who lived only a few houses down from Alex, and within six months they'd married.

She didn't like to sound like a jealous daughter—because she wasn't, she was thrilled to see her mother so happy after a long time being on her own—it was just that Bart came with three daughters of his own, who were all married with babies. And now her mother had grandchildren she loved to spoil, Alex felt she didn't seem to spend much time alone with her anymore.

Alex really liked her new stepsisters and they'd welcomed her into the family from the very first time they'd all met, but she had nothing in common with any of them when so many of the conversations and activities were centred around babies and small children. There was only so much Wiggles a person without their own kids could handle.

She ran her fingers along the top of the lounge. There wasn't much left in the way of furniture or homewares from when she'd lived here; that had all either been sold or donated to charity after her father died eight years ago. She'd replaced it with trendy-looking coastal chic furniture to better suit the holiday rental the house had become. It had been a nice little earner, too, in the last few years. It rarely sat empty, providing her with a side income that had allowed her the luxury of travel.

She let her gaze wander to the large windows that framed a magnificent view of the ocean. She'd grown up with this view and yet she couldn't remember if she'd ever stopped to simply admire it. She'd probably assumed everyone had uninterrupted ocean views from their lounge-room window, and as she grew older she would have been too wrapped up in the latest schoolyard drama to pay it much attention. It seemed a waste to take something so beautiful for granted. *And yet you walked away from it*, she could almost hear her father's gruff voice whisper. She hadn't walked—she'd run, as fast and as far as she could, desperate to leave all the bad memories behind her.

Alex turned away from the window and headed back outside to the car to bring in her suitcase. The sooner she got started, the sooner she could leave.

Sullivan McCoy—Sully to his friends—waved the last guest off the boat before starting the clean-up. It'd been a great trip. The weather had been perfect, and he always felt good when his customers left with a camera full of memories and a couple of fishing yarns to tell family and friends when they got back home. These fishing tours had begun as a side gig for the off season when trawling was slow and had become so popular that it'd pretty much become his full-time job.

The success of his venture gave him the perfect excuse to step back from the trawling side of the business and take a well-earned break from the hectic life that went along with being a professional commercial fisherman. He'd spent years working twenty-hour days, weeks at a time out at sea, which had messed up his relationships and family life. Of course, he still went out on the boat during the crazy season that led up to Easter and Christmas when they earned the big bucks—it was all hands on deck during those times. It usually made up for the less profitable times throughout the year. Regardless of what size catch you came back with, the crew still needed to be paid, on top of the cost of fuel and food and equipment. It wasn't always a great pay day when you owned fishing boats—not like the old days.

The McCoy name had been synonymous with the fishing industry around here for generations. It had also been very well acquainted with the law—and not necessarily on the right side of it, either. In his father's and grandfathers' days, the industry had still been the wild west, where pretty much anything went: no species was off limits, no haul too big.

Sully felt his jaw clench slightly and concentrated on relaxing it. His father had been old-school and, had he still been alive, he'd no doubt be giving Sully an earful about how *he'd* be doing things. 'No bunch of greenie, degree-toting uni students are gonna tell me what I can and cannot catch,' Sully could hear him say. Theo McCoy had been a hard man in every sense of the word. He was tough as old leather and had no time for weakness of any kind. Sully's hadn't been the easiest childhood—his mother had shot through when he was in primary school, taking his older sister with her. She'd died a few years back and he and his sister had only recently reconnected, but they were pretty much strangers with nothing but genetics in common.

Nowadays it was only Sully running the fishing side of things—since his dad and two uncles had all passed. There were a few aunties and a couple of cousins in town, but the majority had moved on to other parts of the country—got out of town to try and distance themselves from the trouble that the McCoy name used to bring around here. Sully too had spent his entire adult life trying to wash his name free of the stains his father had left behind. He'd worked his arse off to ensure his business would be known as the respectable company it was today—a legitimate one that made money legally.

Sully shook off the dismal mood that had descended and began the clean-up. The routine was almost therapeutic. The boat had just spent three days out at sea as a team-building exercise for a group of businessmen. Sully wasn't sure what kind of business they were in, but if three days of fishing, drinking and eating was considered team building, then he was tempted to switch professions.

He glanced up as he heard his daughter call his name and saw her walking down the pier towards the boat. He smiled.

It was hard to believe his baby was nearly eighteen. Where the hell had that time gone? One minute he was being handed a tiny, red-skinned, screaming newborn that he had no idea what to do with, and the next, here she was, a beautiful young woman, all grown up and planning to leave home at the end of January.

Gabby had always been his ray of sunshine in a somewhat less-than-sunshiny life. Even now, with the threat of an after-noon thunderstorm approaching on the horizon, she brought with her a glow. Her dark hair, pulled back in a ponytail, swung with a jauntiness that perfectly reflected her ener-getic personality, and her wide smile filled him with love and pride. It still stunned him that he'd somehow helped create this amazing kid.

'Hey, kiddo,' he said, hugging Gabby tightly as she stepped on deck.

'Hey, Dad. How was the trip?'

'Pretty good. Managed to catch a few decent wahoo and a marlin. How was everything back here?'

'All good. Nothing too exciting.'

Gabby had been working the boat hire and bait shop they ran from the booking office at the marina after school, on weekends and during holidays since she was fourteen years old. She handled customers with a friendly yet competent manner and had saved her wages to buy her own car when she was sixteen. Over the years she'd learned the workings of the entire business: his fleet of trawlers, as well as the boat hire and bait shop that tapped into the area's tourism industry.

She knew as much about the business as Sully did and could probably run the entire operation without him if she had to. He hoped she wouldn't ever have to, though—he wanted more for his little girl than to work in the fishing industry.

They chatted about what had been happening while he'd been away as they fell into the cleaning routine. He paid her extra for cleaning and Gabby had jumped at the chance to earn some more cash before she left home. His heart sank a little as he realised she wouldn't be around to do any of this soon. He'd miss their time together. He knew he was being selfish by wishing she'd change her mind about leaving—after all, he was the one who'd always planted the idea in her head that she could do better than her old man and fishing for a job—but part of him wanted to ground her forever just so she didn't have to leave. Once people left Rockne Heads, they never came back.

He knew from experience.

'So, Dad,' Gabby said a little too calmly as Sully heaved the last of the garbage bags onto the pier. He turned to face her with a guarded expression. 'There's going to be this party on the weekend—'

Sully was shaking his head before she even finished the sentence.

'Dad! Just listen.'

'You know the rule. No beach parties.'

'I'm almost eighteen,' Gabby reminded him, planting her hands on her hips, undaunted by his stern frown.

'I don't care if you're a hundred and five. No. Beach. Parties.'

'You do realise you're being completely unreasonable, don't you?'

'So you've said every time you've ever asked the same question.'

'I wasn't asking a question,' she said flatly. 'I was stating a fact. Dad, I missed out on the Year Twelve afterparty at the formal. That was bad enough, but this is probably the last time I'll get to be with all of my friends at once before they all start heading off on Christmas holidays.'

'So go out to dinner or something. Have a sleepover,' he said with a shrug.

'A sleep—' Gabby stared at her father, exasperated. 'Dad, I'm not twelve! I'm an adult.'

'You're still living under my roof and the rules you grew up with will be enforced until you leave.'

'This place is a prison!' she snapped, storming off, before stopping and turning quickly. 'I don't understand you. I get that there was some stupid tragedy around here a thousand years ago, but it makes no sense whatsoever that I should be punished for something that happened before I was even born!'

'It's not about that,' Sully said firmly, reining in his anger.

'It's exactly about that. You said it yourself last year when I wanted to go to Connor Biscoe's eighteenth,' she said.

'It's about a bunch of hormone-ridden teenage boys sniffing about. No beach parties. End of discussion.'

'Discussion?' Gabby snapped. 'It's never a discussion with you. It's just you saying no to everything fun!'

'That's my job.'

'You make me so mad!' Gabby yelled, stomping away.

Sully watched her walk to her car. She slammed the door and he winced slightly as he imagined having to replace the rubber seals.

He let out an indiscernible sigh after Gabby reversed her little Mazda and drove away. He knew he was overreacting, and yet every time he tried to force himself to be open-minded about parties, that same gut-wrenching helplessness filled him. There was no way he was going to risk his daughter going through that. It may have been almost twenty years ago, but the ghosts of that night still lurked around their little town.

Two

Alex pushed open the glass door and stepped outside onto the covered deck, carrying her cup of coffee. The morning air was cool, but it wouldn't stay that way for long. She'd just missed the sunrise; the intense orange had faded into a paler shade of peach and the sky was turning a vivid blue that promised another hot day to follow. The subtle smell of the ocean filled her lungs and the sound of waves crashing onto the rocks below the headland not far from the house seemed extra loud. Being back in the old house for the first time in so long, she hadn't thought she'd be able to sleep but, surprisingly, when she woke this morning, she didn't even remember falling asleep. When she'd carried her suitcase in yesterday afternoon she'd automatically turned left in the hallway and claimed her old bedroom. Of course, it had changed since then—she'd had the entire house painted when she'd inherited it, and now the candy pink walls she'd so loved as a seven-year-old were a much more grown-up white on white.

A sudden, rhythmic banging interrupted the peace and Alex gave an irritated frown. Out here, with nothing other than the ocean to look at, it was easy to forget you had neighbours behind high fences on either side.

Curiosity eventually got the better of her when the banging continued and seemed to be getting closer so she stood up from where she'd been sitting and walked around the side of the house.

Two women and a man were at the front of her house, juggling what looked like a bunch of signage. The man picked up a hammer and positioned the stake for one of the signs, preparing to pound it into the ground.

'Excuse me,' Alex called, causing all three to whirl around to face her. 'What are you doing?'

'Alex Kelly? Is that you?' one of the women asked, shading her eyes from the glare as she peered at where Alex stood.

'Yes,' Alex said, recognising the woman and the other two people with a silent groan. Of all the people she had to bump into on her first day in town, it had to be Murna Battalex. Everyone referred to Murna as the mayor of Rockne Heads. Not to her face of course, although Alex suspected she'd heard the term and secretly enjoyed it. There were a few other not so polite terms given to her, the most notable being the Old Battle Axe.

'Well, I'll be! Goodness, it must be years since I last saw you home.'

'It's been a while,' Alex said, reluctantly crossing the yard to the picket fence.

'You look exactly like your mother,' Thelma Grant said, shaking her head in amazement. 'Doesn't she, Jonah?'

The man gave an obligatory nod and a small grunt, still holding his big mallet, clearly just wanting to finish his job and go home.

'Can I help you with something?' Alex prompted as three pairs of eyes studied her much like a bug under a microscope. She couldn't really blame them, they were probably quite shocked to see the kid they'd once known suddenly reappear as a thirty-five-year-old woman.

'We're just putting up some signage, dear. We didn't know anyone was here,' Murna said, nodding at the plastic squares at her feet.

SAVE OUR VILLAGE. SAY NO TO ERMON NICHOLADES, the signs read.

'I'm not sure what this is all about,' Alex said slowly.

'They're trying to ruin our way of life, that's what this is about,' Murna snapped.

'We're under attack,' Thelma added, and Alex felt her eyebrows rise slightly.

'From whom?' Alex asked.

'From big corporations trying to buy their way into our valley and destroy our village. They want to make it into the next Surfers Paradise.'

Surely that was going a bit far? Although going by the look on Murna's face, she believed it.

'What are they proposing?' Alex asked. She suspected that, sooner or later, she was going to be hearing about it, so she may as well be properly armed.

'They want to buy up all that bushland on the way into town and tear all the trees down to build a bunch of new houses for a retirement village. They're saying they want to put in over two hundred new homes. Can you believe that? All those new people coming into town? Into our tiny village? Where are they going to park their cars, for starters?'

Alex was still trying to digest the information but found it curious that out of everything she'd just mentioned, parking was Murna's major concern.

'We won't stand for it, I'm telling you! We will fight them to the bitter end!' Thelma said firmly and not without a hint of malice. 'There's a town meeting planned for next week. I trust we can count on your support dear?'

'It's really got nothing to do with me. I'm not a local anymore,' Alex protested. She hoped this property developer knew what he was up against. Listening to a pissed-off Murna and her protest buddies would not be a pleasant way to spend an evening.

'It's got everything to do with you,' Murna said, sounding shocked. 'This is where you grew up, where your family has lived for generations.'

'Yes, well . . . I'm actually back here to put the place on the market.'

Stunned silence greeted her words and for a moment Alex felt uncomfortable. Then she straightened her back. She had nothing to feel uncomfortable about; this was her house to do with as she wished. If she wanted to sell it, she could bloody well sell it.

'What would your father think about that?' Thelma asked with a wide-eyed look.

Alex clamped down on the swell of disappointment doing its best to rise inside her at the mention of her father. He would hate it. 'It really doesn't matter now, does it?' she replied briskly, feeling bad for speaking back to one of her elders, as though she was still a kid and not a grown-arsed woman who had every right to point out how rude they were being. Old habits and good manners died hard, it seemed.

Murna gave a delicate sniff before nodding at Jonah to continue putting up the sign.

'Actually, I'd rather you didn't put one of those in front of my place,' Alex said, feeling the further cooling of the air between herself and the others. Frostbite was becoming a distinct possibility. 'I don't want to get involved in local politics—you know, what with trying to sell and everything.'

Murna held her gaze for a moment and Alex thought she might ignore her request and put the sign up anyway, but the woman turned and, with a wave of her hand, beckoned her two lackies to follow. 'I'm very disappointed, Alex Kelly. Very disappointed indeed.'

Alex headed back inside the house, fighting the urge to run after the trio and defend herself. Why should she care what they thought? Their opinion didn't matter to her.

And yet she couldn't shake the icky feeling their judgy looks had left behind. It wasn't like her reputation around here had been anything to be proud of—half the town had made their opinions loud and clear eighteen years ago.

Sully pushed open the door of the bakery and walked inside to buy his usual order of fresh bread. The owner, Mitch, glanced up from the newspaper he was reading and called a greeting. Sully nodded to two people perched on bar stools at the window bench, eating Mitch's famous pies. Tourists, he instantly thought, not recognising their faces. Once upon a time, you only saw tourists during the Christmas holidays. Nowadays it was pretty much year-round. The caravan park across the street was always booked out and the beach packed with out-of-towners. Not that he was complaining. Tourism had been the thing that had saved his business. Without it, he'd still be stuck doing weeks out at sea catching fish and hoping the market wasn't inundated with whatever he caught, barely breaking even most weeks. Or worse, now that fuel prices had reached an all-time high. Nope—give him a town full of new faces any day.

'Have you heard who's back?' Mitch asked, eyeing his friend carefully.

'No,' Sully said. 'Who?'

'Alex. *Kelly*,' Mitch said.

Sully felt his stomach drop then clench abruptly. He tried to keep his face expressionless. 'No. I hadn't heard.'

'Apparently she's back to sell her old man's house.'

'Really?' That *did* surprise him. The Kellys' beach house was part of local history. It had always been known as the Kelly house, even when Alex had put it up as a holiday rental and named it Four Winds Beach Accommodation.

'Heard it straight from Murna's mouth just a few minutes ago.' Mitch gave a low whistle. 'And she was *not* a happy camper.'

'Who? Murna?' Then again, silly question, Murna was *never* happy—she was always complaining about something around town.

'Yeah. Apparently,' Mitch said, lowering his voice, 'Alex told them to piss off and refused to have a sign in front of the house.' As Sully raised his eyebrows, Mitch hurried to add, 'Or words to that effect.'

'No wonder Murna isn't happy. I'm pretty sure she's the first person who's said no to a sign.'

'I can't work out if she's brave or stupid. Maybe she's just been away so long she's forgotten the golden rule: Don't get on the bad side of Murna Battle Axe.'

'Maybe.'

'Anyway, how was the latest trip?'

'Great. Came back with the same number of people I went out there with, so that's always a good thing. I gotta go, I'll see you tomorrow,' Sully said, collecting his bread and saluting his friend as he headed out.

His gaze automatically went up the road from the shop to the furthest headland where the little white house sat. He wondered if Alex had changed much. He hadn't seen her in almost eight years, not since her father's funeral, and even then they hadn't spoken. He'd wondered if she'd sell the old house, but a few weeks later it was put up as a holiday let. Part of him was relieved—that meant that there was the possibility of her coming back one day. He had to admit he'd pretty much given up on that.

Now that he knew Alex was literally only a few hundred or so metres away, he wasn't sure what to do. Had time eased some of the pain between them now that they were both adults with a hefty chunk of life experience under their belts? Or would she still hate him the way she had eighteen years ago? He wanted to march up the headland and knock on her door right now, but a saner, far more cautious part of him advised against the urge. *Let it be for a few days*, it said calmly. *You've gone this long without seeing her—a few more days won't hurt.*

It made sense—after all, as far as he knew she could be happily married and the last thing she'd want was for her high school boyfriend to turn up on her doorstep unannounced. No, it was better to hang back and wait, see what he could find out about her situation before he got too excited. After all, it was entirely possible she still hated his guts.

To be honest, he really couldn't blame her, after what he'd done.

Three

Alex climbed the two concrete steps that led into the Paragon, the town's small corner store, and let her eyes take a moment to adjust to the dim interior. A deluge of memories washed over her. The old lolly cabinet beneath the high counter didn't actually seem as high as she remembered. There also didn't seem to be the same vast display of sweets either. The one thing that *was* the same, though, was the smell of hot oil and fish and chips cooking.

The Paragon used to be owned by the Stavros family and, in its heyday, had been the best place in town to eat. But the rear part of the building that housed the original cafe and dining area had been closed years ago, so the shop had became a takeaway. As Alex let her gaze wander now, though, she noticed that the once closed-off section had been opened up and there was a second entry from the street around the corner. The store had become a cafe *and* a takeaway.

'Take a seat and I'll be with you in a sec,' a friendly voice called, making Alex jump slightly. She'd only planned to buy a coffee and head back to the house, but curiosity got the better of her and she found herself moving towards the timber booths. She settled herself into one and picked up a menu.

The place had a trendy, American diner–type vibe and had been faithfully restored to reflect the 1950s and '60s style— complete with a juke box and framed posters of Hollywood movie starlets, number plates and Route 66 memorabilia.

'Sorry about that—'

Alex snapped her attention away from the décor to stare at the waitress who'd somehow managed to approach silently.

'Alex?' the waitress gasped, eyes widening and mouth dropping open.

For the briefest of moments, Alex was confused. Then recognition dawned with lightning speed. '*Tanya?*'

'I heard you were back, of course,' Tanya said, 'but I still wasn't expecting you to suddenly appear like this.'

'I've only been back a day. Wow. How are you?' Alex asked, searching the woman before her for a glimpse of the fresh-faced eighteen-year-old girl she'd known.

'Yeah, I'm . . . great. Busy. But who isn't, right?' Tanya shrugged.

'I didn't know you were working here.'

'Why would you? And I own it, actually. As of two years ago now.'

Alex tucked hair that had fallen across her face behind her ear and sat back. The slight chill in her old friend's tone dimmed the momentary excitement of seeing her. 'That's awesome. Congratulations.'

'Thanks. You're not the only one around here who was surprised that Tanya Fox became a businesswoman.'

'I'm not surprised,' Alex said softly. 'I never doubted that you could do anything you put your mind to.'

The women held a silent look for a moment before Tanya cleared her throat and offered a smile. 'Can I get you something? Are you ready to order?'

'A coffee thanks,' Alex said, glancing at the menu. Suddenly she was starving. 'And the Rocky cheeseburger. Actually, can we change the coffee to a thickshake?' If she was going to splurge on a burger she may as well go the whole hog.

'Don't tell me . . . chocolate, right?' Tanya replied and Alex grinned.

'Yep.'

'No worries. I'll get this started for you.'

Alex followed her old friend's departure with a melancholy kind of regret. She hadn't seen Tanya in years—too many to count. Actually, that was a lie. She knew exactly how long it had been. The week before Christmas. Eighteen years ago.

16 DECEMBER 2005, 9 PM

'It's exactly what you need,' Tanya said, overriding Alex's protest as the girls stood in Tanya's bedroom. 'Show him what he's missing.'

Reluctantly, Alex accepted the stretchy, rather clingy, cotton dress her best friend handed her from the wardrobe. 'Obviously he doesn't care what he's missing or he'd have called me by now,' she muttered, toying with the bracelet on her wrist. Sully had collected cowrie shells from the beach and threaded them on a strand of leather. He'd given the bracelet to Alex for her birthday and she treasured it. Not only because it was beautiful, but because he'd taken the time to sit and make it. It was her good-luck charm, and she hadn't taken it off since the day he'd given it to her.

'Go and put that on. I promise, he'll be begging you to forgive him for not calling you after he sees you in that.'

'My parents would kill me if they caught me in this,' Alex said, eyeing herself in the mirror. The soft fabric clung to everything and was short enough for her to realise she wouldn't be sitting down too often.

'Then it's a good thing they're out of town tonight, isn't it?' Tanya said with a wink. 'Oh, come on,' she groaned dramatically as she took in Alex's doubtful expression. 'You're always complaining that you're never allowed to go to any parties. Well, here's your big chance. Have some fun for a change instead of being such a goody two-shoes.'

The comment stung a little—actually, a lot. Alex hated that everyone at school knew her as the 'girl most likely to stay at home and study on the weekend', which, in all fairness, *had* been what she'd done for the last few years. But still. School was over. They'd finished Year Twelve and Christmas was just around the corner. For the first time in forever, Alex didn't have to worry about exams—now her fate was in the lap of the gods. For at least the next few weeks, before she took the next step into university and the rest of her life, she could relax.

She pushed away the thought. Alex's plan to leave Rockne Heads was what had caused the whole *Home and Away* drama between her and Sully, even though things had been tense for the last few months. They'd had to hide their relationship from her parents since she was the daughter of the town cop and he was the son of one of the town's notorious crime families tied up with what was commonly called the 'Rockne Heads Mafia'. The Duncan and McCoy families had connections with a number of dodgy dealings and there'd been allegations of foul play, drug trafficking and even murder over the years. Most notable had been the investigation into corruption within local law enforcement that had spanned a number of decades and had resulted in convictions of not only members of the families but also the town's previous police sergeant, whom her father had replaced.

'Fine.'

'That's the spirit!' Tanya rolled her eyes at Alex's lack of excitement before giving a small sigh and taking her hand. 'I know the last month or so's been hard. All the pressure you've put on yourself with exams and then Sully going AWOL on you, but this is the last few weeks of our youth,' she said, solemnly. 'Everything changes after this, Al. You'll go off to uni and everyone else will leave town and go their separate ways. We won't be kids anymore. We'll have to go off and do grown-up stuff and be all responsible. I don't want everything to change.'

Alex felt her throat tighten at her friend's sad expression. The shine of tears in Tanya's eyes had her blinking back some of her own. Tanya had been the first friend she'd made when she'd started school after they'd moved back to her father's hometown when she'd been seven. Alex and Tanya had been inseparable—more like sisters than best friends—and saying goodbye to Tanya was going to be one of the hardest goodbyes of all. They'd been planning their great escape from Rocky since the start of high school, designing their dream apartment, imagining their exciting, big-city life. It was all they'd talked about, once. The last few years, though, they'd talked less about escaping as the reality of figuring out career options and the pressure of school and study and university sapped all the excitement from Alex's daydreams. It had taken a while for her to realise that her friend was no longer along for the ride.

'I'm not going to university,' Tanya had told her last year. Just like that, out of the blue.

'What do you mean? Why not?' That had always been the plan: they'd apply for the same university, find themselves a flat together and come home for holidays.

'I'm not as smart as you. I don't want to study for another four years. I don't even know what I want to do.'

'You can figure it out as you go. And you are smart!'

'Not book smart.' She shrugged. 'My aunty's giving me a job in the cafe after I finish Year Twelve. I'd leave now, but that was one of the conditions of the job—I had to finish school first.'

'You're going to stay here and work in a cafe?' Alex hadn't meant it to come out sounding quite as judgemental as it did, but she was in shock.

'For now. Who knows? Maybe one day my Prince Charming will ride into town and carry me away,' Tanya had said, waving a hand above her head like a magic wand.

Alex hadn't shared her friend's calm acceptance of her future. In fact, their relationship had started changing from that moment. Alex had poured herself into study while Tanya had been free to party and socialise and enjoy her senior years.

'It'll be okay,' Alex said now, summoning up a bright smile. She hugged her friend tightly as they stared at their reflection in the mirror before them. 'We'll stay in touch. I'll be home every holidays and you can come down and stay with me on weekends whenever you like. We can still go out and have fun.'

'Promise?' Tanya asked, wiping her eyes quickly.

'Absolutely. Whatever else happens in our lives, you and I will always stay friends.'

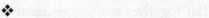

Through the windows of the Paragon, Alex watched the early holidaymakers from the caravan park across the road make the migration through the reserve from their camp sites to the beach. Parents tugged along canvas trolleys filled with beach balls and cabanas, towels and eskies, as they held the hands of squirming, impatient toddlers who were in a hurry to go for a swim. She saw the parents look longingly at the cafe as they went by, knowing there was no way they'd get away with delaying the promised swim to wait for an order. Older couples strolled by, dressed in their resort wear and large sun hats, while a group of teenagers on bikes and skateboards wreaked havoc with pedestrians. The street was bustling, but it was nowhere near the crazy busy it would get in just a few weeks' time, once the Christmas holidays kicked in with full force.

A young boy delivered Alex's meal, interrupting her people watching. She caught something familiar in the kid's face.

'Mum said she'll catch up with you later,' he said.

Mum? 'You're Tanya's son?' Alex asked, realising why he looked familiar. He had Tanya's eyes.

'Yeah.'

'I'm Alex. Nice to meet you,' she said and the boy, who she thought must be about fourteen or so, gave her a quick nod before disappearing into the kitchen. The booths were beginning to fill up and Tanya would have her hands too full for any further conversation this morning. It surprised Alex how much she'd been looking forward to speaking with Tanya again. She hadn't come here to find old friends and 'catch up'. There was very little about the past that she wanted to reminisce about. But seeing Tanya again . . . that had surprised her. She hadn't expected to feel that depth of sorrow for a lost friendship—or the instant joy in finding her again.

The food was delicious, the flavour and presentation second to none. Alex found herself shaking her head in wonder. A place like this in the city—in *any* city, anywhere in the world—would be getting rave reviews. How had Rockne Heads, of all places, managed to hide this little gem for so long?

Tanya was nowhere in sight when she finished her meal, so Alex left the cafe. She was in the process of putting her sunglasses on when she was yanked backwards, and she felt a breeze in her face as a kid on a skateboard streaked past her nose, just about colliding with her.

'Are you okay?' asked a male voice.

Alex turned and lifted her gaze to the man before her and froze. *No. Way.*

It shouldn't have been a surprise—this was Rockne Heads, for goodness' sake, so she was bound to bump into him at some point, only she hadn't anticipated it to be quite so literal.

Sully McCoy. In the flesh.

He'd changed. Which was to be expected—when she'd last known him, he was nineteen years old, a kid really. Now he was a man.

'Alex?' he prompted now, frowning slightly as he looked down at her and she realised she hadn't answered him.

'I'm fine. Thank you.' Though she realised, with some annoyance, that her heartbeat had begun to pick up for some unexplainable reason.

He continued to stare at her, but his frown began to fade. He released her once he was sure she was steady on her feet, and took a small step back. 'Bloody kids are going to hurt someone one day,' he said gruffly.

'It's pretty dangerous, especially considering there's so many young kids and elderly around. I'm surprised Murna's committee hasn't gotten on to it yet,' she said dryly.

She saw his lips twitch a little at that before he tilted his head in the direction of the caravan park. 'They aren't local. Tourists.'

'Hmm,' Alex replied. 'Maybe I'll go over and have a word at the park office on my way home.'

'You can try. There's probably not much they can do. What we need is a copper in town—but we don't have that either. Not like the old days.'

'It does seem strange they closed down the station,' she said, her gaze moving to the little stone cottage at the end of the main street. It held both good and bad memories—good ones of when she was younger and her dad had worked there and bad because . . . Well, she didn't want to recall those.

'Bloody disgrace, really,' Sully said. 'Everything goes through a central switchboard and they send out police from twenty to fifty kilometres away. By the time they get out here—if they even get out here—it's usually too late to do anything.'

As the crow flew, it was probably only a few kilometres from Moreville, the nearest town with any facilities, but the road into Rocky wound its way up the highway and around and under a bridge before following the river that eventually led out to the ocean, making it a long and tricky drive if you weren't used to it, with a lot of sharp bends and narrow sections.

'Have you caught up with Tanya yet?' he asked, looking at the cafe.

'Yes, I was just in there.'

'I bet she was glad to see you.'

Alex flashed a half-smile and shifted her weight slightly. 'She was pretty busy. We didn't really have time to catch up properly.'

'Oh, well. I'm sure you'll find time. How long are you back for?'

'Just a few days. I'm putting the house on the market.'

'Yeah, I heard.'

'Of course you did.'

'Surely you haven't forgotten how fast news travels around here?' he asked, lifting an eyebrow.

'I haven't forgotten,' she said, lifting her eyes to meet his squarely. She saw him blink and then a serious expression fell into place, replacing his earlier laid-back manner. 'I have to go. It was nice to see you again, Sully.'

'Alex. Wait. Do you want to . . .' He paused, then swore softly. 'Would you like to meet up for a coffee, or dinner even, before you leave town?'

His invitation caught her by surprise. Dinner with Sullivan McCoy? The man—well, boy—who'd broken her heart all those years ago?

Yes, a little voice reminded her calmly, *the boy, not the man. That was a long time ago.*

'I'm not sure I'll have time.'

'It wouldn't have to be anything fancy,' he said, then started backing away. 'How's tomorrow night? Say about seven? Meet me down at the pier.'

The pier? Wait—what? Tomorrow? She scrambled to think of an excuse to say no, but he was already walking away.

Alex was still stewing over the conversation when she reached the house. Her breath caught in her chest as she stared at her front door.

Someone had spray painted a word in menacing, bright red paint, which had begun to run in long, gruesome streaks, resembling blood. *Guilty!*

She wasn't certain how long she stood there staring. Eventually, outside sounds filtered into her stunned brain—a lawn mower somewhere down the street, seagulls squabbling over food scrabs nearby. The noises cut through her shock and she pushed open the gate and went inside to find something to clean up the mess.

After googling a solution and a lot of elbow grease, Alex had removed the majority of the graffiti. She'd need to buy some paint to redo the door, but at least the hurtful message was now gone.

The sight had shaken her more than she cared to admit. It was one thing for the town gossip mill to be whispering behind her back but it was another thing entirely when they brought it—quite literally—to her front door. There was no point making a fuss about it though. If she went to the police, it would only draw more attention and that was the last thing she wanted right now.

She just wanted this whole chapter of her life to be over. Was that really too much to ask?

Four

Staying at home the following day had seemed like the safest course of action and Alex worked tirelessly, sorting her dad's stuff into piles to give away or sell. She'd decided to put most of the holiday-let furniture on the local marketplace sites and whatever didn't sell now, she'd include with the house. She didn't want any of it; none of it would suit her new house anyway, with its old-world charm and cottage gardens. The shabby-chic beach house look worked here—not so much in Chilham, Kent.

She'd been working in the study, which had a floor-to-ceiling bookcase that had been built by her grandfather, who'd been a schoolteacher. As a child, Alex had always loved coming in here to play. She'd always been an avid reader and this room had been her retreat. She'd considered leaving it open and giving her holiday-let guests access to it, but in the end it had made more sense to use this room to store her father's personal effects and free up an extra bedroom next door than have a library-slash-study that didn't have any extra bedding. Bodies in beds was the important thing in this business—the more people a house slept, the bigger the bucks.

She sat down on the old leather chair behind the timber desk and placed her hands flat on the surface. She didn't remember where the desk had come from but it was some kind of family heirloom. As a child, she'd loved poking about, looking for its secret hidey-holes. Her father had once shown her the little drawers hidden in strange places, like secret compartments, and they'd often left surprises for each other to find. She'd made drawings of her dad in uniform or of unicorns and rainbows and placed them inside, returning after school to see if they were gone, replaced with lollies or small treats. She remembered the furniture removalists and how they'd all grumble about how heavy the old desk was, every time they'd had to move for her father's latest transfer, and she recalled the relief when they returned to Rockne and the desk was returned to its original space. Her dad and this desk had a lot in common. Both had been dragged around the countryside, and both had ended up back in the house they'd started from.

She missed her dad. She rarely allowed herself to think that thought, but being in here, where she always felt the closest to him, it was almost impossible to ignore. A memory of the last time she'd been home, for his funeral, pushed its way forward.

Her mother had intended to come with her, but she had taken ill a day before their flight and so Alex had ended up flying by herself. Alex had debated even coming. It felt hypocritical to have not seen him for all those years and then come back for his funeral. To this day, that trip was one of the loneliest experiences of her life. There hadn't been many people in the funeral home, mostly police officers and older locals. There was no church service or burial—her father hadn't been into any of that. He'd wanted something simple and low-key, like the man himself. She'd noticed Sully at the back of the small crowd, but only briefly caught his eye.

She'd felt numb, cold, even though it had been a blue, cloudless sky outside. She hadn't shaken anyone's hand or accepted any condolences, she'd simply sat and waited until most of the mourners had left. Then she too left without looking back. Not once.

Her father's ashes had been taken to the cemetery on the headland and put in the ground beneath the small headstone she'd organised with the funeral director over the phone before she'd arrived. The whole thing had felt like some weird dream and still made her feel sad and empty whenever she was silly enough to allow herself to think back to that time.

The relationship she'd had with her father had been a complicated one. It had never used to be—once he'd been her hero and she'd adored him, but when she'd needed him the most, he'd let her down.

She opened the long drawer in front of where she sat. She knew exactly what was in there, because she was the one who'd packed everything into it after the funeral. A waft of tobacco scent floated in the air and she closed her eyes, briefly, savouring the smell she always associated with her dad. There was a box containing three cigarettes and a lighter, a notepad and pen, and two photo frames. The largest photo was of herself and her parents smiling. Well, at least she and her mother had been smiling—her father was wearing that same, no-nonsense, robocop expression that had always terrified her friends and sent many a potential boyfriend running for the hills. The second photo, though, was of her father at the beach, taken just below the headland where their house stood. Her mother had managed to capture the rare moment when her father had forgotten to be a policeman and had slipped into doting father mode, crouching beside three-year-old Alex as she played in a rock pool.

Alex gently set both photos on top of the desk and studied them, letting the past trickle over her. It had been a long time since she'd allowed herself to remember the simpler times in her life and she discovered that, unlike a lot of other memories from the past, these ones didn't hurt.

She tried to cross her legs, but bumped her knee under the table. As she bent forward to rub the sore spot, her gaze fell upon one of the desk's concealed drawers. Tentatively, she pressed her fingers to the underside of the compartment. The latch popped open and she found herself holding her breath as she slowly opened the drawer, the seven-year-old inside of her hoping against hope that she'd find a lollipop her father might have left. The momentary disappointment was quickly replaced by curiosity when the drawer revealed a small blue notebook and a pile of typed pages tied with a tartan ribbon. *The Life of a Small-Town Cop.* By William Kelly.

Her father had written a book? Alex sat back and stared incredulously at the paper balancing on her lap. She didn't move to open it. She couldn't. So she just sat there, frozen. Fear clutched at her insides—something warned her that whatever she found inside would be like a portal, sending her back to the past.

After a few moments, her gaze moved to the notebook. She carefully pulled it out and leaned back in her chair. It was one of her father's police notebooks, used to record interviews, observations and other relevant information while on duty. She flipped through and found various notes in his scribbled handwriting relating to everyday life in a small police station. A lost bike reported, then found abandoned at the beach showers; a neighbours' dispute involving a large tree dropping its leaves over the boundary fence—she couldn't see an address but she was fairly certain that was the couple who'd purchased the house on Grant Street from their elderly parents and then spent the majority of their eighteen months living here involved in a war with the Johnsons next door over practically everything.

She flipped back a page, curious now about the dates. Her heart gave a painful lurch. August, 2005. The same year—

She shoved the notebook and manuscript back into the drawer and closed it firmly. She wasn't going back there again. Not now that she was so close to closing that terrible chapter of her life once and for all.

A loud squeak snapped her attention to the door. She listened intently, her heart thudding heavily.

'Hello?' she called out, then rolled her eyes. In every horror movie she'd ever been stupid enough to watch, there was always that one brainless idiot who called out hello to the serial killer in the house like they expected them to call back, *Oh, hi! It's just me!* Obviously, it was just the old house making noises and if she'd bothered to put on some music earlier, she'd never have heard it.

When there weren't any further sounds—or would-be serial killers calling back a greeting—Alex stood up and shook off the creepy moment to go back to wondering what to do about all the books in the bookcase. Maybe she could have a garage sale, but she'd hoped to avoid anything too involved. Maybe she'd just call up a charity organisation and get them to come and collect most of the stuff. But as she ran her fingers across the spines of the titles sitting on the old shelving, she felt unexpectedly wistful. She remembered her father reading a lot of Wilbur Smith and John Grisham books as well as his homegrown favourites, like Peter Watt and Matthew Reilly. They were all still there, along with some of her mother's collections of Danielle Steel and V.C. Andrews. Higher up were the dusty copies of books her grandparents and great-grandparents had read, along with a 1970s edition of the *Encyclopædia Britannica* and a mind-blowing collection of *National Geographic*s dating back decades. Who was going to want this stuff if she donated it? Was it even worthwhile? But the thought of dumping it just seemed . . . wrong.

Alex gave a frustrated huff and decided to put it on the I-have-no-idea-what-to-do-with-it list and move on.

She glanced at her watch and closed her eyes briefly, letting out a long breath to calm sudden nerves. It was time to start getting ready for this stupid dinner date with Sully. Why on earth had she agreed to something so dumb? *Had* she even agreed? The whole thing had happened so fast some of the details remained a bit sketchy.

With a long, frustrated groan, she finally decided she'd just go and get it over with. After all, they were both adults now. It would be fine.

Five

This is so not fine, Alex thought, forcing one foot in front of the other as she walked down the weathered timber ramp that led to the row of piers where trawlers and other large, pleasure craft–type boats were moored. Her hands felt clammy and her stomach queasy. What on earth was she doing here? She had no idea who this guy even was anymore. Why hadn't she just said no—or better yet, just stayed at home? She didn't want to examine the answer to those questions because part of her was afraid she knew the truth: she was curious. She and Sully had a past and it had ended without closure.

Did that past change anything? No. But then again, she was a little alarmed by the tiny stirrings of awareness she'd felt the day before when she'd been in his arms. *That* had been unexpected.

As teenagers, they'd been like petrol and fire—hormones and youth were a heady combination. Add a touch of drama and a big fat scandal, and the whole relationship had gone off like New Year's Eve fireworks.

Alex wondered where she was supposed to go. All Sully had said was the pier. She'd thought maybe there was a restaurant or something down here—who knew what developments the place had undergone in the time she'd been away?—but she couldn't see anything new, other than a ticket office for fishing trips, boat hire and bait. *The Reel McCoy Fishing Tours*, she read on the signage as she neared the office. Cute, she thought absently.

A girl in her late teens appeared at the window of the ticket office and Alex returned her friendly greeting.

'Are you lost?' the girl asked.

Alex chuckled. 'I think I am. I'm supposed to be meeting someone and I thought we were going to a restaurant or something, but there doesn't appear to be one . . .'

'Who are you meeting?'

'Sullivan McCoy. I take it this is his place?'

The girl eyed her with a little more suspicion. 'Yeah, it is. Hang on. I'll give him a call.'

Alex thanked her and remained in front of the little timber hut, but blanched as she overheard the conversation.

'Hey, Dad. You have someone here to see you.'

Alex found herself studying the young girl closely. *Sully's daughter?* She regretted, yet again, ever coming back to this damn town. She was sick of surprises and sick of memories jumping out at her at every turn. All she wanted was to put the bloody house on the market and close this chapter of her life. Was that really too much to ask?

'I'm Gabby,' the girl said, and Alex shook herself from her thoughts.

'Alex.'

'How do you know my dad?'

The question wasn't asked rudely; in fact, much to Alex's surprise, it simply sounded curious. As she imagined a daughter would be if someone just announced they were having dinner with her father.

'We grew up here together. A long time ago. I'm just back in town for a few days.'

'I thought I knew all my dad's old friends,' Gabby mused.

'I left here . . . before you were born,' Alex said, stumbling on the words slightly. *Dear lord, Sully, where the hell are you?* Maybe it wasn't too late to just leave. She opened her mouth to ask Gabby to let her father know she had to go, but Sully loped around the corner and it was too late to flee.

'Sorry! I had to deal with a bit of an emergency with one of the trawlers.'

'Everything okay?' Gabby asked, concern etched on her Mediterranean features. She'd clearly inherited those from her mother. Alex's mind provided an image of a girl of similar age to Gabby, with full red lips, long, dark hair and exotic, almost slumberous, eyes.

'Yeah—all sorted now. I thought you'd already be gone. Why don't you just close up a bit early and head home,' Sully said.

'I was just finishing up a booking,' Gabby said, arching an eyebrow that was a definite imitation of her father. How many times had Alex seen Sully do that exact same thing? Gabby clearly knew how to make her father uncomfortable and seemed to be enjoying it.

'Gabby, this is—'

'Alex, yes, I know. We've already met. I'll get out of your way. Nice to meet you, Alex,' Gabby said, sliding from her tall seat behind the computer. 'Have fun,' she added as she passed her father.

The two adults stood awkwardly in silence as she left.

'Sorry about that . . . I was planning to meet you before you got this far,' Sully eventually said.

'Are you married?'

'What? No. Why?'

'You were trying to keep your daughter from seeing me.'

'Karla and I split up years ago. She's remarried—happily. Gabby's fine, I just didn't want things to get . . . uncomfortable that's all.'

'Well, that seems to have worked well.'

'Sorry.' He ran a hand through his recently cut hair. It wasn't as shaggy as it had been the day before and the facial hair that covered his chin and top lip had been trimmed short, taming the wild, bushy, sea captain beard. He cleaned up pretty nice. Not that she cared.

'So where are we going?' she asked, breaking a second silence that threatened to linger.

'Follow me,' he said, snapping out of his earlier discomfort and turning on his heel.

'Are these your boats?' Alex asked as they passed by two fishing boats tied to the wharf, bobbing serenely in their bays.

'Yeah. There's another one still out—they'll be gone for a few more days.'

'Impressive. You seem to be doing really well.'

'I do okay. It took a long time to clean up the mess my father left behind, I had to start from scratch, but things are good now.' He shrugged and she knew he was playing down his success.

Theo McCoy had been a scary man. Not that she'd known him personally; he was already in prison when Alex met Sully, and theirs hadn't been the sweet kind of puppy love that most teenagers have—going on dates and spending the weekends having dinner with the parents and whatever else teenagers did when they had a boyfriend. Instead, they'd had to steal moments whenever they could and craft elaborate cover stories—mostly involving Tanya and sleepovers just so she and Sully could spend time together. There was no way in hell her father would have allowed someone like Sully McCoy into his house or—more to the point—into his daughter's life.

'This is it.' Sully stood to one side as Alex came to a stop beside him. The gleaming white boat rising high above her head was impressive. It had *Keepin' it Reel* scrawled across its bow.

'It's huge.'

'Fifty-eight foot,' he informed her like a proud father announcing the weight of his baby. 'This is where my heart truly lies.' He led the way to the gangplank.

'Fishing tours?' she asked, taking in the huge covered deck lined with seating and large ice boxes. They passed by a timber table that sat in the centre of the deck and through a set of glass doors that opened into an indoor lounge area with a kitchen and dining area and a steering wheel console.

'Is this where you drive the boat from? I always thought there was a special room to do that.'

'There is on certain boats. On this one there's also a flybridge upstairs, which is sometimes called the top wheel-house. We usually just call this one the cockpit.'

Alex gave the room an appreciative glance. The white upholstery on the seating that wrapped around a central table gave the interior a bright, fresh look and the navy carpet and timber flooring added practicality. The kitchen was roomy and seemed to have all the mod cons, including a full-size oven and fridge. She had no idea what Sully was cooking but a delicious aroma filled the room, making her mouth water.

'This is great,' she said, surprised by how luxurious it all was. A vast difference from his father's old trawlers, which he'd worked as a kid, and where they'd often sneak away to in order to have some privacy back in the day.

'Do you live on board?' she asked.

'Only while we're out on charters. I have a place just out of town where Gabby and I live. Do you want a full tour?'

'Sure.'

He walked past her into the kitchen and turned off the oven before heading down a narrow staircase off to one side of the dining area.

The first level, a mere three steps down, held four single bunks. One step further down on the second level were another two single beds. They ducked through a steel door that led to a third level where a larger double bed and four more single beds were all made up with navy bedspreads with neatly rolled towels placed at the end.

'Bathrooms are through there.' He pointed to another steel door that reminded her of the doorways she'd seen in submarines in movies. There wasn't a great deal of room, but it was far from cramped and dreary. It felt quite opulent considering it was primarily a fishing boat, albeit for people who were looking for a bit of comfort and luxury.

They turned to retrace their steps and, in the more confined space of the second level, Alex became aware of how big Sully was. A familiar scent filled the room and she was instantly hurtled back to her teens. 'You still wear Brut?' she blurted, then immediately clamped her mouth shut. Why the hell had she said that? She hadn't realised how much she'd missed that smell until now. She was certain she'd never smelled it at any time in the last eighteen years.

He seemed as surprised as her that she'd asked, then a slight grin touched his lips. 'Yeah. I do. How'd you remember that?'

Alex shifted uncomfortably, feeling stupid. 'No idea. Dinner smells good too.' She stilled, her eyes widening slightly before she hastily corrected herself, 'I mean, not too . . . not that you don't smell nice . . . I just meant . . .' *Oh, just stop talking!* the little voice inside her groaned. She worked in public relations, for Christ's sake, and here she was babbling like some lunatic.

He chuckled. 'It's okay, Al. Seriously, I get what you're saying.'

He did? Now she wasn't sure what he understood. She'd just admitted she still loved the smell of the deodorant and aftershave he used to wear when they were together and— even worse, that she remembered he used to wear it. What the hell did that mean? And if he *gets it*, then how come she didn't?

She needed a drink.

'Let's have a drink upstairs then eat. I'm starving.'

Oh, great—now the guy was a mind reader.

'Take a seat,' he said when they were back on the main deck, indicating the lounge area.

She sat in a comfy chair, admiring the clear water with its white sand below—a stark contrast to the headlands either side, with their rolling waves and surf beaches. She thanked Sully when he brought over her wine and a cheese platter. The boat shifted gently on the swell, not enough to disturb the contents on the table, but in a soothing way that encouraged Alex to relax into her chair.

'This is really nice,' she said, reaching for her drink.

'Yeah, it's not too shabby,' he agreed, sipping from his beer bottle. 'You know all about me now, so what about you? What do you do for a living?'

'I'm in PR. I've been working overseas for the last ten years or so.'

'What does PR work entail? You'll have to forgive my ignorance, I'm just a dumb fisherman,' he said with a smile.

'I was mainly working for big companies, writing press releases for new products and doing presentations and writing content for their social media, stuff like that, but two years ago I took a job with the Department of Foreign Affairs for the Australian Embassy in London and I really love it.'

'Wow. Now *that's* impressive.'

Alex gave an off-hand shrug of one shoulder. 'I was looking for a change and this job gave me that opportunity.'

'I kinda have a confession to make,' he said, lowering his gaze to his beer bottle. 'I stalked your Instagram page.'

A nervous laugh escaped as relief rushed through her. Was that all? She hadn't been sure what he was going to say—they had enough history for her to expect anything.

'I bet that was exciting for you.'

'You've travelled a lot, but there weren't many photos of *you* on there. Or mention of your marital status,' he added almost as an afterthought.

'I'm not married.'

'Have you ever been?'

Alex eyed him before setting down her glass. 'Nope.'

'How come?'

'I've never wanted to settle down in one place too long—and I've never found a man who wanted to move around as much as I do.'

'Fair enough.'

The truth was relationships with men had never been easy. She'd shied away from intimacy for much of her early twenties, and after that she'd found it difficult to trust most men in order to have a serious relationship. In the end it was just easier to concentrate on her career and enjoy travelling and embracing new experiences while having the odd casual affair if she came across someone interesting enough. There really hadn't been all that many.

'Gabby seems like a good kid.'

'Yeah, she is. Hard to believe she's almost an adult and leaving home.'

'It's hard to believe you're old enough to have an adult child.'

'Tell me about it,' he said.

'You've done a good job with her.'

'I can't take all the credit. Karla had to pretty much raise her for the first few years while I was trying to get the business up and running—legally.'

Alex felt a small prickle at the mention of his ex-wife's name. It seemed weird to think of Karla as a wife. The last time Alex had seen her, Karla had been a seventeen-year-old who had just announced she was pregnant with Sully's baby. *And that hadn't even been the most devastating event of the night*, Alex thought morosely.

'But she's a pretty resilient kid. Loves the water and boats.' He smiled. 'I'm going to miss her next year.'

Alex shook away the mood that had tried to worm its way in. 'Where's she going?'

'She has early acceptance into Sydney University.'

'You have every right to be proud of her.'

'I am. I might not have done many things to be proud of in my time, but Gabby was the best mistake of my life,' he said quietly. 'I know it probably doesn't mean anything after all this time, Al, but . . . I really am sorry for everything that happened between us. There was so much going on and, as hard as we tried, there was always going to be someone or something trying its best to break us up.'

'You're probably right,' she said, trying for a carefree tone. 'It was a long time ago.'

Although not long enough to forget the shock and betrayal of hearing he'd fathered a child to someone else. Or how that moment had set off a chain of events that had forever changed so many lives.

16 DECEMBER 2005, 9.25 PM

The Rogue Traders belted out 'Voodoo Child' through a set of speakers and Tanya waved as she raced over to join the dancing. Alex sat the song out, too anxious to dance. She breathed in the salty sea smell and tried to calm her jumpy nerves. The ocean seemed to be competing with the music and laughter, the waves roaring and crashing against the rocks on the headland of the beach. Little Beach, as it was ingeniously named, had always been a popular hangout for teenagers, a place to hold parties and other extracurricular activities away from public scrutiny. It was also a popular rock-fishing spot the locals guarded like territorial wolves. Access around the rock pools at the base of the steep headland cliffs could be quite tricky to navigate, which helped limit the number of tourists who might accidentally stumble upon the spot.

Alex wasn't even sure if Sully would be here tonight—he'd been volunteering for more overtime on longer trips out at sea, and they'd barely seen each other or talked for more than a month. He'd been at sea for the last two weeks but was due back today, according to her reliable contacts, namely Tanya's cousin who worked on the same boat. Alex kicked her sandals off and felt the cool sand between her toes—so different from earlier in the day when she'd been down here and the sand had been scorching.

'Hey.'

The deep, quiet voice surprised her. She hadn't seen him approach.

'You came,' Alex said, taking in the tall, lean figure before her like a long cold drink on a hot summer's day. 'I wasn't sure you would.'

'We didn't get back in till late.'

Alex hated this. They were like strangers now. Nothing had been the same since their fight—despite the fact that they'd made up only a few days later. Alex knew part of the blame had been hers. The last few months had been stressful and studying for the HSC had taken over her entire life. She'd worried nonstop, lost weight and pretty much locked herself away in her bedroom during the lead-up to the exams. Sully hadn't understood, having left school years before, and had become impatient with her for constantly cancelling plans. He just didn't get the pressure she was under. She had to do well in these exams. She had to get into university. There was no two ways about it—all her future plans depended upon it. All *their* future plans.

Sully had always been onboard with the plan. He'd been working hard to save up money to make the move to Sydney so they could be together. They wouldn't have to hide their relationship like they did now and she wouldn't have to worry about small-town gossip or her father's rules. And Sully would be away from his father's and uncles' reputations—they could start over someplace where no one knew Theo McCoy, where Sully would be free to make his own mark on the world without people always whispering behind his back about how he'd made his money or ran his business. It wouldn't matter who his father was. It wouldn't matter she was the town cop's daughter. No one in Sydney would care who they were. They could be whoever they wanted to be. But to do it she had to make sure she got the score she needed to get into her degree.

'I missed you,' Alex said now, taking a small step closer, holding her breath a little as she waited to see if he would reach for her.

'I missed you too,' he said, and his eyes softened.

Her heart almost leaped before another voice interrupted and Sully's face took on a startled expression before becoming wary.

Alex turned to find Karla Robinson heading towards them. She didn't really like Karla—they'd never had any kind of altercation, but there was just something about Karla that Alex had never warmed to.

'I need to speak to you, Sully,' Karla announced without even acknowledging Alex.

'Not now. I'm busy,' Sully said. Alex found it strange that he would speak to anyone in such a cold, dismissive tone.

'Now,' Karla insisted, not backing down.

Alex studied the other girl's face. It was almost as though she'd somehow lost some of her youth between the end-of-school celebrations and now. Which seemed ridiculous, and yet a strange, unsettling feeling began to creep up Alex's spine. Something was definitely wrong.

'Go away, Karla,' Sully said.

'Sully, what's going on?' Alex asked quietly. As far as she knew, Karla didn't even know Sully that well—at least, not well enough to be wanting to *talk to him*.

'Nothing,' he said abruptly, taking her arm to lead her away.

'It's *not* nothing,' Karla said, coldly.

Alex dug her heels in the ground, refusing to be led away. 'Sully?'

'Either you talk to me, or I'll tell her everything,' Karla said quietly.

Whatever panic had been driving Sully to shake off this girl seemed to suddenly evaporate and in its place was a weary acceptance—almost as though he were simply preparing himself for his fate.

'Tell me what?' Alex asked slowly.

Karla held Sully's eyes with a determined steeliness.

'When we'd broken up, I did something stupid—but it didn't mean anything, I swear, Alex,' Sully said, turning to her. 'I was planning on telling you about it tonight. To get it out in the open. That's what she wanted to tell you. But like I tried to tell her before, I made a mistake. A bad one. I was drunk, we'd just had that fight and broken up . . . I was a mess, Alex. It's no excuse, I know, but I swear, I didn't even know what I was doing. There was a bunch of us drinking—I don't even know who was there. I barely remember anything about the night.'

'You arsehole!' Karla yelled. She leaped forward, pelting Sully with her fists and crying.

Alex was too stunned to do more than watch in horror. She wasn't even sure she understood anything he was saying. Only, she did. The boy she loved, the boy she'd been making

54

stupid, starry-eyed plans for the future with—the boy she had given her virginity to—had slept with someone else.

The yelling had drawn attention and someone started laughing.

'Knock it off!' Sully snapped, capturing both of Karla's hands in his. 'I told you on the phone to leave me alone. I don't want anything to do with you.'

'Well, too bad!' Karla spat as she struggled to get her hands free. 'Because I'm pregnant and I'm keeping it. *That's* why I've been trying to call, you stupid prick! Maybe if you hadn't hung up on me the other day, I wouldn't have had to track you down here.'

Sully's hold went slack and Karla staggered backwards, her furious eyes glaring daggers at him.

Pregnant. The word spun inside Alex's head. Karla was pregnant . . . with Sully's baby.

'Alex.'

Sully's urgent tone penetrated the heavy fog that seemed to muffle everything around her. Alex snapped her head up to stare at him. She felt her head shaking in denial even as the truth began unfolding inside of her.

'I had no idea . . . I swear . . . I didn't know she was—'

'Pregnant,' Alex said, forcing the word through cold, stiff lips.

'It was a mistake. I've been feeling sick about it ever since it happened. I swear, I didn't mean for it to. I was drunk and upset. I wanted to tell you about it, I just didn't know how. You were studying, already acting crazy over your exams—'

'Crazy?'

'You were stressed,' he corrected quickly.

'So you went out and got drunk and slept with someone else.'

'I wasn't thinking straight.'

'While I was doing everything to make sure we had a future together.'

'You broke up with me!'

'Well, I guess that makes it all okay then,' Alex said, throwing her arms in the air. 'Congratulations.'

'Alex! Wait!' he called as she turned away.

'Don't touch me!' she snarled as he went to reach for her. 'Don't you ever touch me again.'

'Alex, please,' Sully said sadly, defeated. 'Just hear me out. Let me explain.'

'You have. And you're right. We'd broken up. You were free to sleep with whoever you wanted to. But we're over. Go and sort out your mess. You made it—you go clean it up.'

Alex was certain everyone on that beach could hear her heart shattering like a thousand pieces of glass crashing to the ground as she walked away. She needed to be alone, to hide and get far away from everyone and everything. There were too many things thundering against her head like a damn jackhammer, desperately trying to break in and overrun her thoughts.

She sank down behind a rock and covered her ears to block out the laughing and sneering, the gasps and snide remarks. It was too much. Her tears fell unchecked and the sound of the waves crashing against the nearby rocks beat in time with the ache in her heart, vibrating through her chest. Nothing had ever hurt this much.

Six

'Did you cook this?' Alex asked as she watched Sully deftly move about in the small kitchen—or galley as he had corrected her earlier—serving up their meal. The chicken Kievs were golden brown and oozing just enough garlic butter to make her mouth water. He served them with crispy scalloped potatoes and steamed beans.

'Yep . . . well, not from scratch, but I threw them in the oven.' He grinned. 'Surprised?'

'I guess I am. I don't know why. It's not like men don't cook. I guess you just didn't when we knew each other.'

'I had to learn how to do a lot of stuff I didn't do back then,' he said, glancing at her before turning his attention back to their meal. 'I grew up pretty fast once Gabby came along.'

'I imagine you would have,' Alex agreed. It was hard to think of the boy she'd been in love with suddenly becoming a father. 'Is there anything I can help with?' she asked.

'You can pour us more wine, if you like.'

Glasses filled, she followed Sully outside to a small table on the deck and sat down. A gentle breeze had picked up as the afternoon sun sank low in the sky. She loved this time of the day—just before dark, when the heat gave way to a balmy summer evening.

'This is really good,' Alex said after her first bite. 'I'm impressed.'

'Wait until you try dessert.'

'You cooked dessert too?'

'Well, technically it came out of a box from the freezer, but Sara Lee has never failed me yet.'

They shared a smile, though Alex was still bemused by this grown-up version of the person she'd known so long ago.

'So why are you selling the house? Why now?'

Alex took a sip of her drink before answering. 'I found a house I want to buy in Kent.'

'So it's permanent, then? You living overseas?'

Alex shrugged. 'I guess.'

There was a small silence before he murmured, 'Fair enough.'

'So what's the story behind Murna and her posse? Are these developers as bad as she's making out?'

'Depends who you talk to,' Sully said. 'The developer has some big ideas—but is hardly the conglomerate giant

Murna and the committee are making out. But it's a pretty big project and it'll bring in a lot of people. I think they're talking a hundred homes, so that's a considerable population spike in a short time. The group *is* raising some valid points, but you know Murna—if there's a chance of drama, she'll be charging in at the front of the pack.'

Alex gave a small chuckle at the image of the rather round woman sitting on a gallant steed, holding up a sword. 'What's your position on it?'

Sully seemed to ponder the question, and Alex found herself respecting that. He'd always had a quiet, thoughtful way about him. He was a listener and a thinker, rather than someone who offered an opinion just for the sake of hearing their own voice.

'Like everywhere else at the moment, we've got a housing crisis. Rent's gone through the roof and people are being kicked out of rentals in favour of a higher bidder, and house prices are insane, as you're no doubt aware,' he said. 'All that's a real issue in a small town. I think even though this over fifty-five community won't be of any obvious benefit to families and younger people, it will most definitely free up some houses in town. I mean, think about it—Murna is jumping up and down shouting, "We don't have any more room for newcomers", but there's a considerable number of residents in big houses who would absolutely jump at the opportunity to sell up and buy into a smaller home in a secure village with all the amenities at their doorstep. The one thing

Rocky lacks is services like transport and community access for the elderly. We both know of people who are in their eighties, still living in the homes they've been living in all their lives. A lot of them are like prisoners. They can't drive and they aren't physically stable enough to navigate steep driveways or walk to the shops, so a place designed with everything they need onsite plus the added bonus of having companionship and social activities is a huge drawcard. In return, a number of places in town would be freed up for sale or rent to younger families.'

'I imagine there'd be some added business bonuses to bringing in more people too?'

'This place needs development. It has for years, but you can't even say the word around here without risk of verbal attack.'

Alex could only agree. Heaven forbid the town allowed a service station to be built so you didn't have to drive all the way to Moreville to fuel up.

'This community action group is out of control. Development doesn't always mean high-rise building and concrete jungles. Like it or not, even Rocky has to move into the future at some point. But it's like a bunch of these sea-changers have bought up and moved in and now they're trying to build a wall to keep everyone else out.'

Alex nodded. 'Smells a touch hypocritical.' Despite herself, she'd taken a look at the Save Rocky Community page the night before just to see what all the fuss was about but, after almost pulling a muscle from all the eye rolling some of the comments had caused, she'd shut down her computer. There had to be a happy medium somewhere; a commonsense approach to bringing in the developments that would benefit the community.

'I'll walk you home,' Sully said, as they rose from the table.

'There's no need,' she said, shaking her head. 'Seriously, I'll be fine.' She could see her house—well, its roof at least, behind the houses built on the east side of the headland across the road from hers. It was a good thing she'd decided against driving, considering they'd polished off the better part of two bottles of wine. The hill to her place was going to be a killer, but the night was so balmy and bright that she was willing to put up with a bit of exhaustion.

'I'm walking you home. I wouldn't expect a guy to let my daughter walk alone at night, I'm sure as hell not going to let you.'

'How very caveman like of you.'

'Since when is basic safety caveman like?'

He had a point—and she was honestly grateful that he was sensible enough to think of her safety. If only it had been anyone except Sully McCoy offering. Too many things tonight had been bringing back old memories.

'You're right. I'm sorry. Thank you.'

Her apology seemed to throw him off guard, like he'd been preparing himself for a bigger fight over it.

Alex brushed past him and made her way off the boat. There was the slightest hint of a breeze in the air as they started the steep ascent towards her house at the top of the hill. She loved the sound of the ocean at night, when everything else had gone to sleep and there was no sign of modern life, that's when the ocean could roar to its heart's content. The boom of the waves crashing against the sand sent a surge of energy through her. The footpath hugged the headland and beach below, and as they neared the plateau where the small lookout was, they paused. Much to Alex's chagrin, *she* was the one who needed to catch her breath. Sully seemed barely affected by the exertion.

'I think I need to join the gym when I get back,' she managed between breaths.

'You're just a bit out of practice.'

Once, she used to run up this damn hill and barely break a sweat—a *long* time ago. The salty smell of seaweed carried on the breeze, making her body tingle with long-forgotten memories of her childhood. She closed her eyes, feeling the hot cement of the path under her bare feet, the drying sand on her skin and the coolness of a towel wrapped around her bikini-clad body, hair still wet from a swim.

'You seem a million miles away.'

Sully's soft words jolted her eyes open. 'I guess I was.'

'You looked like you were seventeen again.'

Alex gave a little scoff at his words and stepped away from the wooden rail she'd been leaning against. 'I must remember to stand around in the dark more often so I look younger.'

'You still look the same to me,' Sully said with a gentle simplicity that made her pause.

Standing there under a bright moon, holding each other's gaze, Alex felt the strangest moment of déjà vu. It really did feel like she'd stepped back in time to when she was seventeen and life had been like one of her teenage romance novels. Until the romance had turned into a nightmare.

Another face flashed before her—not Sully's—and the carefree butterflies and sunshine feelings disappeared, replaced by an icy touch that stabbed painfully at her heart.

'It's getting late. I need to get home,' she said, turning away to continue walking.

'Hey, wait up. What's wrong?'

'Nothing. I've still got lots of sorting to do tomorrow.'

'I can lend you a hand if you like.'

'No, thanks.'

'I imagine it's a big job—emotionally speaking,' Sully said, keeping up with her brisk pace with annoying ease. 'Going through old memories, selling the house and all that. It must be hard.'

She'd thought she'd dealt with all of that years ago, but an unexpected lump formed in her throat. 'Dad and I weren't close—hadn't been for years. Then he and Mum got divorced and everything kind of fell apart.'

'I think he went through a pretty rough patch after . . . everything. He kept to himself the last few years. I don't think he left the house much.'

'Apparently.'

'You know, he was in a really tough spot. I often thought about it afterwards. You were his daughter, but he had a job to do.'

Alex stopped abruptly and turned to face him. 'Exactly. I was his daughter,' she said. 'He should have known me better than anyone. He should have *believed me*.'

'I'm sure he did—'

Alex shook her head. 'He didn't. I saw it in his eyes when he looked at me. He believed what everyone else in this stupid place believed,' she said bitterly. 'That I killed Jamie Duncan.'

Seven

Sully leaned back slightly at her blistering words. It was as though the past had come hurtling towards him, hitting him square on the chin.

All night he'd let his mind wander through the memories, touching on every good moment he'd ever had with Alex when they'd been kids. Nothing was as potent as your first love. Those heady, sweaty, nerve-wracking moments when he'd first worked up the courage to ask her out, knowing that she was way out of his league but spurred on by sheer love-sick bravado. The heart-racing moments when they'd shared their first kiss and the mind-blowing, life-altering days after they'd first made love. He'd felt young again.

Alex Kelly had been his first love—his only love. There was no point denying it. He'd married Karla out of a sense of duty and because he genuinely wanted to be a father and step up to claim his responsibility. Maybe it'd been a knee-jerk reaction or a way to prove that he was nothing like his old man. Either way, deep down inside, he knew he'd had his doubts about leaving town with Alex as they'd planned and everything that had followed had been his fault.

'I never believed that,' he said softly.

He almost flinched at the disbelieving look she threw at him.

'I didn't. Alex,' he said, reaching out to hold her arm. 'You seriously think I could believe you were capable of something like that?'

He let her arm drop when she tugged at it impatiently. 'All I heard was people yelling at me and calling me a murderer. Not once did I hear anyone yelling over the top of them and saying I was innocent.' She turned away.

She was right—gossip and theories had spread through town like wildfire. Scary, really, how their sleepy little town of usually calm-headed, laid-back people could suddenly turn into a lynch mob. An image of a frightened Alex being led into the police station replayed in his head and his gut clenched. He'd wanted to push his way through the crowd and hold her, protect her from the anger Jamie's family had been throwing at her. Then he remembered the rumours: she'd been with Jamie that night. His mind had tortured him with all the things 'with Jamie' implied. Jealousy had surged through his body, holding him back from rushing into the crowd.

'What happened that night, Alex, between you and Jamie?'

The alarm and fear that flashed through her eyes were quickly replaced with anger.

'I know it was a long time ago, and I don't have any right to ask . . . but thinking of you and him at the time—' he added, and instantly regretted bringing it up when he saw her eyes narrow dangerously.

'You want to know if I slept with him? Seriously? After what you did, you think you have a right to be angry about whether or not I slept with someone else? You got another girl pregnant!'

'We'd technically broken up,' he offered weakly, knowing full well it didn't lessen the sense of betrayal.

'All of five minutes before, but hey, sure, whatever makes you feel better about yourself.'

'For the record,' Sully said, a little more forcefully, 'I didn't feel good about it. I regretted it as soon as it happened. And I had no idea she was pregnant until that night on the beach. I'd been feeling so guilty for being with someone else that it didn't even cross my mind I could have got her pregnant . . . That side-swiped me completely.'

'You weren't the only one!'

'You had every right to be hurt that night. I just don't understand why you'd have picked Jamie, of all people. That wasn't like you at all.'

He saw her lift a shoulder but noticed her eyes were not reflecting the same off-hand dismissal. There was something deeper there—almost like grief. Which made no sense.

But before he could question it, Alex had started walking once more and he knew the topic was closed.

They reached the front of her house and she stopped abruptly and turned to face him.

'Thank you for walking me home. I'm fine now. Goodnight.'

'Alex, I didn't mean to upset you . . . I guess there's been a bit of unfinished business between us after all this time that needed to be aired.'

'It was eighteen years ago, Sully. We were just kids. None of it's important now.'

Somehow her softly spoken words hurt more than if she'd yelled at him. 'You were important to me, Alex.'

She pulled a face before shaking her head slowly. 'It's the past. Nothing can change it and you can't go back.'

'Sometimes I wish we could. I would have done things differently.'

'No, you wouldn't,' she said gently. 'If you did, you wouldn't have your daughter and I can see how much she means to you.'

'She means everything to me.'

'Then everything happened for a reason.' She smiled but it held a tinge of sadness, making Sully's heart squeeze painfully. 'Thank you for dinner. It was good to see you.'

'We can do it again. I've got an overnight trip tomorrow, but I'm back home Wednesday night.'

'I don't think that's a good idea. We said everything that needed to be said. I don't plan on hanging around town any longer than necessary. I'm hoping to be done by the end of the week.'

'If you change your mind, you know where to find me,' Sully said, surprised by how gutted he felt from her knockback.

'Goodnight, Sully,' Alex said, unlocking the door and stepping inside.

'Night.'

He stood there until she closed the door behind her.

Eight

Alex noticed the Paragon was a lot quieter at this time of the afternoon. She ordered a coffee from the girl behind the counter and found a booth to sit in, then took out her phone to check her emails.

She looked up with a smile of thanks on her face as her coffee was placed on the table. But the expression froze before widening into something happier as she saw who'd delivered it.

Tanya hovered by the booth. 'I haven't had a chance to properly catch up with you. Am I interrupting?'

'No, not at all, please sit for a while, if you have time?'

'I'm the boss, I have all the time in the world.' She grinned, then thanked the waitress as she delivered a coffee to her employer. 'I hear you've caught up with *a lot* of people since your return,' Tanya said, watching Alex over the top of her cup.

Alex's surprised eyes met Tanya's, before she rolled them and gave a small snort. 'Wow. The gossip mill has gotten even faster over time.'

'You didn't seriously think anything had changed, did you?' Tanya asked, raising her eyebrows in mock surprise. 'So?' she prodded impatiently.

Emotion clogged Alex's throat before she forced it away and let out a shaky chuckle. It was as though, with a snap of the fingers, the last eighteen years had suddenly melted away and they were just two best friends prying the latest news out of each other.

'I'm assuming you're talking about Sully?'

'Of course I'm talking about Sully!' Tanya said, in an eager rush that made Alex laugh.

She shrugged. 'We had dinner together, caught up on old times and that's it.'

'Nothing else happened? No spark reignited?'

'Sorry,' Alex said, shaking her head as she ignored a niggle of guilt over telling a little white lie. 'What about you? You've got kids . . . I feel stupid asking, but are you married? Do I know them? We've got a lot of ground to cover here.' She was sad to realise she had no idea what her former best friend had been doing for the last eighteen years.

'*Was* married,' Tanya said, 'and you didn't know him—he moved to the area after you left. We have three kids, all boys, and we split up about five years ago. He decided family life wasn't for him and has since remarried.'

'Oh no. I'm sorry that happened,' Alex said.

'The divorce part was okay—we hadn't really been getting on after the third baby came along. And, quite frankly, he was useless around the house and I was pretty much a single mum,' she said with a small scoff. 'The thing that makes me furious though—more for the boys than myself—is that, once he remarried, he went on to have another two kids with her. So basically, he left a family only to go and start a new one with someone else. Men!' she said disgustedly, shaking her head.

'Oh, wow.'

'Right?'

'What a dick.' Alex couldn't summon the words to say anything constructive.

'Yep. But, I think, in the grand scheme of things, the boys have a much healthier home life without a negative influence sitting in a lounge chair drinking himself stupid.'

'You've done a remarkable job. It can't have been easy to take on a business while raising three kids singlehandedly. Is your mum still in town?'

'Yeah. I bought our house from her a couple of years ago so she could move in with Aunty Bet to take care of her when she got sick. She's still the same—smokes too much, likes a drink at the bowling club a few times a week and plays bingo. That's about the extent of her day.'

Tanya's mother hadn't been your typical stay-at-home mum the way Alex's mother had been. She didn't like to cook or clean the house, so Tanya had done most of that while her mother spent the majority of her time down at the club. Luckily Tanya had had an extensive circle of aunts, uncles and cousins, so she'd always had somewhere to go if things got too out of hand. That was also why she'd spent so much time at Alex's house.

'I heard on the grapevine that you've been living in the UK. So do you have a nice Englishman back home, then?'

'No.'

'How come?'

'I don't know really,' Alex said with a surprised laugh at her friend's bluntness. She'd forgotten how forthright she could be. 'I guess I've been concentrating on my job a bit too much to have time to spend on a boyfriend.'

Tanya chuckled. 'You make it sound like having a man is like being a responsible pet owner: "I can't have a puppy because I don't have the time to walk it and house train it",' she said in a toffee-nosed accent.

'I don't sound like that,' Alex protested.

'You do have a little bit of a fancy accent. Only sometimes, though. There's still hope you haven't completely turned into a Pom yet.'

'Heaven forbid!' Alex said, dryly.

'But seriously, don't you miss being back here?'

'Here? In Rockne?'

'Yeah, or just back in general. I can see how living overseas might be pretty exciting for a while, but . . . don't you get lonely?'

Alex thought about it. 'I've got Mum and Bart—she's remarried,' Alex added and briefly filled Tanya in on her stepfamily situation.

'Yeah, I heard that. But I mean—people *other* than your mum?'

'There's lots of other people,' Alex said lightly.

'But it seems like you're not very interested in finding anyone? I guess I'm wondering what's keeping you over there if it's not a guy? Your mum seems settled and happy, but what about you?'

Alex opened her mouth to answer then abruptly shut it. She'd never really thought about that particular question before. 'It's an amazing place with so much history and . . . well, there's my job,' she said, frowning as she wondered if her answer sounded as flimsy as she thought it did.

Tanya sipped her coffee but didn't comment, leaving Alex to contemplate why she suddenly felt so confused by such a simple question.

'I've found the most adorable little cottage to buy,' she said, unlocking her phone and scrolling through to find the photos.

'It looks like something out of a Beatrix Potter story,' Tanya said, admiring the photo. 'Holy cow!' She suddenly leaned forward and dragged the phone closer. 'Is that how much it is?'

'Yeah. It's in a pretty popular spot—anywhere close enough to commute to London is a bit pricey.'

'In Australian dollars that would be—'

'Yes, a lot, I know.'

'Are you expecting to get that much from the house here?'

'No. Well, not really . . . but hopefully a tidy sum to put towards it.'

Tanya chewed on her bottom lip quietly as she stared at the photo. 'Not that I don't think you haven't thought this all through . . . but . . .' She looked up at Alex. '*Have* you thought this all through? That seems like a hell of an investment for a house.'

Alex bit back a surge of irritation as she picked up the phone. 'I have thought it through. Property is a sound investment—especially over there. Prices are only going to continue to rise in these sought-after places. Besides, moving to the country is something I've wanted to do for a long time now.'

'You could move back here,' Tanya said, putting her cup down. 'If you wanted country, you don't get more small town than Rockne Heads. If you wanted a farm, you could always buy somewhere out of Moreville.'

Alex gave a small smile. But Rockne Heads wasn't Chilham, Kent. And that was the dream.

Sully took the heavy container of fish and ice from one of his deckhands and stacked it on the wharf beside him. The trawler had not long come in and they were a man down so he had come down to lend a hand. It was a decent haul, which made the fact that he was going to be feeling the results of all this lifting tomorrow a little less painful.

One of the Duncan boats was also unloading across the dock and Sully could hear Tom Duncan swearing at one of his workers. He silently shook his head. There was something to be said about moving with the times. Sully had grown up at the tail end of how things used to be done, where verbal abuse—and occasionally physical abuse, like a slap up the side of the head from his father—had been commonplace, a way to enforce lessons.

Nowadays there were workplace standards, although clearly the Duncans had decided to ignore the memo. They did things their own way—always had, always would. If anyone else treated an employee the way Tom was right now they'd probably worry about getting a visit from Fair Work or some other governing body. Not the Duncans. Employees didn't report over there. Not if they wanted to stay in one piece. The Duncans were still old-school in their handling of disputes.

And being part of the Duncan family didn't earn you any special privileges either—they were always fighting and squabbling among themselves. Sully reckoned that if it wasn't for Russell Duncan holding the reins their whole business would have imploded long ago. Russell ran the family and the company with an iron fist, but he was known to occasionally look the other way where Tom was concerned. Sully hated to think what was going to happen once Tom was placed in charge. Where Russell had mellowed over the years, Tom had only become more fiery. At least with Russell there was still a code of conduct of sorts. He was a tough, sometimes brutal, man, but he was at least a man of his word.

Sully and Russell had formed a truce some years ago, bringing back stability to a community that for generations had been divided into either the Duncan or the McCoy camp. Brawls had been commonplace between the fishing boat crews, and out on the water it was nothing short of a territorial war. When the sea could earn you big bucks, greed was a mighty motivator. But those days were all but gone— now it was a case of if they didn't all work together and fish responsibly then the whole industry would collapse and no one would have a business. Russell at least had grasped the logic in that, and after he and Sully had made their grudging treaty the violence and warring had stopped. Mostly. There was still no love lost between Tom and Sully, though, and Sully didn't trust the younger Duncan as far as he could throw him.

'Heard your girlfriend is back in town, McCoy,' Tom called when Sully had finished unloading and was heading back to the office. 'She would have been smarter to stay away.'

Sully turned to the beefy-faced fisherman. 'She has just as much right to be here as anyone else.'

'She gave up that right when she messed with the Duncans. We don't forgive and we don't forget.'

'I hope that wasn't some kind of threat.'

Tom's lips twisted as he chuckled briefly. 'I don't make threats. I just tell it how it is, mate, you know that.'

Sully took a step closer and held the other man's almost piggish eyes. 'So do I. And if I find out anyone's messing with her, they'll regret it.'

'I'm shakin',' Tom scoffed.

Sully held his stare levelly for a moment longer before turning away. He'd developed the skill of keeping his cool over the years, especially since his business had started taking off—reputation and respect was everything in this industry and something he held in high regard as he tried to distance himself from his family's past. There might be a truce between the McCoys and the Duncans, but there was a very real, very savage part of him that would love the opportunity to beat the living shit out of Tom Duncan should the occasion ever arise. He wasn't proud of it, but it was there, watching and waiting. He could feel it now, clenching and unclenching its fists, ready and willing to spring into action.

Nine

As she drove out of Rocky, and eventually found herself back out on the highway, Alex realised yet again what a pain it was for locals to get anything done. She checked the fuel gauge on the car and added another job to her mental to-do list—*don't forget to find a service station.*

As she took the exit from the highway and drove into Moreville, a flood of memories washed over her. The bus trips home after school, the early morning weekend sports, hanging out in town with friends. Where Rocky was tucked away behind the mountains, Moreville had once had the main highway running through it, until the bypass opened. The bypass didn't seem to be having too much of an impact on the town though; there were no car parks in the main street and Alex had to do a lap around the main town block to find one.

Moreville serviced the farming sector of the valley Rockne Heads was part of, its population made up of the outlying arms of the river and their communities. The town had the major facilities: a few stores, lots of cafes, hairdressers and beauticians, as well as two larger chain supermarkets to choose from. While Rockne Heads had the small grocery store for the basics, its pricing was well and truly aimed at the tourist market, so most people still drove to Moreville to do their weekly shop. Unless, of course, they didn't drive, in which case they were forced to buy all their supplies at an exorbitant price.

Alex took her time walking up the main street, headed for the real estate office. She was pleasantly surprised to find a few small boutiques had opened since her last visit, but there was little else. She didn't remember the town being quite this small when she was growing up—back then they'd had a shoe shop, a few different clothing stores, a jeweller and giftware stores. Maybe she'd just been spoiled, living in London for so long. It was quite the culture shock to come back and remember what living in a small rural town was like.

When she reached the real estate she stopped outside the display window, noticing there were plenty of sold stickers slapped across photos, which was a good sign. It had only been a few short weeks ago that her friend Holly had jokingly suggested Alex buy her mother's cottage after they'd been visiting one weekend. For some reason, the conversation had stayed with Alex all that evening and into the next day, and she'd realised she had an insane urge to actually do it.

Holly thought she was crazy. 'Why on earth would you want to move all the way out there to live? It's like an hour and a half commute each way? And what about living out in the middle of nowhere? It's so far from everything.'

It was true—until now, Alex had been the quintessential London girl, loving everything about the hustle and bustle of the city, the museums and the shopping, restaurants and theatre. But lately she'd also realised she preferred a quiet night at home. She'd begun turning down invitations from friends to go out, craving instead a glass of wine and a night on her lounge. And she could change some of her hours and work from home if she really wanted to. Something about the little cottage with its thatched roof and twin chimneys, its pale blue window frames and front door and the gorgeous cottage garden inside a white picket fence pulled at her with surprising strength.

Chilham, with its narrow lanes and timber-framed Tudor houses, the woodland and open countryside surrounding it, reminded her a lot of . . . here. Except for the history attached to the buildings, it was very much like the place she'd grown up in.

She found this sudden desire to head for the country difficult to explain to anyone else—didn't understand it herself, really—but she knew she was no longer happy living in the city and she desperately craved the peace of rural living. The sale of the beach house would give her close to the amount she needed and she'd get a loan for the remainder.

Tanya's concern flitted through her mind and Alex shrugged it off. She'd done the sums—she wasn't completely stupid. She knew it would be tight and she'd have to watch her pennies if she wanted to make the big move away from the city, but she could keep chooks and grow her own vegetables to save some money. She wouldn't starve as long as she managed to keep her garden alive—and the animals, she supposed. How hard could it be?

She gave a decisive shake of her head and pushed the doubt away. She'd be fine.

Yet there was something confronting about being here today. Actually putting her family home on the market seemed very . . . final.

She'd miss this place. The thought made her sad, a feeling that caught her by surprise. So much that had happened here, the pain and the grief, had overshadowed the good memories, but somehow this time more of the good things had started to return. As hard as she tried to suppress them, they'd still managed to wriggle in.

But it didn't change anything. She'd returned to tie up loose ends and she supposed all these annoying emotions were just part of that process. She didn't like complicated emotions. In fact, she didn't *do* complicated emotions. They were messy and unnecessary and she'd had more than her fair share in the past so there was really no need to experience them again. She'd rather just get through all this and go back to her new life. It was business, that's all. It's just a house. People buy and sell houses every day.

Taking a deep breath, Alex pushed open the door and walked inside.

Twenty minutes later, she walked out, having secured a time for the estate agent to come out and do a valuation. It felt different from how she'd imagined it, less exciting somehow.

You don't have to go through with it, the little voice piped up, surprising her. So much so that she actually stopped walking and the man behind had to swerve around her.

Don't go through with it? Was she crazy? Of course she was going to go through with it. She'd had to argue with her boss to get the time off to fly all the way over here to deal with the clean-up and sale. She had to go through with it, otherwise it was just . . .

A well-earned break? the voice suggested.

It was true Alex had been feeling a little burnt out lately. Maybe that was what had been behind the sudden urge to find somewhere quieter to live. And yet, it wasn't that sudden, it had been building for a while. She'd been working well-paid but long-hour jobs for the last few years—the bigger the company, the higher the stress and pressure to get results. The London job was supposed to be a bit of a shift to take away some of that burnt-out feeling, but there was a certain amount of pressure and stress tied up with that job as well. Part of it was Alex's own work ethic and the fact she was a bit of a perfectionist and maybe just a tiny bit of a control freak. Delegating was all well and good until you had to give up control and discovered you had the urge to take over so it was done right. She did need to learn how to step back a little bit more and stop trying to do everything. Hers just didn't seem to be the type of career where that was going to happen. There was too much depending on the outcomes to risk taking her eye off the ball.

No. She was doing the right thing. She'd have the house valued and then she'd sign the paperwork to list it for sale. She'd just do it. Rip it off like a band aid and everything would fall into place.

The air had lost its crispness by the time Alex had dressed the following morning. She'd planned on walking into town, but after a brief inventory of the fridge decided she'd better take the car and do a small grocery shop. She knew from experience that losing circulation in your fingers as you carried multiple bags in each hand while tackling the headland hill was not recommended. She thought about heading back into Moreville, but decided the round trip would only cut into her day and she needed to get that damn library sorted.

She realised the flaw in her decision as soon as she stepped through the grocery shop's door.

'Alex. How nice to see you again, dear,' Murna said from where she stood by the fruit display.

Damn it. There was no way Alex could pretend she hadn't heard her and keep walking—she was positioned across the aisle, effectively preventing her, and anyone else who may be in the store, from getting past.

Alex smiled, dragging forth her professional diplomatic face. You didn't work in the embassy and not learn how the pros could fake a polite greeting or two. 'Good morning.'

'Doing a spot of exploring are we?'

Hold it together, she warned herself firmly. *Ignore her patronising tone and just smile.*

'Just doing a spot of shopping so I don't starve.'

'Oh, well, you must try the Paragon. Tanya Fox bought it. I believe you and Tanya were once good friends?'

'I was in there the other day. It seems to be doing really well, which is great.'

'Well, we did suggest that Tanya consider doing something a little more *in keeping* with the quaintness and tradition of the village when she took it over,' Murna said with a sniff. 'I'm not sure about this American diner thing.'

As far as Alex could recall, she'd never heard Rockne Heads ever referred to as a village when she'd been growing up, but clearly *quaint* and *village* was the direction the newly formed Save Rocky Community Group had decided upon.

'Actually, I remember my gran talking about the Paragon,' Alex said. 'When she was younger, American food and décor was all the rage. So really, Tanya only restored what was originally here. But that was probably before your time.'

'Before a lot of people's time, I'd say,' Murna quipped.

Alex nodded. 'True. Only the locals would probably remember.'

The jab went completely over the woman's head. 'Yes, well . . . there's getting fewer of us every day. Not to mention how many more locals they'll push out of town if they get their way with this new development.'

'I'm not sure you can stop progress,' Alex said, hoping to wrap up their conversation and move on.

'We have so far, dear. At least the wrong sort.'

Alex wasn't sure what to say to that: *At what cost? Maybe?* She really didn't have a dog in this fight. She wasn't a local anymore and once she sold the house she'd have cut all ties with the town. She shouldn't care. Only, a small part of her *did*. The town risked closing itself off from multiple advantages if it refused to move with the times and it was the vulnerable of the community who would suffer, not the people who bought in when prices were far cheaper and no longer had a mortgage nor needed to work nor had children in school. Keeping the town small suited that group just fine, but it was almost arrogance that a select few in town with the loudest voices were able to dictate the rest of the population's future.

'Maybe the meeting will be a great opportunity for everyone to hear what the developers are proposing straight from the horse's mouth, without all the wild assumptions that are being made around town and on social media. It's probably not as bad as a lot of people are making it out to be.'

Instantly, Alex saw the woman's eyes narrow suspiciously and her friendly manner disappear.

'It must be a little strange for you, coming back after all this time. Stirring up all those old memories and such,' Murna said, peering at Alex as though watching for a reaction of some kind. 'That *was* a terrible business back then.'

Oh, hell, no—she was *not* going down that rabbit hole this early in the morning. 'It was a long time ago.'

'It's funny how people remember things, though. Especially the locals. They have very long memories.'

Was that some kind of veiled threat? Or was she imagining the slight malice behind the words?

Alex decided she wasn't going to bother finding out. 'Well, I better get moving. Lots to do.'

'Yes, I'm sure you have. Nice to bump into you again, dear. Take care.'

Alex tried to shake off the uncomfortable feeling of Murna's beady eyes following her departure. The town could remember all it wanted—she wasn't some scared seventeen-year-old anymore. This time they wouldn't be able to intimidate her.

Stepping out of the grocery store, a heavy bag in each hand, Alex headed for her car. The humidity was terrible and she could already feel sweat running between her shoulder blades. It was barely ten in the morning.

From the corner of her eye, she noticed two men walking across the parking lot, but didn't bother looking at them until she heard a low snigger.

'You've got a hide,' one of the men said, raising his voice as he neared.

Alex felt her limbs go tingly and stifled the urge to run. There was no mistaking who these men were—Duncans. She'd recognise that neckless, stocky build anywhere. It was the same as—

Alex hurried to her car, wishing she'd found a closer park. *Just get in the car and you'll be fine. It's broad daylight—they can't hurt you*, she reminded herself, feeling a little faint.

'Oi! I'm talkin' to you, girl!' the man called again, but Alex refused to acknowledge him, reaching the car and fumbling to press the right button on her remote. She found it and climbed in.

'You've either got a huge set of balls on ya, or you're the dumbest bitch around, comin' back here.' The man slammed his fist on the bonnet of her car and Alex flinched, then slammed the door shut, flicked the central lock and started the vehicle.

She couldn't avoid eye contact completely as she tried to reverse out of the spot, and could see that the one doing all the yelling was Tom. He was a few years older than her and had only gotten scarier with age. The other was Chris. She'd gone to school with him and although he was smirking, he'd remained quiet, standing back slightly. For the briefest of moments she locked eyes with him. Alex thought his gaze softened a bit. Then Tom leaned closer to the windscreen, making her jump.

'Murderin' bitch.'

Alex froze, feeling the colour drain from her face. There was only pure hatred burning in the man's eyes, almost drilling into her through the glass. She put her foot down on the accelerator and the car surged backwards, causing the men to shrink away in order to avoid being run over.

She didn't look in the mirror, she couldn't. Her heart felt like it was missing beats and, when she pulled into her driveway a few minutes later, her hands were shaking uncontrollably. Terrified that they'd follow her, she grabbed the groceries and ran inside. She locked the door, then raced around to double-check the rest of the doors and windows. When she was done, she sank to the floor of her bedroom and hugged her arms tightly around her legs, dropping her head to rest on her knees.

She wasn't sure how long it took for her heart rate to settle and for the shaking to stop, but when she finally got awkwardly to her feet she was stiff and sore and filled with a nauseous dread. She thought all this had ended eighteen years ago.

When would that nightmare of a night ever leave her alone?

Ten

Sully finished drinking the glass of water he'd poured and stared out through the sliding doors that overlooked the bush. He'd bought this block of land as an investment after he and Karla had divorced. His life had been spent out on the ocean and salt water practically flowed through his veins, but the bush . . . Out here, surrounded by tall trees with only the sound of birds for company, well, that was something altogether different. This soothed his soul. Building his dream house and being able to focus on his boat-building hobby had been an unexpected bonus.

'Dad, you do remember what's happening today, don't you?' Gabby asked, walking into the room and eyeing his work clothes.

'No. What?' He did a frantic mental calculation of dates. It wasn't a birthday of any sort.

'The town meeting with Ermon Nicholades,' his daughter said flatly, staring at him as though she were the adult and he was the teenager. 'You *are* going, aren't you?'

'I wasn't really planning on it.'

'You *have* to go. We need all the support we can get. They can't just come into town and think we'll all lie down and let them walk all over us.'

'You do understand that they're only building houses, right? Not skyscrapers.'

'For now, maybe . . . but we can't let them get their foot in the door,' Gabby said with a nod.

'You know, you're sounding more and more like Murna every day.'

'The action group is made up of more people than just Murna, Dad. A lot of young people want to get involved. I thought you'd want to be more protective of our future. You've lived here all your life.'

'Yeah. I have. And if I thought there was anything in this proposal that I needed to protect the town against, I'd be standing shoulder to shoulder with Murna and the rest of them, but there's not. I can only see positives.'

'It's what they aren't saying that's the concern,' she said, folding her arms across her chest.

'Gab . . . Look, I'm glad you feel like you need to stand up for something, really, I am. As long as you're doing it with an open mind and not being caught up in all the propaganda and fearmongering. You have to be able to weigh up both sides of the argument fairly.'

'They're here to make money—lots of money—and they don't care about communities. It's the bottom line they care about. You think a big corporation is coming to our little town simply out of the goodness of their heart?'

'No,' he said patiently—far more patiently than he was actually feeling at the condescending tone his daughter had just used towards him. 'Of course their plan is to make money—that's business. And maybe you're right, maybe they don't care about the community, but the reality is, if it wasn't something that people wanted then they wouldn't have so many developments all over the country, would they? These communities are what a lot of older people want, so why not bring one here?'

'Because of the ripple effect that dumping a huge site like that in a small town like ours will cause.'

'Okay, so there'll be ripples. Some of those ripples will be beneficial for people here. New jobs. New people. Growth. Tourism—'

'Added strain on our infrastructure.'

'Fair point,' Sully acknowledged, 'and that's something that needs to be addressed. I'm fairly certain that a company as big as this one would have already looked into all this and at least have offered some kind of solution.'

'This is why we need to go to the meeting,' Gabby declared almost triumphantly, and Sully muttered a silent curse as he just realised he'd talked himself into a corner. 'I'll drive,' she said, sending him a smug grin.

Just how he wanted to spend his day off.

The surf club, situated in the park reserve, had always been a gathering place for groups and private events. Its prime location, nestled in against the headland rockface overlooking the main beach, was a developer's dream, but tonight the seating was facing away from the windows to focus on the small stage area, where a long table had been set up. A number of men and women dressed in business suits waited patiently behind the table for the crowd to quieten and take their seats.

By the time Alex got inside she discovered it was a full house with standing room only, which suited her fine, as she hoped to make a quick exit and that was far easier to do standing close to the door. She spotted Tanya and a few people she recognised in the centre of the audience but didn't attempt to catch their eyes. She'd rather not draw any attention to herself by squeezing her way along the rows of already seated locals.

On the other side of the room sat a group of Duncans—surly and intimidating and taking up the entire back row. Alex felt herself shrink instinctively, but none of them seemed to have spotted her. She made sure she remained out of their line of sight. They would be unlikely supporters of Murna's cause. She didn't kid herself that they were here out of any community-minded spirit, though—their reasons would be purely self-serving; namely, to stop any more outsiders coming in and sniffing around their dealings.

The hundred different conversations around the room finally settled once the spokesperson for the company stood up and welcomed everyone to the meeting.

'Ermon Nicholades is a small company that prides itself on its community-focused projects. We're not a worldwide conglomerate like many of the other big-name players in this field—all our profits stay in the community. We are focused on wellbeing and environmentally sustainable building. Our villages are created to live in harmony with the natural environment, and our planning and building decisions take into consideration the environmental, social and economic situations of the areas we build in. Put simply, we are not a one-size-fits-all conglomerate.'

The presentation was slick and professionally produced, showcasing the company's projects and revealing a futuristic draft concept of what their new over 55–living community would look like.

Alex was suitably impressed. The development looked amazing.

The atmosphere in the room, although quietly respectful as people listened, felt somewhat hostile once the presentation ended. Alex supposed the people fronting the meeting were probably used to that kind of response whenever a new development was announced in a smaller community. Still, she couldn't help but feel slightly sorry for them as the questions from the crowd began.

'We can't cope with the holiday population as it is— how is bringing in more people going to help the situation?

Water, sewerage and infrastructure are already at capacity,' one man yelled.

'What about traffic coming into town? Our roads are already stuffed,' someone else added.

'And there's not enough parking for locals,' another piped up.

A woman in her early sixties with a tightly pulled back grey bun and dressed in a business-like skirt and suit jacket, calmly stood and nodded sagely. 'My name's Margaret Catling and I'm the general manager of project sales for the development,' she said smoothly. 'I hope to answer all your questions, but one at a time.'

Margaret spent the next half an hour explaining the benefits their project would provide the community as well as a long list of success stories from other communities where they'd developed retirement villages.

'And what about the doctor shortage? Do you know how hard it is to get an appointment around here? Up to two months is the standard waiting time. Two months to get an appointment with your doctor? And you want to bring in more people who'll be needing medical treatment?' a younger woman demanded from the front of the room.

'Unfortunately, this isn't just a local problem. GP shortages are happening everywhere in regional Australia. And we agree, this isn't acceptable, which is why a medical centre is included in our community.'

'For your residents, I assume?' Murna replied.

'Yes, which won't add to the pressure on your local resources.'

'It doesn't help us, though, does it?' a man yelled.

'It's not their job to fix the medical system,' a young woman called back, sparking a further debate about whose responsibility it was, until Margaret intervened and got everyone back on topic.

Interesting, Alex thought. It seemed not everyone here was against the development.

'Our company understands that sometimes the introduction of a development such as this one, despite the fact we value environmental sustainability and take great care in designing our houses and landscapes to blend with and complement the environment we build in, can cause some extra stress on the greater community surrounding us. Which is why we plan on being as inclusive as possible. We have a design team working on walking and cycling tracks that will link our community to the town and provide public access and leisure activities. We hope to contribute to the upgrading of the main road into town, along with council and other bodies responsible, to improve access for locals as well as our community. And, of course, there are a number of opportunities for local employment. Once we're up and running we'll need groundskeepers, cleaners and kitchen staff, just to name a few. The construction will include a number of local trades as well as the added custom this in turn will bring to town to support established businesses.'

The woman was saying all the things that the locals had hoped to hear and yet Murna and her team were like a pack of fox terriers, refusing to let go of the arguments surrounding the lack of housing for families and the ongoing impact of a population explosion in the area.

'All these rich, elderly people coming to town,' one woman, dressed in a pair of denim overalls and sandals, threw out scathingly, 'taking up valuable housing and pushing out local people. What gives them the right?'

'How dare hard-working retirees even think about living out their best years in paradise. Shame on them!' someone from the front of the room announced drolly, raising a few chuckles in response.

'Our younger people need housing!' the woman in overalls shouted back.

'Did it occur to anyone that maybe some of our local over fifty-fives might want the kind of lifestyle that's on offer and be among the buyers of these new homes? And that, by doing so, they'd be freeing up established properties for new buyers?' a man down the front, sitting with his arms folded across his chest, said calmly.

'You don't know that'll happen,' overalls woman declared.

'I know I'm definitely interested,' the man shot back. 'I currently live in a five-bedroom, two-storey house that's way too big for my wife and me now that the kids have all left town. I don't want to leave Rockne Heads, and the opportunity to buy something on a level block with all those amenities attached? That's lookin' pretty good to me right now.'

'Only the wealthy will be able to afford to buy into it. What about families? What about young people? How is this development going to help them?' another woman yelled out from the back.

'It's called a flow-on effect,' a middle-aged woman in the centre of the room piped up. 'I buy into the development, which then frees up my house for someone else.'

'Maybe not everyone is in a position to buy your house,' a man sitting beside overalls woman piped up. 'Some of us rent.'

'Maybe it'll be an investor who buys my house and then they'll put it up for rent,' the woman countered.

'You can't guarantee that, though,' he said defiantly. 'And anyway, once this thing goes ahead, the whole vibe of the village will change.'

'They aren't changing anything about the *town*. They aren't building a skyscraper or an eyesore—it's all surrounded by bloody bushland on the outskirts of town. You wouldn't even know it was in there,' an older man put in.

'That's the other thing.' Murna stood back up quickly. 'The wildlife. We've been fighting for a corridor to be declared so that koalas and other native animals have safe passage the entire length of the local coastline.'

'A corridor? How are you planning on doing that?' a woman asked from the centre row. '*The town* sits smack bang in the middle of where you want your corridor. Your house, included, Murna,' she pointed out. 'What are you planning on doing? Moving the whole town?'

'We don't intend to remove any more of the bushland than is absolutely necessary,' Margaret cut in swiftly. 'As you saw in the package we put together, the appeal of our communities is the peace and tranquillity they offer. Destroying the native bushland would go against everything we're hoping to achieve. We have an excellent track record of working closely with environmental groups and ensuring we do things the right way.'

'Sure you do,' Murna scoffed rudely.

Margaret sent Murna a calm yet direct look. 'We welcome you to inspect the environmental policies we've already put in place. We hold ourselves and our reputation to a very high standard—we would take serious offence if it should be unjustly criticised.'

Alex's gaze swivelled back to Murna to see the woman purse her lips resentfully at the lightly veiled threat. It seemed to put an end to that particular line of conversation.

The meeting continued for a further twenty minutes or so before it was wrapped up and a date set to get back to the community with further updates. Alex had been suitably impressed by the professionalism the developer had shown. They hadn't been arrogant or cocky and they'd appeared to listen to the concerns raised with genuine interest. If they managed to come back with suitable arrangements for how to tackle some of these concerns, then Alex couldn't see how Murna and her followers could have any arguments with the development, other than they just didn't agree with progress coming to Rocky.

Sadly, progress eventually came to everywhere. Pretty much no part of the country was untouched by some form of progress or development. The key was to make sure it was the right kind of progress and beneficial to the majority.

'Hey.'

Alex stopped as Sully approached her outside the hall. She hadn't seen him since the night they'd dined aboard his boat.

'I didn't know if you'd be here or not,' he said, holding her gaze lightly, a friendly smile on his lips.

'Murna made some interesting comments the other day and I was curious to see what the developers had to say.'

'I heard you sent her packing when she tried to put a sign up in your front yard.'

'I simply *requested* that she not put one in my front yard.'

'Not how I heard it,' he teased.

'You should know by now to cut any story you hear around here in half and divide it by five,' she said dryly.

'I kinda like the idea of you being rebellious and tough.'

'Really?'

'Yeah, although it does make me feel a little threatened. Murna still scares the hell outta me.'

Alex bit back a smile at the thought of a big, tough fisherman being intimidated by little old Murna. 'It was nice to see that at least the developer wasn't threatened.'

'I don't imagine developers would be easily threatened.'

'Yeah, I suppose not. There were some interesting points raised on both sides, though.'

'Sitting on the fence, are we? That's the diplomat coming out in you.'

'Maybe. Not that it's got anything to do with me,' she said, turning to walk away.

He fell into step with her. 'Well, it should. This is still your hometown.'

'Used to be. Not anymore.'

'I don't think it's as easy as deciding you don't belong to a place anymore, Al,' he said quietly.

'Sure it is.'

'You're able to forget all the good memories of growing up here just because of a few bad ones?'

If only he knew just how bad the bad ones were. 'Apparently I can.'

'That's kind of sad.'

Alex stopped and looked at him. 'That's life, Sully. Sometimes people grow up and they move on from their past. It's called maturing.'

'Well, if that's maturing, then I guess I haven't got there yet, because I wouldn't give up the only good memories I have of this place just because a few bad ones got in the way—not for anything,' he said calmly, holding her eye, before leaving her to continue walking home alone.

16 DECEMBER 2005, 11.30 PM

The night wore on and as long as Alex didn't let herself think about Sully, she could pretend she was having the time of her life.

'Who knew you could be so much fun.' Jamie Duncan had come over and started dancing with her not long after Sully left the party. Jamie was a good-looking guy. He was never short of female company and had a natural swagger that she had to admit was pretty sexy. At some point—she couldn't recall when—Jamie had put his arms around her. She could feel his muscular body against her own as the music continued to pound the air around them. She leaned backwards and let him hold her as she took in the world that had been turned upside down, before she was being pulled back upright and Jamie's hot breath began tracing delicious tracks of kisses down the side of her throat. She wanted to block out the pain and what he was doing felt so good.

'Let's go somewhere quieter. Let me make you feel better. Make you forget all about Sully and what he did,' he whispered roughly against her ear and Alex could do nothing more than nod. She was clammy and hot from dancing and she smelled like smoke from the camp fire. She needed to sit down someplace cooler.

'Al!'

She stopped when Tanya called out to her.

'Are you okay?'

Her friend had found her earlier while she'd let the tears fall and had comforted her the best she could, but they'd separated once they'd returned to the party.

'She's fine,' Jamie called back, without stopping. 'I'll take care of her.'

'Al?' Tanya called again.

Alex waved a careless hand in the air. 'I'm fine.'

Did her words sound a little slurred? She couldn't be sure, but probably. Not that it really mattered. That lovely, floaty, I-don't-care-about-anything feeling was back and all she wanted to do was sit down and maybe even take a little nap for a bit.

Jamie led her further up the beach and they climbed over a few rocks, Alex mainly stumbling and being half-carried by her knight in shining armour, but eventually they came to a small clearing of sand. Waves crashed onto the rocks, showering them with a spray that soaked Alex's dress. The water was refreshing against her hot skin.

She momentarily thought about Sully and tears threatened to invade her drunkenly gathered peace, so she pushed the thought away. She'd give him a bit of his own medicine. See how *he* liked it when he heard about her sneaking away to fool around a bit with someone else. She wasn't going to sleep with Jamie, though—she didn't want to rub it in Sully's face that much. She also had far more respect for herself than that, but she knew talk would get back to Sully tomorrow about who she'd been dancing with and that they'd been all over each other. That would be enough.

'Take one of these,' Jamie said, digging out a packet of small pills from his pocket. 'It'll help you forget all about McCoy.'

She stared at the bag, tempted, but reason kicked in and she shook her head. 'No thanks,' she said when he shook the bag.

'Come on,' he coaxed, then shrugged when she continued to shake her head. 'Your loss.' He took out a pill and swallowed it before shoving the bag back into his pocket. Alex had heard the talk about beach parties and drugs—the two kind of went hand in hand—but she'd never actually been offered any before.

'Here, I'll help,' Jamie said, when she tugged at the wet top of her dress, which was sticking to her skin.

Before she could protest, he reached down and took the hem of her dress, lifting it up over her head in a swift movement, leaving her standing before him scantily covered in now see-through underwear. When she went to cover her chest with her arms, he pulled them away.

'Don't hide now. I've been watching you all night—those tits of yours bouncing about. Now I get to see them.'

His words immediately cut through her buzz. This wasn't how it was supposed to be going. She tried to take her dress from him, but he dropped it to the ground and grabbed her, his fingers digging painfully into her upper arms.

'Let me go!' she yelled, squirming and twisting, but his grip only got harder. He slammed her up against the nearby rocks and she felt the sting of sharp oyster and limpet shells scratch her back.

She screamed, but barely had the sound passed her lips when it was followed by a hard slap to the side of her head that made her ears ring and then she didn't scream any more.

She felt the hard wet sand beneath her back as Jamie pushed her to the ground. In a way it felt almost soothing against the scratches, until the sand began rubbing into them as his weight pushed her down. She couldn't move—she could barely breathe. Alex felt the hot trail of tears that ran down the side of her face and she begged silently for it to stop.

When Jamie rolled away, everything inside Alex screamed at her to get up, but she couldn't make her legs move. Jamie lay on his back, one arm over his face as he caught his breath. Her eyes moved to the rocks—large, black shadows, like crouching monsters, looming behind them. Something moved.

A chill crept over her skin and nausea swelled inside her. She had to move. Now. The urgency shocked her into action.

She didn't know why—all she knew was there was something evil in the night and she had to run.

17 DECEMBER 2005, 12.15 AM

The needle-like sting of the water falling from the shower head onto her back helped take Alex's mind off the pain everywhere else as she sat on the floor of the shower and cried. She'd scrubbed herself almost raw as soon as she'd got home, discarding the ripped remains of her clothing, which she'd hastily gathered and tugged on at the beach, before stepping under the hot water, desperate to rid herself of any remaining memory of Jamie Duncan and his filthy touch.

How could she be so stupid? She was an idiot. She'd willingly walked away from the party with him. She'd put herself in the very situation her parents had ever warned her *not* to put herself in. Nausea returned as images flashed through her mind. She stared at her legs and arms, covered in red marks and scratches. They'd be bruises soon.

Alex dragged herself back up to her feet and took the soap once again, lathering up the cloth and scouring her skin until the hot water went cold and she was too exhausted to stand up any longer. No matter how hard she scrubbed, she still couldn't get rid of the sensation that he was all over her.

She dragged herself to bed, wrapped in only a towel, and climbed under the covers, willing oblivion to come and take her away.

Eleven

Alex walked into the Paragon and smiled as she caught Tanya's eye from behind the counter. She spotted a table for two across the room and made a beeline towards it, passing a larger table with a group of people. Too late, she recognised the anti-progress, anti-everything gang were having some kind of tactical meeting, with Murna in full preacher mode. Alex couldn't turn around and leave, so she continued past the group.

'Has anyone heard anything about that land over on Hadley's Headland? I've noticed a bit of activity going on lately—cars driving in and out, and they've put that monstrosity of a padlock on the gate. Can you imagine? We've had access to that land for years and now suddenly someone's decided no one else can use it.'

'Wasn't it bought recently?' a tall willowy man in striped cheesecloth pants and an open-neck linen shirt asked.

'Apparently. But still, it's been vacant for years. You can't just suddenly lock it up and tell people they can't walk their dogs in there anymore.'

Well, technically, you can, Alex thought, *if you own the land.*

'They would have paid a fortune for it, with those views,' a bird-like woman said, before taking a dainty sip from her teacup.

'I heard it was a celebrity who bought it,' a third woman added, her riot of red, curly hair bobbing as she nodded.

'I heard it was one of the Hemsworths.'

'Oh, great. Just what we need,' cheesecloth man moaned. 'Look what happened up north. A bunch of celebrities moved in and the cost of living skyrocketed. Locals were forced out of their own towns. Well, if they think that's happening here, they've got another think coming.'

Alex concentrated on not rolling her eyes. *Here we go. Murna will be adding 'Remove all celebrity types from purchasing property' to her hit list.*

The little bird lady tsked. 'It's not right.'

'Ready to order?' Tanya asked, coming to a stop beside Alex and placing a small bottle of chilled water and a glass on her table.

'Ready to stop biting my tongue. Honestly, how do you listen to all their crap all day and not snap?'

'You get used to it. I usually don't pay them any mind. They mean well.'

'Do they? 'Cause from an outsider listening in, it sounds like they're doing more harm than good. The other day they were blaming sand erosion on the beach on the influx of holidaymakers to town—*next* to a table of holidaymakers. That's the kind of thing that does damage to things like your business.'

Tanya sighed. 'Yeah, I know. I don't think we're the only coastal community that has a love–hate relationship with tourism, though.'

'What do you mean?'

'Well, the thing is, yeah, businesses need the tourists to earn a living, but there's a big downside too. During the holiday season, the tourists considerably outnumber the locals, so locals get pushed out of their cafes and restaurants. They can't get a car park in town. They suddenly have a million people on their usually empty beaches and there's more noise with so many families and kids about. It can be a huge inconvenience.'

'But holidays have always made this place busier. We used to love it—it was exciting with all the hot new guys coming to town for a few weeks over Christmas,' Alex reminded her friend, wiggling her eyebrows as she remembered Tanya finding a holiday romance with a boy from Sydney when they were fourteen.

'It was busy back then but nowadays it's completely over the top. They expanded the caravan park a few years ago so it's doubled the number of bookings it can take and it's always at capacity.'

'Then maybe the answer is investing in some new businesses to cater for the numbers. Create more local jobs. But then, Murna and her crew would make it their mission to stop it.'

'There's no simple fix unfortunately.'

'Yeah, but sitting back and not trying to fix anything is also not the answer.'

Tanya twisted her lips wryly. 'Welcome back to life in Rocky.'

After Tanya took her order, Alex poured herself some water and pondered their conversation. It was funny—as a kid she'd never really given anything like this a second thought, but now that she was, she did recall her parents grumbling about the crowds and the tourists who came to town around holiday time. She hadn't thought anything of it and had always liked when their small town came to life—everything took on a new energy. There were new faces around and everyone always seemed relaxed and happy because they'd escaped their everyday work life and were on holidays. Not to mention all the extra stuff that always happened to take advantage of the crowds—the markets and the food festival the town was famous for and that drew people from everywhere, and the fireworks display—it all happened around peak holiday time. They made up some of the best memories of her childhood.

Alex noticed an older woman at the counter had struck up conversation with a younger woman as they waited for their takeaway orders. Alex recognised the older woman as Mrs Burtrum, who'd been a friend of her mother's and part of the local CWA. She waited for a break in their conversation to catch Mrs Burtrum's eye to say hello.

'I think Murna runs a book club,' Mrs Burtrum said, looking up to search the cafe before waving her hand in the air. 'Murna.'

Murna had been talking and seemed annoyed by the interruption as she looked up.

'This young lady was just enquiring if there were any book clubs in town. You still run one, don't you?'

'I do, but we're full,' Murna replied briskly.

'Full?' Mrs Burtrum repeated with a confused frown.

'Yes. We have enough people. We're not taking any new members.'

'Oh,' Mrs Burtrum said, clearly taken aback by the blunt dismissal as Murna returned to her conversation.

'Actually,' Alex said, drawing the attention of the two women at the counter, 'I'm hosting a book club tomorrow night. I'd love it if you could come along.'

The woman's surprised smile drew a weak one from Alex in return. She had no idea where her outburst had come from, but after listening to Murna waffle on, witnessing her self-righteous attitude just now had been the last straw.

'How lovely, Alex, dear.' Mrs Burtrum nodded approvingly. 'I didn't even see you sitting over there. How are you, darling?'

'I'm really good, thanks. You're invited too of course, Mrs Burtrum,' Alex said, standing up to join the two women, and this time her smile was far more confident. 'Seven pm.'

'Gloria, you RSVP'd to the committee planning meeting tomorrow night,' Murna butted in unexpectedly. 'And you were bringing the sandwiches.'

'Oh. So I am. I'll drop them off on my way. Do make my apologies for the meeting, Murna,' Mrs Burtrum said before calmly turning her back on Murna.

'Alex Kelly,' Alex said, introducing herself to the bemused woman.

'Terri . . . Gordon. It's great to meet you. Ah, whereabouts will the meeting be?' she asked nervously.

'At my place. I'm the white house at the top of the headland. You can't miss it.'

'Thank you, I'm really excited,' Terri said, her smile broadening as she took her coffee from Tanya and waved goodbye.

'Are you in a rush to head off?' Alex asked Mrs Burtrum. 'I've got a table.'

'I have an appointment soon, but I'd love to catch up. I've been meaning to pop in and say hello,' Mrs Burtrum said, taking a seat at the table. 'It's been such a long time since I've seen you. I keep in touch with your mum, of course, and she fills me in on how you've been going, but it's just so nice to see you back here again.'

'It's . . . strange being back.'

'Yes, well, it would be, I suppose, after everything . . .' The woman's words trailed off then she brushed the awkwardness away like an irritating speck of dust. 'But look at you.' Her wide smile crept back onto the face that still looked so familiar even after all this time. In fact, the woman seemed to have barely aged. 'Living in London! How exciting.'

'Sometimes I still pinch myself,' Alex admitted.

'It must be wonderful,' Mrs Burtrum said in a dreamy tone. 'I've always wanted to go there, but I still haven't gotten around to it.'

'You should. There's so much to see. I'd be happy to play tour guide if you ever do decide to come over.'

'Oh, that would be lovely!'

'Coffee's ready, Mrs Burtrum,' one of the waitresses called.

'Oh, that's me, pet. I better go.'

'See you tomorrow.'

'Interesting. I don't recall you mentioning anything about a book club meeting the other day,' Tanya murmured as she delivered the burger Alex had ordered.

Alex shrugged. 'The idea just came to me.'

'Hmm . . . This new Alex is a lot feistier than the old one.'

'I just don't like seeing people being excluded.'

'So a book club, huh?'

'Will you come? I've never hosted a book club before. I have no idea what I'm doing.'

For a moment, Alex thought Tanya might refuse, but she smiled and gave a small nod.

'Sure. Why not? It could turn out to be a riot.'

'Well, probably not, with only you, me, Mrs Burtrum and Terri.'

'Leave it with me, I'll round us up a few more readers and we'll make a party of it.'

'Okay,' Alex agreed, before adding a cautious, 'but not too many . . . I mean, it's not going to be a street party or anything.'

'Don't worry, I've got it all under control,' Tanya said, collecting the empty water bottle and heading out the back.

Oh, dear. What had she done? She was supposed to be packing, not hosting a party.

She glanced at Murna's table and saw the woman getting to her feet to leave. For a moment she held Alex's eye before giving a haughty sniff and leaving the cafe, disciples in tow.

Later that day, Alex carried a basket up and down the aisles of the little supermarket, tossing in an assortment of soft cheeses and dips before heading next door to the bottle shop for wine. She still couldn't believe she'd actually volunteered to host a book club. She should have just let Murna do her thing instead of letting the woman's attitude get the better of her.

Outside the bottle shop a thin woman dressed in a wraparound sarong and a white singlet top leaned against the wall, smoking a cigarette.

'Hey. You're Alex Kelly, aren't ya?'

Alex braced herself. 'Yes,' she said slowly.

'You probably don't remember me. I'm Cassie Newton.'

She'd been younger than Alex at school, but looking at her now, Alex was shocked at how different Cassie looked. Her long thin hair hung unwashed and unbrushed around a thin face and the hand that was holding the cigarette to her mouth seemed unsteady. Her blue eyes narrowed as she blew out a long slow stream of smoke.

'Oh. Hi. I remember you from school,' Alex said, trying for a smile, still unsure if this was going to be a friendly exchange or not.

'You've certainly stirred the pot comin' back, haven't ya,' the woman remarked, dropping the cigarette butt to the ground and stepping on it before immediately lighting another.

'Have I?' Alex asked.

'You should hear the Duncans goin' off about it.'

'I can imagine. Nice to see you, Cassie,' she said, taking a step away.

'He was a piece of shit,' Cassie said.

'Sorry?' Alex eyed the woman quizzically.

'Jamie. You did the world a favour, if ya ask me.'

Alex was too surprised to immediately reply, feeling like an owl as she blinked at the woman. 'I didn't do anything.'

Cassie shrugged and tilted her chin back to blow smoke into the air above them. 'Whatever.'

To argue the point would only make her seem as though she was being defensive, so Alex bit back another denial and walked away.

Cassie's comment stayed with her for the remainder of the trip home. It was odd, to say the least. There were very few people who had ever come out and said how they really felt about Jamie at the time. Since his death, he'd been elevated to near sainthood—at least by his family—and the rest of the town had suddenly forgotten about the fact he'd had a substantial police record and was by no means an angel.

18 DECEMBER 2005, 9.30 AM

Saturday had been horrendous. She'd been vomiting almost nonstop since the early hours of the morning and her head throbbed relentlessly. Everything ached, and her back pulsated where the rocks had left deep scratches, a constant reminder of what Jamie had done. She'd found it hard to sleep; as soon as she allowed herself to relax, memories of being held down and pushed roughly into the sand would wake her, casting her into that dark, horrible moment again and again. She was exhausted, drained from crying and lack of sleep. By late afternoon, though, she'd managed to stop throwing up and had dragged herself to the shower and got dressed then forced down a few dry crackers.

She'd ignored her phone ringing. There was no way she was up to talking to anyone about the night before—even Tanya—so after typing in a short message that she was hungover and sleeping, she turned the phone off and hid it in the bottom of her drawer. But Alex's silence hadn't stopped Tanya, who had come over to see her. Alex had ignored the knocking and stayed in bed. She couldn't face anyone yet—not even her best friend. It was too soon.

By Sunday morning, though, she'd had to pull herself together, because her parents were due home. Her dad had gone straight to the station on arrival and Alex, still nursing a whopper of a headache, had pleaded the onset of a cold and gone back to bed.

Now Alex groaned as the phone beside her rang. With a resigned sigh, she answered.

'It's about time! Where the hell have you been? I've been calling you.'

'I was hungover,' Alex said in a low voice, mindful of her mother somewhere in the house.

'I was worried about you. You took off without saying goodbye on Friday night,' Tanya said.

'Yeah, I ... was pretty drunk. I didn't want to bother you. I just went home.'

'So have you heard?'

'Heard what?'

'About Jamie Duncan.'

Instantly, Alex's focus cleared. 'What about him?' she asked slowly—almost fearfully. Had someone found out?

'He's dead. His body was found this morning.'

'What?' Alex couldn't feel her lips and her fingers had begun to go tingly where they clutched the phone tightly.

'I know! It's crazy. We only just saw him Friday night and now he's ... dead.'

Oh my God, oh my God, oh my God. Dead?

'Al? Did you hear me?'

'Sorry? What?'

'I said, did you see anything?'

'Me? Why would I have seen anything?'

'Well, you were with him that night. Was he acting weird or anything?'

'I don't know,' Alex said hastily, 'I wasn't with him long . . . I felt sick so I went home.'

The other end of the line went silent briefly. Then Tanya said, 'Al, you probably should know . . . people are talking.'

'About what?'

'Well, with all the stuff going on with Jamie, you know, everyone has their own theory about how he died. There's a bit of talk about you from the party and everyone who was there.'

'Me? What would I have to do with it?'

'I'm just saying, people saw you with him that night.'

'I don't understand. That was two days ago.'

'He's been missing since Friday night. Alex, I think you might have been the last one to see him alive.'

18 DECEMBER 2005, 11.40 AM

Alex heard her father's police four-wheel drive pull up in the driveway and her heart began thudding painfully inside her chest. The front door opened and then there was murmuring in the kitchen before the heavy black boots her father wore to work thudded along the hallway and came to a stop outside her bedroom.

Alex's heart momentarily paused its panicked beating, and she closed her eyes almost in defeat as the knock rapped on her door.

She'd grown up seeing her father in uniform—it had always made her feel safe and a little proud. Although at home he always seemed a bit gentler somehow, he was never too far from the no-nonsense, reserved demeanour he used at work. That softer side was nowhere to be seen today. Bill Kelly was wearing his gun and his baton and he wasn't smiling. For the first time in her entire life, Alex didn't see her dad standing in front of her, it was just a policeman—intimidating and terrifying.

'Alex, I need to ask you some questions.'

Alex swallowed and nodded, biting back the urge to cry. She walked past him to the kitchen and sat down slowly, hiding the wince of pain the action caused.

'Did you know James Duncan?' her father asked, getting straight to the point.

'I know of him,' Alex said. Her mother hovered in the background, fussing about as she made a pot of tea.

'Where were you Friday night?'

'At Tanya's,' she said calmly, holding her father's gaze. 'Having a sleepover.'

'Were you both there all night?'

'That's what a sleepover implies,' she said.

Her father slammed the table with his hand, making her jump. Her mother dropped a teacup. 'This isn't a game, Alex. Where were you Friday night?'

She knew that he knew exactly where she'd been and that she'd been linked to Jamie at the party. There was no point trying to deny it, so she lifted her eyes and met his firmly.

'I was at a party on Little Beach.'

'Were you with James Duncan?'

'Yes. As were lots of people.'

'Were you with him alone?'

Alex fought to keep the rising panic from her expression. 'For a while. Yes.'

'What time was that?'

'I don't know. I wasn't wearing my watch.'

'What time,' her father demanded.

'I don't know!'

'Alex, this is important. *Think*. I need you to tell me a time.'

Alex shook her head in frustration but did her best to think back to the hazy events of that night. 'I don't know, maybe sometime before midnight? Just after? Why?'

She saw her father slump in his chair and close his eyes.

'Bill?' her mother asked, taking a nervous step towards the table.

'What happened?' her father asked, after apparently finding some last strands of calm.

'What do you mean?' Alex's chest squeezed painfully again.

'What happened when you were with the Duncan boy?'

'Nothing. We just . . . talked. He'd been drinking.'

'Were you?'

'A bit,' she admitted. 'I'm almost eighteen,' she added with a touch of defiance.

'Almost isn't eighteen, though, is it? Was he inebriated?'

Only a policeman would use that term. 'Not really. But he'd had a fair bit.'

'And then what? Did you leave together? Go somewhere else?'

'I left him there and went home.'

'He was alone?'

A memory of that dark shadow flashed through her mind again and she gave a slight shiver. 'Yeah.'

'You're positive there was no one else . . . no other witnesses?'

'Witnesses? To what?'

'To his possible murder, Alex,' her father snapped. 'His body was found in the water by his family and they're claiming he's been murdered. He's been missing since Friday night and everyone we've spoken to so far has said the last person he was with *was you*, Alex. So I'm asking you again. Are you positive that he was alone when you left him?'

'Yes,' Alex stammered, frowning. 'At least, I think so. It was dark—I don't know.'

The long sigh her father let out was anything but encouraging and Alex nervously picked at her fingernails.

'I need to know everything that happened that night, leading up to you coming home.'

Slowly, Alex replayed the bits of the night she could remember, leaving out the fight with Sully and what happened when she was alone with Jamie. She knew from the look on her father's face that he was aware she wasn't telling him everything. She was fairly sure the police had a rule about family interviewing family even if this was in their kitchen instead of at the station. There was probably a lot to be said for having someone who knew you so well asking the questions and looking for the truth.

'Did something happen that night you want to tell me about?' her father asked after sitting in silence when she'd finished speaking. His voice had softened slightly and Alex bit down hard on the inside of her lip to keep from telling him everything. There was no way she could ever tell her father about what Jamie Duncan had done to her. He would never look at her the same way ever again. The humiliation of anyone ever finding out would be too much to handle.

So instead, she shook her head and hardened her heart. 'I drank too much and I felt sick. Jamie was lying on the ground. I think he fell asleep. I left him there and went home.'

'Had he been in a fight with anyone that night?'

'Not that I saw.'

'So when you left him, he was sleeping. But completely fine?'

Alex nodded, wondering what other information her father seemed to have.

'If you know anything else, you need to tell me now, Alex.'

'There's nothing,' she told him irritably.

He sighed again, then stood up. 'Okay. You're going to have to come down to the station and make a statement.'

'Oh, Bill, surely not? She just said she didn't know anything.'

'Monica, she was probably the last person to see the kid alive. She's a witness and we need her to make a statement. That's all. Get your things, Alex.'

There was a small crowd gathered at the front of the police station by the time her father pulled up. Alex heard him swear under his breath.

'Don't say anything, just get inside, okay?'

Alex nodded, but her eyes widened slightly as three burly men, all Duncans, approached them.

'We wanna know what's going on. What have you lot found out?' a grey-haired, round-faced man wearing a black beanie demanded, stepping in close to her father.

'Russell, I told you, we're getting statements from everyone who was at that party. Once we've got those together we should have a better idea about what happened.'

'We already know *something* happened and everything points to *her* knowing what it was.'

The man pointed his podgy finger at her and her dad hurried her along with a hand on her back, making her wince and arch away in pain. She caught her father's brief glance, but didn't stop moving. Once inside, she was led into an office and told to wait for an officer to come and take her statement.

By the time she'd finished, the crowd out the front had grown. Alex shrank against her father as he led her to the four-wheel drive. The crowd mostly consisted of Jamie's family—and none of them was happy. A reporter shoved a microphone towards her after asking why she'd been taken into the station and if she had any information about Jamie and what happened to him.

'Get that thing out of her face,' her father growled, pushing the microphone aside.

'Sergeant Kelly, is your daughter being questioned for the murder of James Duncan?'

'No, she is not. She's simply giving a statement, like everyone else who was at the beach that night. And this is not a murder investigation. The coroner is yet to examine the body. Get your facts straight before you go around stirring up trouble.'

'My son was murdered!' Russell Duncan yelled from the crowd. 'We know it and so does everyone else.'

Alex clenched her hands together tightly in her lap to stop them shaking as she stared out the windscreen at the sea of angry people. She caught sight of a familiar face near the back and the tears she'd fought so valiantly began to fall. *Sully.* All she wanted was to feel those strong arms around her.

Then she remembered they were no longer hers to have, and the tears fell faster.

Twelve

Alex opened her computer and sorted through her emails. Technically she was on leave and she'd resisted the urge to check into work too often, but there had been a few small details that the perfectionist in her wanted to keep an eye on. So far, though, it seemed her replacement had everything under control. Maybe Alex wasn't as indispensable as she thought she was? The idea should have been slightly more alarming to her. Once, she would have flown into a panic and started questioning why things were running so smoothly without her. Now she only felt relieved that she didn't have any problems to try and untangle from the other side of the world.

A text message beeped, drawing her attention away from the computer. She picked up her phone. *Tanya better not be cancelling on me for tomorrow.*

There's something you need to see, the message read. There was a link included.

Curious, Alex opened the link and found herself staring at the front page of the local newspaper, posted on a Facebook group.

LOCAL ROCKNE HEADS FAMILY DEMAND JUSTICE, the headline screamed. The page featured a large photo of Russell Duncan and his wife, Maureen, who cradled a photo of James to her chest. They looked sombrely at the camera, while their son Tom stood behind them.

> *Local parents Russell and Maureen Duncan say they are planning to petition the courts to have their son's case reopened eighteen years after his tragic death. The family of the late James Duncan, who fell to his death after a beach party in 2005, have always insisted that their son was murdered and have never accepted the coroner's report that ruled his death as accidental.*
>
> *'There were just too many unanswered questions and delays with the body being examined. Vital evidence could have been lost by the time the coroner performed the autopsy—police stuffed the investigation up at every turn and our son's killer got away with murder,' Mr Duncan said.*
>
> *Police have declined to comment on the matter.*

Alex put her phone down as a million different emotions raced through her. Why would they reopen the case? Why now? It made no sense.

She suspected her return was the most obvious reason. But it had all happened eighteen years ago. And her father was dead—there was no longer any reason to continue their war on him for his part in ruining the Duncans' drug business. Why couldn't they just accept that their son had died in a tragic accident, not helped by the fact he was drunk and under the influence of God only knew what drugs he'd taken.

Alex fought to control the return of the helplessness she'd drowned in so long ago. She was over feeling powerless and scared. She wanted to curl up in her bed under the covers and block it all out.

19 December 2005

Alex hadn't slept. How could she, when the whole town had apparently decided she was a murderer? It was a nightmare. If only she could sleep, then maybe when she woke up she'd realise it had, in fact, been some terrible, ridiculous nightmare.

Only it wasn't. Just on two o'clock in the morning, a rock had come through their front window, spraying a shower of glass across the living room floor. By the time her father had gone outside, the car had disappeared, but there was no doubting that it had most likely been one of the Duncans.

At six o'clock, a police car from Moreville pulled up outside and a detective came to the front door.

Alex sat on the edge of her bed, listening anxiously to the low conversation in the living room.

'Bill, we can't be seen as showing any favouritism just because she's your daughter,' the female detective was saying when Alex came out of her room. 'The Duncans are making a noise about it.'

'The Duncans are nothing more than a bunch of thugs who think they're untouchable. No one's going to listen to them, Jackie.'

'The superintendent is. This station has already had one corruption investigation and he doesn't want the headache of dealing with another one.'

'There's no corruption going on in my station,' her father said stiffly. 'They can bellow and carry on till the cows come home. I've got nothing to hide and neither do any of my officers. My daughter is being treated like any other witness.'

'Yes, but we have no leads, and the coroner's time of death points to Alex being the last person who saw him before he died.'

'*Died* being the operative word here,' her father snapped. 'Until that report comes back, we don't even know if there *is* a crime. We don't know how he died.'

'Agreed. However, we still have to look like we're doing something in the meantime. Looking at all avenues. Especially since we have a potential suspect who happens to be the police sergeant's daughter. You see how it looks, Bill?'

'I don't give a shit how it looks, detective.'

'We need to make sure—for Alex's protection as well— that we're doing everything we can to properly investigate the family's claims.'

'She's already given a statement.'

'We'd like to take her back in.'

'Why? Just to make some kind of show for the bloody Duncans? I don't think so.'

'You were there when she gave her statement, Bill. She might not be involved in the kid's death, but there's definitely something she isn't telling us.'

Her father gave a weary sigh. 'I'll bring her down.'

'That's fine, but you won't be sitting in on the interview.'

'She's my kid.'

'I understand that, but I think we have more of a chance to get to the bottom of whatever she's hiding without her father—the cop,' she added pointedly, 'in the room. Look, Bill, I get it,' the detective said, lowering her voice further. 'It rubs the wrong way to be giving the Duncans any special treatment, but like you said, we're waiting for the coroner's report and all this is just for show to keep them happy so they stop throwing around all this corruption crap.'

'I'll go in with her,' her mother's quiet, yet firm voice piped up. Until now, her mother hadn't said a great deal, but there was a strength Alex hadn't heard very often, echoing through her voice now.

Alex closed her eyes, struggling to hold back a rush of panic. How had everything gone so terribly wrong? All she'd wanted was one night to let her hair down and have fun. She should have just gone home.

She breathed in a long, steady breath then blew it out silently. She could get through this. She had to. She'd just tell them everything she'd already told them and then she could climb back into her bed and pull the covers over her head and pretend that stupid party had never happened.

'Alex, I know you've already given us a statement about the party and when you last saw Jamie, but we just have a few more questions about something else that happened that night.'

Alex eyed the female detective warily. Detective Rushton had a no-nonsense kind of aura and looked almost mannish in her ill-fitting black pants and jacket. They hadn't charged her with anything—there was no crime so far. At least, not until they had some kind of evidence that suggested Jamie's death wasn't an accident. Her mother gave her hand a reassuring squeeze. Alex just wanted to get this over with.

'There've been a few reports of an argument earlier in the evening between Sullivan McCoy and Karla Robinson. Were you present during this?'

'Yes.'

'Did you hear what the argument was about?'

'What's that got to do with Jamie?'

'Possibly nothing. But can you answer the question?'

Alex shrugged. 'She'd been trying to call him and he hadn't been answering her calls.'

'Were they a couple?'

'No,' Alex said, as her stomach dropped and a wave of despair washed through her once more.

'Then why were they arguing?'

'It's got nothing to do with me. Why don't you ask them?'

'We have. At least, we've asked Karla. Sully seems to be out at sea, but we'll be talking to him as soon as he arrives back in port.' The detective tilted her head slightly. 'Karla said the argument was because she believes she's pregnant with Sully's baby.'

Alex clenched her jaw and lowered her gaze to the tabletop. She could feel the prick of hot tears forming on her lower eyelids and fought to keep them at bay.

'Alex, were you and Sully a couple?'

'What has any of this got to do with anything?' Alex snapped. 'You're supposed to be working out what happened to Jamie.'

'There's a possibility that the two situations are connected.'

'What?' Alex asked frowning.

'If Sullivan McCoy was your boyfriend, and you and Jamie went off alone, then that could give Sully a motive. Maybe after you left Jamie, Sully confronted him.'

Alex shook her head quickly. 'Sully left the party after he and Karla spoke. Besides, we'd broken up weeks ago. He isn't my boyfriend,' she said and heard the emptiness in her voice. It really was true—she and Sully were no more.

'That's something we need to confirm with Sully once we speak to him,' the detective said almost breezily. 'But it is something we need to look at. Look, I personally don't think this was a murder, as such. I think,' she said, drawing circles on the table with her finger, 'something got out of hand and it was an accident. Either a fight or an argument between Jamie and Sully or maybe Jamie did something that frightened you and you acted in self-defence. Maybe you pushed him or he slipped and fell off the rocks . . .' She left the sentence dangling, watching Alex expectantly from across the table.

Alex returned the woman's stare quietly.

'Alex, I'm trying to help—I *can* help. No matter what happened that night, I can help you, but you have to tell me.'

'I told you what happened. Jamie was alive. I left him on the beach and went home.'

'What about Sully?' Detective Rushton added, eyeing her almost slyly. 'Could he have been angry enough to hurt Jamie if he knew you two had left the party alone?'

'Like I said, we weren't together anymore, and he'd already left the party by then.'

A knock came at the door and Alex looked up to see her father, his face grim but determined. 'I'm taking her home now.'

The detective tossed her pen on the notepad before her and leaned back in her chair to give a drawn-out sigh. 'Fine. We're done here anyway.'

On the short drive home, the interview played over in Alex's head. Sully? A suspect? He would never— Then she remembered she'd never have thought he'd ever sleep with someone else either and look what happened. Still, it concerned her that they might be trying to pin Jamie's death on him somehow.

'How long have you and the McCoy kid been sneaking around?' her father asked as they pulled up outside the house.

Alex swallowed nervously. 'A few months.'

Her father's silence frightened her more than his policeman face. 'I've seen kids around this place get into trouble and do stupid things and I always thought to myself, thank God I have a good kid. 'Cause there you were, sitting at home, studying to make something of yourself. But all this time, you were hanging around a no-hoper like Sullivan McCoy. I thought I knew you, Alexandra.'

'Sully isn't a no-hoper, Dad. He's not like his father.'

'He will be. They all become their fathers around here. There's nothing else for them to do.'

'I hope I don't,' she said, angry that her father would never change his stubborn mind once it was made up about something. 'I hope I don't become angry and bitter and only see the bad in everyone instead of the good.'

'You have no idea what these people are capable of—what they have done, Alex.'

'Other people. In the past. Not Sully. You're not even trying to give him a chance.'

'I know exactly who he is. Just like I know exactly what he's going to become. I just thought you were smarter than that.'

'He's a good person.'

'Does a good person get another girl pregnant?'

Her father's comment stole the breath from her lungs. She could only stare at him as the pain seeped from her heart into the rest of her body, until it came out in a stream of tears. Her father's furrowed brow smoothed slightly, but she reached for the door and clambered out before he could say anything more. There was nothing more to say. Sully and she were over and the future she'd had planned was gone.

Thirteen

Alex groaned at the persistent knocking on the front door. She wanted to ignore it and hope whoever it was went away, but it seemed that wasn't going to happen.

'I knew it,' Tanya said, standing in the doorway.

'Knew what?' Alex asked, her irritation momentarily forgotten.

'That you'd react this way after seeing the Duncan story. You've been hiding under your bed, haven't you?'

'I wasn't hiding under my bed,' Alex said defensively.

Tanya gave a rude snort as she walked in carrying two takeaway coffees, leaving Alex to close the door.

'Here,' Tanya said, handing her one of the cups as she settled herself on the lounge.

'Thank you,' Alex muttered, the last of her indignation deflating. It was hard to stay annoyed when someone brought you coffee.

Neither woman spoke as they sipped at their coffee.

Eventually, Alex gave a small shake of her head. 'I don't understand it. Why won't they let it go?'

'I guess because it's their son. I mean, I'm certainly no huge fan of the Duncans—they've always been trouble—but they're always going to mourn the loss of their child.'

'I get that. I mean, I don't have kids, but I'm not a complete monster—I understand losing a child would be horrendous. I just don't understand why they'd continue to insist it was anything other than a stupid, horrible accident.'

'After everything happened,' Tanya said, 'they were pretty vocal about some of the stuff they reckon the police didn't follow up. I guess, from their point of view, once the coroner said there'd been no murder it would feel like they hadn't been heard.'

'What wasn't followed up?'

'I can't remember now—there was something about a witness who'd heard shouting or someone arguing that night, but the police didn't interview them because they didn't come forward until after Jamie's death was ruled an accident.'

'I didn't hear anything about that,' Alex said slowly.

'How could you, when you'd already taken off?' Tanya replied.

Well, that hurt.

'Look, I think because it's getting close to the anniversary of when it all happened and the stupid rumour mill's firing up again with your arrival back in town, a heap of bad memories have been brought up and they're lashing out.'

'But I wasn't the one who did anything,' Alex said, standing up abruptly. 'It was Jamie the saint, who everyone's feeling sorry for.'

'I probably wouldn't go around saying that out there. I mean, the guy did die. His life ended before it'd barely begun.'

'Maybe he had it coming,' Alex said, walking to the window.

The silence that followed hung heavily between them.

'Alex, that night, when you went off with Jamie,' Tanya said, quietly. 'Nothing . . . happened, did it?'

Alex wanted to let the words tumble out until she didn't have any more words left, but she bit down on her tongue until the urge passed. Nothing good could come of digging that up now.

'Nope.'

'It's just that . . . I've always worried that I let you walk away from the party with him.'

'You didn't let me,' Alex said without turning around. 'I told you it was okay, remember?'

'Yeah, I know . . . it's just that, ever since, I've had this feeling—'

'It was a moment of rebellion.' Alex schooled her features into a smile. 'Nothing else. I was angry at Sully. I guess it was a stupid thing to do and, in hindsight, I wish I'd just gone home instead of becoming the last person to see Jamie before he died.'

'I just wanted to make sure you were okay,' Tanya said, standing up. 'For what's it worth, I don't think the Duncans have got much hope of reopening the case. Everything's going to be all right.' She smiled and Alex hoped she was right. 'Don't hide yourself away, Alex. You've done nothing wrong, remember?'

Alex nodded and this time her smile, weak though it may be, was genuine. 'Thanks for the coffee.'

'No worries. But don't expect it to be home-delivered tomorrow. You have to come into the cafe for the next one.'

Alex watched her friend walk down the front path. She was grateful she had Tanya in her life again.

Her smile faltered as her gaze fell on a car that was parked on the street. Tom Duncan was watching her through its open window. For a moment she was too scared to move. Then she stepped back inside and shut the door behind her firmly, leaning against it as she fought to control the hammering in her chest.

Sully stopped as he watched the Commodore cruise past him before the driver revved the engine and took off with a squeal of tyres and the smell of burning rubber. Tom Duncan. He wondered what the hell he'd been doing up here, then he realised. Alex. He jogged the remainder of the distance to her house and banged on her front door.

He heard a whimper and his instincts went into overdrive. 'Alex? Are you in there? It's Sully.'

There was silence before he heard the rustle of something on the other side of the door and it opened a crack.

Alex peered out at him.

'Are you okay?'

The door eased open and she cleared her throat, nodding quickly. 'I'm fine. You just . . . surprised me. I wasn't expecting you.'

'I just saw Tom Duncan. Was he here?' He wanted to ask, *Did the bastard touch you?* but pulled back on the need to ensure she was safe.

'He drove past. I think he was just trying to rattle me again. It worked,' she said, tucking a strand of hair behind her ear with a hand that shook.

Sully's jaw clenched. The thought of anyone terrifying Alex that way made his blood boil. 'Again? Has he done this before?'

'Not really. He just yelled at me the other day in town.'

'Why didn't you tell me?'

'Why would I?'

'Because I could have said something to him.'

'I don't want you getting involved,' she said, her words sounding a lot firmer.

Well, too bad. He was getting involved. There was no way he was standing by and allowing a prick like Tom Duncan terrorise a defenceless woman.

'Sully. I mean it,' she said, obviously reading his expression correctly. 'This has got nothing to do with you. I don't want you getting mixed up with the Duncans.'

'It wouldn't be the first time. We go back a long way.'

'I know. Which is why I don't want you getting involved in this. You don't need that kind of trouble.'

'The Duncans aren't the crime syndicate they once were. They may have been mixed up in some pretty heavy stuff at one time, but nowadays they're nothing. They're all too wasted and broke to do anything more than make a lot of noise.' It was almost sad how far the family had fallen, but he supposed that's what happened when your entire family got caught up in using the drugs that they were supposed to be selling. He had no time to waste feeling sorry for them, though. They'd had a chance to turn their life around just like he had, only they'd chosen not to.

'It's fine,' Alex said in a clipped tone. 'Can I get you something?' she asked as she led him to the kitchen.

'No, I'm okay, thanks.' He would have killed for something strong to drink if he was being honest, but it was probably too early in the day for that. 'I take it you saw the newspaper?'

'Yes.'

'There's no way they'll reopen that case. There was no case to open in the first place.'

'I know.'

He didn't like the way she was avoiding his eyes. He hated seeing her like this. It reminded him way too much of another place and time. But this was different, he thought, stomping on those memories. This time he was a grown man, not some scared, dumb-arse kid who'd let his girlfriend down.

'Look, don't take this the wrong way, but . . . do you want to come and stay at my place for a few days till all this dies down?'

He watched her blink in surprise.

'I'm sure that won't be necessary,' she said. 'It was a shock, and the whole Tom thing earlier . . . I can't imagine there's any reason to be worried about it turning into anything more. Like I said, he was just trying to rattle me.'

'You said it wasn't the first time. I don't think we should take any chances.'

He watched as her shoulders straightened. 'I'll be fine. Thank you.'

'Do you want me to stay here, then? On the lounge,' he hastily added when he saw her eyebrows raise.

'No. I don't think we need to go to those lengths. I overreacted earlier. Seeing him caught me off guard. I'm perfectly safe here. Besides, I have a lot to do before book club tomorrow night.'

'Book club?' he echoed. He must have missed something.

'Yes. I somehow managed to create a book club in the cafe,' she said.

'Bringing a bit of culture to Rockne Heads?' he asked.

'I don't think Rocky's ready for that.'

'We've got culture coming out of our ears. They had an art exhibition at the surf club last month. Charged people to get in and drink champagne and everything,' he said, keeping a straight face.

'I stand corrected.' She smiled and he felt a warm ripple in response. He'd thought he'd always remembered her smile, but even his best memories hadn't prepared him for the real thing.

'Anyway, I should have plenty of stuff to do to keep me busy enough to forget about Tom Duncan.'

Sully didn't believe she was over the fright of moments before, but clearly she didn't need his help. Other than sleeping on her front verandah, which he didn't think she'd appreciate, there was nothing much else he could do but accept that she was fine.

He glanced at his phone as it rang and swore silently. 'Sorry, I need to take this.'

'Sure.'

Sully snapped out an abrupt hello and listened to the skipper on the end of the line. Great. Another breakdown he didn't need right now. 'Okay. I'll get hold of someone. Come back in as soon as you can,' he said, ending the call, his mind already racing with a million things he needed to get lined up before the boat came back into port. Damn it, he really didn't need another delay right now, he needed the boats out there catching fish before the season ended.

'Sorry, Al, I need to get some stuff sorted. If you need anything, no matter what time day or night,' he said, holding her gaze sternly, 'you call me okay?'

'I will. Thanks, Sully.'

He hesitated then turned away just as his phone started ringing again. He muttered a curse under his breath before letting himself out the front door. What was that old saying, he wondered, half-listening to the gruff voice on the other end of the line . . . Time and tide wait for no man? Something like that. Never a truer word had been spoken in the fishing industry.

Fourteen

Alex must have slept at some point, because she woke the following morning, stretching with a yawn. She made her coffee and took it to the window while she soaked in the ocean view. The draw of the sparkling ocean and the blue skies above was too strong to resist and, after downing her coffee, she tugged on her shoes and headed outside. Some fresh air and sunshine would help clear away the remaining cobwebs of dread she carried around after the previous day.

At some point during the night, she'd decided both Tanya and Sully had probably been right—there really wasn't any reason to think that the Duncans would manage to get Jamie's case reopened after all this time, especially since there was no logical reason to do so. Besides, even if they did, she was innocent. There was no evidence she'd been involved, because she hadn't been anywhere near the headland when he'd fallen. She knew her anxiety had been a knee-jerk reaction to reliving the horrible few days when the whole town had been in a feeding frenzy, with her as the main meal. It wasn't like that now.

She kicked off her shoes as she reached the cold sand and wriggled her toes, closing her eyes and breathing in the salty air. She could almost feel the stress slipping away. She'd missed this.

Her phone interrupted the tranquillity and she looked down to see a FaceTime request from her mother.

'Hi Mum,' Alex said when the screen filled with a blurred, dark shadow. She gave a small chuckle. 'Mum, it's a video call, take it away from your ear.'

There was a moment of muffled conversation before Monica's face appeared and her cheery smile filled the screen. 'Silly me. I thought I just called you.'

'Never mind, it's nice to see you instead,' Alex said, and meant it. She and her mum had always been close and still lived within walking distance of each other, although the majority of their talking seemed to be done via the phone these days. Life with a brood of step-grandchildren to spoil and a newly retired husband to travel with kept Monica Chatsby busy.

'Where are you, darling?'

Alex briefly turned the phone around to show her mother the view.

146

'Oh, it's still so beautiful. I do miss those beaches sometimes.'

'Yeah, not a lot here has changed.'

'I guess that's the beauty of it.'

'I'm not so sure,' Alex said. 'I mean, growing up, I don't really remember feeling like we missed out on anything. But I don't know, unless you're here on holidays, there's really not a great deal to do.'

'All it took to keep you and your friends happy was the beach. You'd disappear all day.'

Alex smiled at that. How times had changed. No parent in their right mind would let a kid go off for a whole day unsupervised these days, getting up to God only knew what. Not that she'd ever really done anything. She'd never really been that rebellious as a kid—not compared to some of the kids she knew.

'I bumped into Tanya and Mrs Burtrum the other day,' Alex said.

'Oh, how lovely. Do give Gloria my regards. And how is Tanya? It was such a shame you lost touch with each other.'

'She's doing great, actually. She owns the old Paragon cafe. We're having a book club tonight.'

'Book club? In Rockne Heads? Well! Things have gotten fancy out there, haven't they.'

'I'm not sure how fancy it'll be, but it should be fun.'

'How's it been . . . with the house?'

'Harder than I'd been expecting.'

'There's a lot of memories tied up with that old house.'

'There are. But, onwards and upwards,' Alex said, forcing some determination into her voice.

'Maybe just allow yourself some time. Don't rush through the process,' her mum said.

'What do you mean?'

'Darling, there was a lot going on when you left Rockne, and the last time you were back was your father's funeral. Those things were both very emotional and I'm not sure you've ever properly dealt with either of them. Maybe this is a good opportunity to just . . . take it all in and process.'

Alex didn't want to process any of it. She just wanted to leave the past in the past where it belonged.

She saw her mother's expression soften before she smiled. 'I know it's not what you do, but just . . .' Monica paused, seemingly choosing her words carefully. 'Think about it. You've needed some time away. Maybe being back in Rockne is where you'll find your focus again.'

Mum and her new age crap. Next she'd be telling Alex to ground herself and listen to some shamanic drumming while she meditated.

'You know, Gloria tells me there's a lovely meditation yoga that she goes to through the week. Maybe you—'

'Ah, Mum, I better get going, I've got a bit of stuff to do before this book club thing tonight. Love you. I'll give you a call in a few days.'

'Okay, darling. I love you too.'

She felt bad cutting her mother off, but she really wasn't in the mood to hear another lecture about dealing with her emotions and all the touchy-feely stuff that went along with it. She'd dealt with her trauma. She was fine.

She wriggled her toes in the sand and looked down, then rolled her eyes. She was not grounding herself, she was just barefoot in the bloody sand and it only felt good because it was the beach! There was no spirituality seeping into her body.

She pulled on her shoes and marched back up to the house.

Alex dragged a few extra chairs into the living room and arranged them into a circle. Eyeing her handiwork critically, she decided it looked passably book-clubbish and headed into the library to select a few books she could use as props on the coffee table to at least make an effort towards the evening's theme.

As she scoured the shelves, her gaze stopped on the spines of a few family photo albums. She slid them out, placing them on the desk. The thinner books that had been leaning against them toppled from the shelf and Alex bent down to retrieve them, shuffling through an assortment of family history booklets and one by the local historical association about the history of Rockne Heads. She turned the last book over and saw that it was the yearbook from her final year at high school. She'd forgotten she even had that. She hesitated briefly before opening the booklet to flip through its pages. Memories flooded back as her gaze fell on a collage of photos taken throughout their last year of school: swimming carnivals, mufti days, excursions and school discos. Her eyes halted on one photo and she peered closer, noticing a group of faces smiling from the dance floor. One face in particular jumped out—Jamie Duncan.

Her throat clenched shut and her breath hitched. Seeing his face had been so unexpected—what had he even been *doing* at the school dance? She saw his arms wrapped around Tiffany Ennis and vaguely remembered something about them dating at one stage. He wasn't even going to school then. He must have somehow sweet-talked his way into the school hall that night—or snuck in, more likely.

Her eyes fixed on the face in the photo and she felt that familiar pins-and-needles sensation threatening to start in her fingertips. Those dark eyes and that smug, arrogant smile—

She shut her eyes tightly in an attempt to block the image from her mind. Jamie no longer had the power to hurt her.

She took a deep breath and opened her eyes, forcing herself to look at him. He was just a twenty-year-old kid, she told herself firmly. She was an adult now. She concentrated on his face, trying desperately to see him for what he was: a guy who was barely out of his teens. Yet still, somehow, she was hurtled back in time. She was still that terrified seventeen-year-old, unable to stop him hurting her.

She slammed the book shut and dropped it in the bin beside the desk. She didn't want to keep a reminder of that year.

She quickly grabbed a few novels for the table, uncaring what they were, and left the room.

❖

'Where are you off to?' Sully asked, looking up from the invoices he was working on at his desk in the office as his daughter walked past wearing make-up and a dress.

'Just a small gathering at Ameil's place.'

'A small gathering?' Sully echoed with a frown. 'That's not code for a party is it?'

'It's a small gathering.'

'How small?'

'I don't know—a few people from school.'

'Are her parents going to be there?'

'Yes,' Gabby said with a huff. 'We'll be suitably chaperoned at all times because heaven forbid we might actually be almost grown adults or something.'

'*Almost* being the operative word.'

'You do realise I'll be leaving soon and I'll be going out to parties at some stage?' she replied, her hands on her hips. 'How exactly do you plan on monitoring me then?'

He'd had a few thoughts on the subject, but he knew she was right. There was no way he could watch over her once she flew the nest and the idea was enough to make him break out in a cold sweat. It wasn't that he didn't trust his daughter—far from it. She was one of the most responsible, sensible people he knew, and that included many adults. It was the unknown that terrified him. All the what ifs and things that could go wrong. She'd been his entire world for eighteen years and letting her go out into the world was a huge thing for him. The world was a big place and she'd only known this very small corner of it. Here she was safe, protected. Out there . . . well, anything could happen. But he was trying to deal with it. It was just taking a little time.

He saw her glance at the newspaper on his desk and resisted the urge to bury it under the paperwork.

'Is it true? What they're saying around town about Alex? Did she really have something to do with that guy's death?'

'No. She didn't.'

'People are saying that there was a cover-up.'

'People obviously have nothing better to talk about. It was ruled an accident and Alex had nothing to do with it.'

'So you and her used to go out together?'

'Yes. For a while.'

'Before Mum?'

'Yeah.' He wasn't sure if Karla had told Gabby anything, but having a one-night stand and regretting it with every fibre of his being wasn't one of his prouder moments in life. It was definitely something his daughter didn't need to hear about. 'You better get going or you'll miss out on your *gathering*,' he said lightly, hoping to sidetrack the interrogation.

Gabby was clearly not going to let a prime opportunity to flee the house without a further lecture go astray and dropped a kiss on his cheek before waving goodbye.

Sully stared at the photo of the Duncans, his eyes eventually coming to rest on the frame Mrs Duncan held. He just wished this whole thing would stay dead and buried in the past where it bloody belonged. Jamie's death had caused nothing but grief and heartache back then and it was only going to do the same again now, if the case was reopened. He hoped to God it wasn't.

Fifteen

Despite herself, Alex was actually excited about the evening.

Tanya knocked on the front door and Alex had a fleeting moment of déjà vu as she opened it to discover her best friend standing on the other side. How many times had Tanya stood in this very spot after school or on the weekends, picking up Alex to head down to the beach or to hang out in her bedroom and listen to music and discuss school gossip?

Terri walked up the front path shortly after and Alex showed her into the lounge room.

'I've never been to a book club before. What do we actually do?' Tanya asked, sipping her wine as she sat down.

'Well, in my last book club, we mainly just drank and ate cheese,' Terri said, reaching for a cracker and slicing into the soft brie on the platter in front of her.

'Isn't the whole purpose of a book club to actually talk about books?' Tanya asked.

'Well, we can do that too,' Terri said, 'but the cheese and alcohol are the most important part.'

'Somehow I don't think Murna would run her book club like that,' Tanya said thoughtfully.

'God, no,' Alex said, taking her seat beside Tanya. 'You'd probably get banned if you hadn't read the required pages.'

'She is rather . . .' Terri paused, searching for a word to describe Murna.

'Terrifying?' Tanya suggested.

'Yes, kinda.'

'She always has been. Even as kids we used to be scared of her.' Alex grinned at Tanya.

'If she ever spotted you somewhere you shouldn't be or doing something you shouldn't be doing, your mum would know by the time you got home,' Tanya said.

Alex chuckled. 'You got grounded for smoking behind the hall in the reserve after school, once.'

'And you didn't!' Tanya exclaimed with mock outrage.

Alex grinned again. 'Clearly Murna didn't spot me. But even though she appears to take great delight in meddling in *absolutely everything*, I suppose she has the best interests of the community at heart.'

'That's true. And as annoying and pretentious as they can be, she and her posse *have* got a lot of things done around the place,' Tanya said. 'They're just a little . . . full-on *all* the time.'

'So both of you grew up here?' Terri asked.

'Yep,' Tanya said.

'My dad came from here, then moved away, then brought us back here later. I met this one in primary school,' Alex said.

'What brought *you* to town?' Tanya asked Terri, leaning back in the lounge.

Terri chewed the last of her cheese and cracker thoughtfully before answering. 'A man. My boyfriend moved here for his job, but that didn't work out. He moved back to Sydney and I decided I really liked it here, so I stayed.'

'What do you do for work?' Alex asked.

'I'm a graphic designer. I can work remotely, so I can live pretty much anywhere I like. What about you?' she asked Alex.

'I work with the Australian Embassy in London.'

'Wow. So what are you doing here?'

'I'm packing this place up to put it on the market.'

'You're selling it? But why? It's amazing.'

'My life's in the UK now. It's time I moved it on.'

The woman stared at her as though she'd lost her mind and Alex fought to reassure herself she was making the right decision. Of course it was the right decision.

Two of Tanya's cousins arrived next, followed by Mrs Burtrum.

'Come on in, Mrs Burtrum.'

'Enough of this Mrs Burtrum stuff, you're a grown woman now. Call me Gloria.'

Alex glanced at Tanya in surprise. 'Okay.' But it seemed almost impossible to force out the name. She'd been brought up in a household where you always addressed your elders as Mrs or Mr.

'I haven't been in here since . . . well, goodness, it must be at least ten years or more,' Mrs Burtrum—*Gloria*—continued, after she settled on the lounge and accepted a glass of wine. 'You've done a wonderful job with the decorating. I quite like the décor.'

'Thanks. I wanted a simple beach theme for the guests.'

'I still remember how it used to look,' Tanya said with a slight wistfulness in her voice. 'It was always so homely. Not that it isn't nice now, it's just . . . different.'

Alex knew what her friend meant. When this had been a home. With a family. But that was a lifetime ago. Another life.

'Well, I wasn't sure what you had planned tonight, Alex,' Gloria said, 'but I took the liberty of bringing along a few books that I've recently read and thought maybe it would be nice to see what everyone else has been reading.'

'I was just about to suggest the same thing,' Tanya said.

'Oh? What books did you bring?' Alex asked, scooping some brie onto a cracker. She wasn't game to look at Tanya as she did her best to at least seem like she knew what she was doing.

'I'm curious to see what books Gloria's been reading,' Tanya sidestepped smoothly.

'This was a very . . . enlightening read,' the older woman said, withdrawing a rather daunting-sized book.

'*War and Peace*,' Michelle, Tanya's red-headed cousin, read out loud.

'Yes, it's a classic.'

Michelle's sister, Amanda, took the book from Gloria and opened it to skim a few pages. 'It looks . . . ah, confusing. I can't even pronounce half of these names.' Where Michelle was tall and quite slender, Amanda was shorter with dark hair.

'It's Russian. They do take a bit to get used to.'

'And you've read this? The whole thing?' Tanya asked.

'Well . . . oh. No. I didn't manage to finish it,' Mrs Burtrum said, sounding defeated. 'This was on Murna's reading list.'

'Good grief,' Tanya muttered, eyeing the thick book with something akin to horror. 'We're not reading this kind of stuff are we?'

'I don't think we'll be reading anything Russian,' Alex said.

'Thank goodness,' Gloria said with relief. 'I've actually hated every book we've been given to read so far.'

'Why do you keep going if you're not enjoying it?' Alex asked.

'I don't know. It's a social outing, I suppose. I like to keep busy and there's not a lot to do if you don't have a driver's licence anymore. It can feel a little bit isolating, living out here sometimes.'

'Is there any kind of community transport?' Alex asked.

'Oh, yes, there is, but you know, it's sometimes not convenient and you don't feel like being a problem, asking people to take you places all the time.'

'This is what I don't understand,' Alex said, sitting back with her drink after topping up everyone's glasses. 'Rocky's gotten so much bigger over the last few years but there still aren't enough basic services in town.'

Tanya shrugged. 'I think we're stuck in the middle—not quite large enough for businesses to invest in but too big for existing infrastructure.'

'I'm really hoping this new development gets the go-ahead,' Gloria said, taking a large sip of her wine. 'But don't let Murna know I said that.'

'You'd be interested in a place there?' Alex asked.

'Absolutely. They have onsite activities and a medical centre . . . their own transport. I was reading through the brochure the other day. It sounds perfect for someone like me. I mean, I have lovely neighbours—at least on one side. I don't know the ones on the other side, they're younger and don't seem to be around very much. It's not like the old days, when everyone in town knew each other. I think I'd enjoy having people my own age living close by. It would make me feel a lot more secure. But if Murna gets her way, that won't happen.'

'You know, Murna is just one person—she doesn't actually have the power to shut down a major development,' Terri said, sounding confused.

'Try telling Murna that,' Amanda scoffed.

'*How* does she have that kind of power?' Terri asked.

'She knows people. She's that squeaky wheel they always talk about, getting in the faces of everyone. Unfortunately, she's also gotten in with a lot of the newer transplants to the area, who have backgrounds in government and politics and environmental areas. They know how to write grants and find *and fund*,' Michelle added pointedly, 'high-profile legal teams. They've got the current local council running scared.'

'It's a real shame, because I think this development is something we actually need,' Terri said.

'Sadly, I think they aren't seeing it for what it could be. They're seeing it as a precedent—that if this gets through, it'll just open the door to bigger things,' Tanya pointed out.

'I fear they'll get their wish. I know I, for one, will have to sell up and move into Moreville someday soon, when I can't manage my steps anymore. I'll miss this place terribly when I do, though.'

Alex shook her head sadly. It shouldn't have to come to that—people who'd lived here all their lives having to move just because a handful of people in town refused to acknowledge that some progress would be good for the town. It just didn't sit right.

'Has anyone else read anything good lately?' Terri asked.

'God, I haven't read a book in . . .' Tanya frowned as she tried to think. 'Probably when I was nursing my youngest— and that was eleven years or so ago.'

'What about you, Amanda and Michelle?' Terri asked.

'I think the last book I read was when *Fifty Shades of Grey* was all the rage. That's going back a bit now, but I did enjoy those,' Michelle said as she wiggled her eyebrows.

'Seriously?' Terri asked doubtfully.

'Oh, come on. Like you didn't read them.' Amanda chuckled.

'I didn't,' Terri protested.

'Yeah, right,' Michelle drawled. 'There's no way we were the only ones.'

'I did read the first one,' Terri admitted.

'See!' Amanda chortled.

'Oh, all right,' Alex said, 'yeah, I read it . . . and watched the movies.'

'You dirty perv,' Amanda said with almost a note of approval.

'We don't care if we're the only ones on the planet who haven't read them, do we, Gloria,' Tanya sniffed, then turned her head when the older woman didn't immediately agree. 'You've read them too?' she gasped.

'Well . . . I did,' Gloria admitted, nodding her head quickly, 'I can't lie. But do *not* tell Murna.'

'Mrs *Burtrum*!' Michelle said, sounding shocked, but laughing at the same time.

'We get old, dear, we don't go blind. No harm in a bit of a trip down memory lane.'

A new burst of laughter exploded around the room as drinks were rapidly refilled.

'Memory lane? Are you telling us you were into all that stuff?' Tanya was still looking somewhat shocked by the whole thing, which seemed kind of funny to Alex, considering Tanya was always the one leading *her* astray in the past!

'Well, you don't think your generation and this latest one invented sex, do you? I was young once!'

'I guess we can safely say we don't have to censor too many of our upcoming reads,' Terri said.

'God, yes, bring on some romance—the spicier the better, I say,' Gloria said. 'I'm sick of these literary snobs turning their noses up at romance and women's fiction. Murna would have a pink fit if anyone suggested anything like that—it has to be something depressing *and with artistic merit*,' she finished, mimicking Murna's articulate tone.

'Here's to romance and smut!' Amanda toasted.

'Romance and smut!' the rest of them echoed, laughing.

'I don't know about smut, but I really do love a good romance—makes me think back to the days when we all dreamed about who we'd end up marrying and where'd we be living,' Tanya said. 'Thank God for romance novels—at least they don't disappoint, unlike men!'

'This is true,' Michelle added.

'Oh, as if you can talk!' Amanda scoffed. 'You and Adam have been together for years and you're still as lovey-dovey as the first day you met. You don't need romance novels to keep you going.'

'What about you, Gloria?' Tanya asked. 'Was your first love like a romance novel?'

'Harold Hicks. He was lovely. A real good-looker too. I was the envy of every girl in my year when I made my debut. He was so handsome.'

'Your what?' Terri asked, tilting her head.

'My debut. It's a coming-out dance.'

'Coming out,' Terri said, glancing across at the rest of them uncertainly.

Tanya chuckled. 'Not *that* kind of coming out.'

'A debutante ball is when you're presented to society for the first time. You didn't have a deb ball when you were sixteen?'

'No. Not where I came from.'

'We didn't do ours either, they'd kind of started losing their appeal by the time we came through, but my older cousins all made theirs,' Michelle said.

'It was the most wonderful night.'

'Did you and Harold end up getting married?' Terri asked.

Gloria reached for her glass and took a sip before shaking her head. 'No. My father didn't really like him and Harold ended up moving away, so that was the end of that,' she said with a forced cheerfulness that didn't do anything to hide the obvious pain the memory had caused.

'I'm sorry, Gloria,' Alex said, reaching over to squeeze her hand gently.

'It's all right, I wouldn't have found my Gerald if I'd ended up with Harold.'

Alex didn't remember Gloria Burtrum with a husband and hadn't realised she'd lost him so early on.

'And what about you, Alex? Who was your first love?' Terri asked.

For a moment, Alex froze. 'Oh . . . no one.'

The other women went quiet and a weird awkwardness fell over the room.

'Did I miss something?' Terri asked nervously.

Tanya shook her head. 'Not at all. Alex had a torrid love affair with a bad boy, but it ended when she left for uni. He's still in town, though, so that's kinda . . . weird.'

'Oh. Sorry,' Terri stammered. 'I didn't realise it was a touchy subject.'

'It's not,' Alex said, trying to reassure her. 'Really, it isn't. It's just that he, ah . . . ended up with someone else and we broke up before I left town.'

'Oh.'

'It's fine.' Alex waved a hand and pulled a face.

'You know that he's not married anymore, right?' Michelle said, receiving an elbow to the ribs from Tanya. 'What? I'm just saying.'

'I'm sure she's aware,' Amanda said. 'She's been home long enough to have heard that by now.'

'I am aware.'

'See?' Amanda retorted.

'He's still pretty hot,' Michelle added.

'Yes, well. I'm not staying long enough to really care how hot he is,' Alex said.

'There's a hot eligible guy in town? How have I not known about this?' Terri asked.

'I think you'll be wasting your time,' Michelle said. 'So far, no one has successfully managed to turn the head of Sullivan McCoy. It's almost as though he still pines for a lost love or something.' She cast an innocent look at Alex.

'You've been reading far too many romance novels,' Alex said dryly.

'That does sound rather romantic. Do you think it could be true?' Terri asked. 'I mean, maybe you should find out?'

'He is *not* pining for me, I can assure you. He's probably too busy with his business and his daughter.'

'So he's financially independent too—'

'Who wants more wine?' Alex asked, jumping up to get another bottle.

'I overheard some women talking the other day in the grocery store about some kid who died at a party. They were having a great old time coming up with conspiracy theories. Does anyone know what it was about? I couldn't loiter around the vegetable section without looking conspicuous. Was there really a murder here?' Terri was asking as Alex reached the doorway on her way back.

'It wasn't a murder,' Tanya said quickly.

'It was an accident and it had nothing to do with Alex,' Michelle added.

'With Alex?' Terri almost gave herself whiplash as she spun around to stare at Alex.

'A guy fell off the headland after a party and died,' Tanya said. 'It was years ago.'

'So why is everyone talking about it now as though it only just happened and is some big, unsolved mystery?' Terri asked, looking between Tanya and Alex.

'Because I'm back in town and they have nothing better to do than gossip.'

'Surely if the police closed the case that should be the end of it?'

'My dad was the police sergeant here at the time,' Alex said. 'A lot of people believed the police covered up a murder because an officer's kid was involved. If only they knew how way off they were about that,' she muttered. Then she sighed as she saw Terri's confused expression. 'My father always believed I had something to do with it.'

Terri gasped. 'Why would he believe that?'

'I have no idea. But he did. I overheard him tell my mum the night before we left.'

'Oh, Al,' Tanya said sadly, touching her arm lightly.

'Surely over time he realised his mistake?' Terri asked.

'Nope. After he and my mother divorced, I never saw him again.'

'That's so sad.'

It was, Alex thought dismally. She and her father had been alike that way—both stubborn and neither knowing who should make the first move, so neither of them had and that had been that.

Tanya stayed back after the meeting to help clean up.

'Al, I know you probably don't want to bring up everything again, but talking about what happened earlier . . . I just . . .' Her friend's words seemed to falter as she placed the glasses in the sink. 'I wasn't a good friend to you back then,' she blurted, turning her devastated face to Alex.

'What?' Alex frowned. What on earth was she talking about? Tanya had been her only friend.

'I should have been here—I wanted to come around. I mean, I did come, but your mother said you were too upset for visitors, and then when it all got really bad, my mum wouldn't let me come and see you. She didn't want us getting mixed up in all the media stuff.'

'I get it. It was pretty crazy.'

'I've just always regretted not being able to stand by you, you know? But if I knew you were planning on just taking off without a goodbye, I probably would have made more of an effort.'

'I wasn't planning it. It just happened. Mum and Dad had this massive fight and it was all over me and what I'd done—supposedly done. It didn't even matter in the end if I'd done it or not—I'd managed to somehow ruin Dad's reputation and my parents' marriage.'

'You weren't responsible for their marriage ending, Al. You were a kid. It takes more than what happened to end something like that—they clearly had issues you didn't know about. It wasn't your fault.'

Alex had considered this. She'd never been able to fully convince herself because there'd been nothing she could remember about her parents' marriage being rocky. Sure, they'd had their share of arguments, but it had only been over trivial things like her father leaving his clothes on the floor and her mother not emptying the kitchen bins until they were overflowing. Nothing she could blame when the scandal became the last straw.

'None of that matters anymore,' she told Tanya gently. 'We were both just kids. It was a situation that was way out of anything we had any control over.'

'I'm just so happy you came back. I've missed you.'

'I've missed you too.'

They shared a tight hug and Alex felt her throat tighten with emotion. How had she managed all these years without her best friend? How would she manage when she left?

The sudden emptiness that thought sparked inside her allowed a tear to escape and she quickly wiped it away as they pulled apart. She didn't want to lose her best friend again.

Sixteen

After Tanya left, Alex sat staring into the straw-coloured liquid of her drink. She held the crystal glass up to catch the light and found herself reflecting on the conversation about her father. Why *had* he believed for all those years that she'd had something to do with Jamie's death? Surely it hadn't just been the fact she didn't tell him about the rape. Admittedly, she was a terrible liar, but that had been different—she wasn't lying about anything, she'd been genuinely trying to block the episode from her mind. Had her behaviour really been so obvious and suspicious enough to make him believe she'd somehow been involved with that much certainty? Surely not.

Tipping her head back, she drained the contents of her glass and set it on the coffee table, then got to her feet purposefully. If there was an explanation, then she knew it was going to be in one of two places: the notebook or the manuscript. She'd been afraid to read through them before, but now she had no choice—she was not going to spend the rest of her life wondering. She couldn't.

In the study, Alex picked up the police notebook and began turning the pages.

> Location: rock pools at Little Beach. No visible footprints remaining due to tide. No signs of any disturbance due to tidal activity.

There was a list of names and as Alex read down them, she didn't see any that she was overly familiar with. She figured these were possibly suspects her father had been looking into as part of the initial investigation into Jamie's death. A couple of names she vaguely recalled, but only in passing. Danny Vincent was a guy she remembered driving an old car—one that had been done up—but she didn't know enough about cars to know what kind, just that it was loud and he'd seemed pretty proud of it. He worked for one of the fishing trawlers and she did remember seeing him at the party that night. Beside Danny's name her father had written: *seems to have suddenly started spending cash around town and recently purchased an expensive vehicle and motorbike.* There was a large question mark beside the comment as though maybe he was planning to look into it further. A few of the other names had similar comments about sudden spending habits but most of them also had 'alibi verified' written underneath.

She flicked through the book and stopped at a page that had her name at the top. Underneath was an outline of her statement with a few phrases underlined and question marks written in the margins. Her father had been picking apart her statement to find out if she'd lied?

Part of Alex realised he was a police officer first and foremost and a good one—fair and just—but was also known around town for being tough when needed. He didn't believe in pussyfooting around the truth and he wasn't the one you went to if you wanted something sugarcoated; Sergeant Kelly believed in telling you how it was. But still, staring down at the page before her now, Alex couldn't help but feel a little angry that her father hadn't just taken her word for it.

But you hadn't told him everything, that little voice reminded her pointedly, and Alex closed her eyes against a rush of pain. She pushed it back down. Of course she hadn't told her father everything. How could she have told him she'd been so stupid as to place herself in that kind of position? She knew better. He'd *taught* her better. She'd been so caught up in rebelling and then so hurt over Sully—

No. She couldn't have faced her father if he'd known the truth. She couldn't have endured seeing that disappointment in his eyes. It was bad enough that she'd dragged him through all the bad publicity in the first place . . . But in that she felt justified. When it came to Jamie's death, she'd had nothing to hide. But having everyone find out what Jamie had done to her earlier that night? No way. There was no way *in hell* she would have survived the public scrutiny of that—or her parents' grief and humiliation.

She understood this notebook was a document that could be called into question during a court hearing or referred back to for information if need be, so it had to be clinical in its detail, but it still hurt that her father had written nothing in the notebook that actually declared his belief that she was innocent.

Her gaze strayed to the drawer where the manuscript still sat. She gingerly picked it up, letting out a shaky breath. As she turned the first page after carefully unwrapping the ribbon that secured it, Alex felt a wave of foreboding grow in the base of her stomach. Something told her that once she read whatever was in here, she'd never be able to unlearn anything about her father or life as she knew it.

The Life of a Small-Town Cop

I was a good cop. I always saw clearly that line between right and wrong, with no grey in between. I stared down criminals who'd made a living killing people, I'd stood strong in the face of temptation and taking the easy way out, unlike many of my colleagues at the time.

I prided myself on being honest in my career as a cop. I loved my family and my community. But in the end, it was my daughter who would become my downfall.

Alex felt a cold trickle of fear run down her spine. She turned the page and continued reading, scanning the pages, feeling her heart drop as she delved deeper into this memoir-turn-confession of a policeman who had also been her dad.

The first few chapters were about growing up in Rocky over fifty years earlier and the people who'd lived and died in the area. It was a much simpler time, and a tad more politically incorrect, but she enjoyed taking a trip back in history to witness how her father had seen the world as a kid. He'd never told her anything like this growing up. She'd only heard a few off-hand 'when I was a kid' kind of lectures, nothing as in-depth as the stories he was telling in his book.

Time ticked away silently in the background as Alex continued to read, the pile of discarded pages growing at a fast pace. The manuscript moved on to entering the academy and some of the people who'd influenced his early career, followed by his first station posting and stories of city policing in a time when corruption had been at its peak.

In their quiet neck of the woods, it was the fishing industry that was her father's main concern. For a long time, it had been a largely unregulated industry worked by hard men in even harder conditions and, once the drug trade got its hooks in, the money, power and addiction issues made being an honest cop in Rockne Heads a dangerous occupation.

Alex paused as she finished a chapter that had dealt with Sully's father and his arrest. Her father had learned that he'd had a target on his back and there'd been a number of near misses made on his life. He'd feared for the safety of both Alex and her mother on a few occasions and had written how torn he'd been when choosing to run or to stay. Alex had had no idea how scary that time had truly been—a testament to her father's ability to stay tight-lipped about the slightest detail. Although she couldn't help but wonder if, by writing this memoir, he'd felt a rush of relief at finally being able to let out everything he'd been holding in for so many years. Why hadn't he sent this to her to read before he'd died? Admittedly, his heart attack hadn't been expected, so maybe he'd been waiting for the right time . . . But look where that had gotten him.

Through the stories, Alex finally understood her father's stand on cleaning up the system, as she'd sometimes overheard him saying to her mother. They'd moved to Rocky at a time when the old ways were being stomped out and replaced with the new and it hadn't earned her father many friends either at work or in the community. She hadn't realised the pressure and emotions her dad must have been experiencing in those days. Now, as an adult, reading her father's words was confronting.

Alex fell asleep at some point in the early hours and woke with a stiff neck from sitting awkwardly in the office chair. She dragged herself to bed, but picked the manuscript back up later the next morning and read all afternoon. How had she been his demise? She sure as hell couldn't stop reading until she found out. Her father couldn't lead with a statement of that significance and not reveal how.

The chapter that dealt with Jamie Duncan's death began with a phone call her father received while he and her mother had been out of town, telling him that they'd found the body of Russell Duncan's son and he'd better get his arse back to town pronto. *I don't know why, but as soon as I heard the news of the Duncan boy's death, my gut warned me that everything was about to change,* her father had written.

He spoke about arriving at the station and heading to the location where the body was found. Because of who the family was, he and the other police involved were instantly wary of the potential of foul play. On the surface, Jamie's death looked like it could well have been accidental—the stupid, pointless death of a kid who'd had the rest of his life ahead of him. A kid who'd died because he'd been walking around the rocks while too drunk to see. And maybe, if he'd been anyone else's kid other than Russel Duncan's, that would have been true.

Alex's heart thudded heavily at the first mention of her name. In his notebook, her father had sounded professional, detached even, just as she'd mostly remembered him at the time, but here, there was a change. He introduced her as his daughter, his little girl, and wrote about how it seemed she'd grown up overnight without him even seeing it. He'd learned of her attending the same party Jamie had been at and spoke of how scared he suddenly was that he could no longer seem to protect her from the world. Alex blinked as tears stung her eyes. She hadn't expected to read anything like this from her father.

The story moved on to their exchange before she'd given her statement and told him where she and Jamie had been. She relived the arrival at the police station and the crowd that had gathered. The fear her father had felt for his daughter's safety but couldn't show. Knowing now the extent of the animosity the families like the Duncans had towards her father for the work he'd done in trying to stop the illegal activity they'd been involved in, she understood why he'd been so stressed and short-tempered. At the time, she'd felt the anger from the family, but hadn't realised the full potential of the situation the way her father had. The Duncans were the people who'd already threatened Bill Kelly's family—and now they were hell-bent on seeking revenge.

I went down to the location where Alex had been with the Duncan kid. I went down as a father, not a cop, and already I knew I was headed down a slippery slope. This was possibly a crime scene. If the kid's death was deemed suspicious, then it would most definitely be a crime scene. I should have called it in, had the place photographed at the very least, but I didn't. Not yet. I wanted to see it for myself—put my mind at ease that Alex had told me the truth. But something told me she wasn't telling me everything that happened that night.

It was a secluded spot, dark and out of sight from the rest of the beach, partially hidden at the foot of the headland. This was a place you went to if you wanted privacy. My blood began to boil at the thought

of what some dickhead kid had planned to do with
my daughter.

There was nothing to determine what had gone on
there—no footprints or tracks. The tide had come
and gone a number of times before the body had been
discovered, washing away any evidence that might have
been left behind.

I continued to make my way around the headland,
looking for anything that might have been left behind
as some clue as to where he'd fallen into the water.
From the condition of the body, it was impossible to
tell if the injuries on his face and torso had been
from the rocks or if he'd sustained them earlier. The
coroner being caught up on another job and the stuff-up
with finding someone to fill in at short notice was a
delay that wasn't helping. We had no idea if this was
going to proceed as an accidental death or a homicide
investigation, but my gut was telling me there was more
to this than an accident.

I knew the kid and the family and I had my suspicions
that the Duncans were already recruiting the next
generation into the family trade—and not the fishing
one. Drugs had been resurfacing after a lull and we'd
been running an undercover op into finding the source of
the new influx. Sources were saying it pointed to this
area and Jamie Duncan was top of my list of suspects,
only I couldn't prove anything. Was this some kind of

internal war? Were the Duncans under attack from a rival? Was Jamie's death linked to drugs?

I approached a track that led from the rocks up onto the headland itself and decided to follow it as Jamie's most likely direction. The path was bordered by thick brush and sand, and I came to a clearing, a blind spot that widened slightly halfway up the track, where I noticed something on the edge of the path. A shoe. The same kind that was currently sitting on the foot of the kid laying in the morgue.

I called it in. This was evidence that Jamie had come this way, probably on his way home. I looked around and noticed how close it was to the edge of the headland. There were no fences, no safety rails up there, just a goat track that locals and fishermen had been using for generations to get down onto the rocks and beach below. Had being drunk or on something made Jamie stumble and fall to his death, eventually washing up on the rocks below with the tide? Or had his death been something more sinister?

As I looked around for more evidence, I spotted a dark patch of colour on the ground and went over for a closer look. Blood, soaking the ground around a jagged rock about the size of a man's hand. Bingo, I thought. The murder scene and weapon. As I inspected the scene before me, I knew, instinctively, what had happened. Someone had used the rock to hit Jamie in the back of the head then he'd either stumbled his way to the edge of the headland and fallen over, or he'd dropped and someone threw him over to cover it up.

I was feeling pretty excited about the discovery until something else caught my eye. I took out a plastic evidence bag from my pocket and bent down to pick it up. It was a string of cowrie shells made into a bracelet. I recognised it immediately and my stomach dropped. Alex had worn the bracelet religiously for the last few months until today, when I'd noticed it was missing. It'd been a source of irritation, knowing that it had most likely been a gift from a boy, but Alex had refused to admit who it was from. There was no mistaking it—her name engraved on the silver clasp, stared up at me defiantly.

What the hell was it doing up here? And more to the point, why had my daughter lied to me about the last place she'd been with the Duncan kid?

Alex remembered the news that they'd located the spot where they thought Jamie had fallen from, but there'd never been any mention of her bracelet being found there. If it had, there'd have surely been mention of it when she was questioned.

Alex heard her heartbeat loud in her ears. Her father had found her bracelet at the scene of Jamie's death. But surely that was impossible . . . Because she hadn't been wearing the bracelet by that time.

16 December 2005, 10 pm

Kelly Clarkson's single 'Since U Been Gone' was playing and Alex belted out the lyrics with gusto as she danced centre stage, almost tripping over in the soft sand but caught by a set of strong arms. Her spinning head momentarily cleared as she stared up at a thunderous-faced Sully.

'You need to go home,' he said.

'You need to leave me the hell alone, Sullivan McCoy,' she threw back at him. She thought he'd left ages ago. When she'd come back to the party after allowing herself a good solid forty-five-minute cry, Alex had decided to do what any rational, recently heartbroken girl would do and drink herself into oblivion. So far it seemed to be working— she'd stopped crying and started dancing and was feeling much better. She knew tomorrow would be another story, but she wasn't thinking about that now. She was finally at a beach party, and this was probably the last time she'd ever see the kids she went to school with before they all went their separate ways and became responsible adults . . . Well, some of them maybe, she'd conceded, thinking about the group of guys who'd been testing the theory about igniting farts with a cigarette lighter.

She pushed out of Sully's arms and staggered slightly as she made her way to the esky where Tanya had put their drinks earlier.

'You've had enough to drink, Al. Come on. You're going to be feeling like absolute shit tomorrow. I'm taking you home,' Sully said, standing beside her.

'I'm already feeling like shit. Didn't you hear? My boyfriend just knocked up someone else,' she snapped. 'What are you even still doing here? I don't want to see your stupid lying face ever again.' Her hand reached for her bracelet and a fresh wave of grief and anger washed over her. 'And you can take this stupid thing back.' She threw the string of shells at him.

He caught it against his chest. 'Alex.'

'Don't,' she snarled. 'Just. Don't, Sully. Leave me alone.'

'You're not even going to listen to my side of it?'

'Did you sleep with her?'

The bluntness of her question seemed to surprise him and he faltered before managing, 'Yes, but—'

'Then that's all there is to it. I don't care if you were drunk. You left me and went straight to her—drunk or not, makes no difference. You're going to be a father. It's over. It was over the minute you decided to drink yourself stupid and sleep with Karla Robinson.'

'And that's it? We throw away everything we had over one mistake?'

'Are you going to turn your back on that baby?'

He flinched, and Alex knew everything she needed to.

'I didn't think so.'

'That doesn't mean we have to be over.'

'Yes, it does,' she said sadly. 'Your life is here now. Just leave me alone, Sully. I can't do this anymore tonight.' She wanted to go back to the light-headed nothingness she'd had before he reappeared and sobered her up. She didn't want to think about how sad she was or how much she still loved him, she just wanted to drink and forget it all for a bit longer.

Opening the bottle in her hand, she held his disapproving gaze as she took a long drink, then she turned away and moved back into the crowd.

When she glanced back, he was gone.

Seventeen

Alex chewed her bottom lip. She was so close to the end, and despite her stomach churning at the emotional roller-coaster the manuscript had been, she knew she needed to finish it. Hopefully she'd find some kind of closure.

So I did what any father would do—yet something I vowed I would never do. I threw the bracelet away and never spoke of it to a single other soul until this moment. Over my years serving as a police officer, I'd seen pretty much everything, including the lengths to which parents would often go to cover up for their kids when they were in trouble: giving false alibis, even trying to pay off officers to drop charges against their little darlings, which in my experience only encouraged further bad behaviour the police and justice system

would have to deal with at some later stage when young
Freddy turned into a full-blown criminal.

Yet, there I was, doing exactly the same thing—and
not just covering up some kid taking a car on a joyride.
This was potentially murder and my daughter knew a
hell of a lot more about what happened than she ever
told anyone.

I listened to the theories being thrown around about
the blood and the rock and kept my own suspicions to
myself. The detectives went back and forth over the
whole murder or accident aspect. Detective Rushton was
leaning towards a second person being involved, but
the other detective, Jorgenson, wasn't so sure. After
all, they'd combed the site and hadn't turned up any
other evidence. Naturally, they didn't find the bracelet.
Within a day of the rock's discovery, the coroner had
sent their report over and, despite checking the head
wound for anything suspicious, it came back that the
time spent in the water meant there was no evidence in
the wound that could be used to ascertain if the injury
had been from an attack. There were enough drugs in his
system to support the theory that he'd simply fallen,
hit his head and stumbled in a daze to his death.

Once the coroner came back with the accidental death
verdict, I tried to convince myself that none of it
mattered, and yet I could never shake that gut instinct
I'd had as soon as I saw the kid, that there was

something not right about the situation. As much as I hated to admit it, the Duncans were right. That kid did not just fall off the headland.

Was it murder? I believe it was. But then I had to factor in the possibility my own daughter had had something to do with it. Was she capable of murder? I don't believe so. But the instincts that have served me well during my whole career and always pan out told me something happened that night. Perhaps it was self-defence, provoked by a moment of insanity or rage, that caused Alex to pick up that rock and hit Jamie in the head, causing him to fall. Either way, it was still a homicide. Manslaughter, at least, but something that was serious and held grave consequences. And I had covered it up.

I'd like to say I moved on, put it out of my mind and got on with my life, but my punishment for my part in perverting justice was to lose my family and for the job to which I'd once dedicated my life to become something I simply tolerated.

My retirement was more the end of a sentence than the end of a career. I am a man full of regret and great sadness that I was unable to reach out to my daughter in the years that followed, due to pride. Maybe I wrote this memoir as a way to atone for some of the things I've done in my life. A way to set the record straight.

Sully was doing routine maintenance on his boat when he looked up and noticed Alex walking towards him. 'Hey, how's the packing?'

'I need you to tell me the truth about something,' she said.

The grin faded from his face. 'Okay,' he said, folding his arms across his chest.

'The night of the party. Were you ever alone with Jamie?'

For a moment he didn't say anything. Then, 'Come on aboard.' He hitched his head in the direction of the gangway.

Alex made her way to the outdoors lounge area where he stood. She took a seat. 'Can I get you a drink?' he offered, and she shook her head.

'I just need you to answer me.'

'Why? What does it even matter now?'

'Because if you did, that changes a lot of things.'

'Like what?'

'Like the fact you lied to the police!'

He took a seat across from her. There was no point in denying it now. 'It was self-preservation, I guess.'

'Did you have something to do with Jamie's death?'

Of all the things he'd prepared himself for Alex to ask, this had honestly not been one of them.

'Of course not,' he said, but her expression did not waiver. 'I swear,' he added when she continued to hold his gaze, her eyes doubtful. 'Where is all this coming from? Why would you bring this up now?'

'Because I found something my father wrote about the case. He found the bracelet you made for me up on top of the headland. The same one I remember giving back to you earlier that night.'

Fuck. The bracelet. Sully's mind raced as he unwillingly went back to the night in question. He'd only realised he didn't have the bracelet a few days later and figured it must have fallen out of his pocket at the party. Weirdly, he still sometimes found himself looking for it whenever he walked along the same stretch of beach. Which was stupid, because it'd been lost eighteen years ago and would have been long gone by now. Or so he'd thought.

'Your dad found it?' he asked.

'Apparently.'

'And you think I had something to do with Jamie being killed because that bracelet was found nearby?'

'It does seem like a bit of a coincidence.'

'Except I didn't. Yeah, I confronted him. I came back to find you. I was worried you were drinking too much and angry at myself for walking away and leaving you there. When I came back, I found out you'd gone off with Jamie. I went looking for you. I found Jamie—alone.' Sully wasn't sure what might have happened if he'd actually found him with Alex—he'd already been in a state just thinking about what that jerk could have been doing. He'd heard enough talk to know the guy was a pig where women were concerned and he sure as hell wasn't going to let him touch Alex.

'What happened?'

'We had words. I hit him. I left.'

'You hit him? With a rock?'

'What? No!' he said. 'I hit him with my fist.'

She seemed to be digesting this information with far more deliberation than he thought necessary. 'Why did you hit him?' she asked.

'Why do you think?' Sully snapped then did a double take when he saw her expression change to something very much like fear. 'He was talking shit about . . . everything.' Sully pulled the breaks on that train of thought. He hated to admit it, but one stupid conversation with a guy off his head on drugs and alcohol eighteen years ago shouldn't have stayed with him for so long—nor have the ability to still make his fists clench, as they were doing now. He made an effort to unclench his hands and calm down. The things Jamie had said were only to stir Sully up—the guy had never known when to shut his damn mouth at the best of times.

'Look, he and I were never friends. I couldn't stand the guy. But he was alive and breathing when I left him. I should have told the cops that, I know . . .' He paused. It hadn't been one of his finer moments and he still felt ashamed of himself when he recalled how much of the fallout Alex had taken. 'But with my family's reputation and everything, I knew the cops wouldn't believe me if I told them the truth. So I kept my mouth shut.'

'I can't believe you lied all this time.'

'I didn't lie about anything. I didn't do anything wrong. I didn't have anything to do with Jamie's death. If he fell off that headland—or jumped,' Sully added pointedly, '—that wasn't on me. Or you.' Everyone knew how hard Jamie used to hit the party drugs—if it hadn't been for the Duncans making such a big deal about Alex being the last person to be seen with him, no one would have questioned the fact the idiot had clearly stumbled to his own death over that headland. But the juicy scandal and rumours had been too much of a temptation to resist in a small community, where the slightest hint of drama or excitement was always catapulted into something much bigger for entertainment.

'My father died believing I had something to do with Jamie's death,' Alex said quietly, looking at Sully with an expression so raw that it momentarily stole his breath away.

'What do you mean?'

'He got rid of evidence at the scene to protect me. He went against everything he stood for because he believed I was the one up there. He believed someone attacked Jamie that night—that he didn't just fall.'

'Surely after the coroner ruled it accidental, though, he would have realised you had nothing to do with it.' He found it difficult to believe her own father would think she was capable of lying, but more importantly, that she'd ever be capable of doing anything that would hurt someone. She was the gentlest soul Sully had ever known . . . well, at least back then. She'd certainly found a confidence she'd never had as a teenager, and she was definitely far more worldly and wise than when she'd lived here.

'I think he would have, if he hadn't found that bracelet.'

'Al . . . Look, I'm sorry if anything I did contributed to that, but if your dad suspected you had anything to do with

Jamie's death, then that's on him. Because anyone who knew you would know there's just no way you were involved. No matter what evidence Bill thought he'd discovered.'

'Believing I lied to him was enough. He wouldn't have been able to let that go. He had to have everything figured out.'

'Then I feel sorry for him. If you two were estranged over that, he missed out on having an amazing daughter in his life.' Sully couldn't imagine ever cutting Gabby out of his life, no matter what she'd done. It took a special kind of arrogance to believe your values and principles were more important than your child.

Alex seemed taken aback by his words but gathered herself quickly. 'You still should have told them the truth,' she said stiffly, as she stood up to leave.

Her words hit a sore spot inside him. He knew his behaviour had been selfish—to a degree. He still believed he would have somehow been hung out to dry by the cops. It was no secret her old man had had it out for a lot of the old fishing families.

'Was he lying?' he heard himself call.

She paused and turned back to look at him. 'Was who lying?'

'Jamie,' he said bluntly. 'When he said you'd let him . . .' He couldn't finish the sentence. He wanted to take back the words that had haunted him for so long, but it was too late. They were already out.

He watched her face pale and inwardly swore. It was true—the bastard hadn't been lying. All these years Sully had somehow managed to tell himself that Jamie had been taunting him, trying to get a rise out of him . . . But even now, Alex could never lie—nor arrange her face to conceal one.

'I bet your father didn't know about that. I guess we both had things to hide that night, didn't we?' He felt like a jerk—he really did—but he hadn't expected something that had happened that long ago to still have the power to hurt so much.

He wanted to apologise, but he didn't.

He couldn't.

Eighteen

Alex listened as the ring tone sounded on the other end of the phone and her mother's cheery voice answered.

'Hello, darling, I was just thinking about you.'

'Mum, did you know that Dad wrote a book?' Alex hadn't slept well and her emotions were all over the place since reading that stupid manuscript and speaking with Sully yesterday. She realised she'd sounded short and quickly apologised. 'Sorry, Mum, it's just that I found it in his desk.'

'No. I didn't know. He never mentioned he ever wanted to write one.'

'Mum, he really believed I had something to do with Jamie's death,' she said and her voice cracked as she felt hot tears run down her face.

'Oh, sweetheart.'

Alex heard a long, empty sigh on the other end before her mother spoke again.

'Your dad was a complicated man. Actually,' she said, 'that's not true. He wasn't complicated. He was very simple: there was right and there was wrong. And that was it.' There was only the slightest edge to her usually gentle tone. 'He was never capable of compassion. He lacked it. His father was the same—he was a very distant man and your father's upbringing wasn't filled with a great deal of affection. I think that's what somehow attracted me to him in the beginning. We were complete opposites. I had this need to fix Bill or something,' she said with a gentle, almost helpless, laugh.

'But I remember him, sometimes, when he was different.'

'When you were born, he did soften. You were his pride and joy. He did love you very much, Alex. I just don't think he knew how to handle something so emotional. He was torn between his duty and being a father. I think, with everything going on, he just didn't know how to put into words what he wanted to say to you. I did beg him to try, but there was so much going on.'

'I've always felt guilty that I was the reason you and he ended up divorced.'

'It was never because of you,' her mum said firmly. 'I know we've talked about this, but you have to let that go. It wasn't your fault.

'Your dad and I had been having trouble for a number of years before all that happened. It was just the final straw—not the reason. In fact, I carry a bit of my own guilt about it, if we're being honest.' Her mother sounded sad. 'I think I jumped on that whole thing as my excuse to finally do what I'd been too scared to do—to actually leave.'

'Really? Things were that bad before?' Alex asked.

'It was hard being an affectionate person when my partner wasn't,' her mum said, picking her way through the words. 'I knew what I was getting into when I married your father— although, in my youthful innocence, I truly believed I could change him. Melt that part of him inside that hadn't had any real love and show him what a loving partnership looked like. And to some extent I think he did soften, a little bit. At least it felt that way, until we moved back to Rockne. That's when things changed. I knew the moment we got back there that he was never going to leave again. There's something about that place for people who've been born and bred there—they just can't seem to stay away. It sucks them back in somehow.

'I gave up my dreams of travelling and exploring new places when I decided to marry your dad, and I thought it was a fair deal once I had you and we moved around to different postings and met new people . . . But then when we went back to Rockne and I realised that was where I was going to live for the rest of my life, I think I started to regret it. I was an outsider—I didn't fit in. This was before a lot of the sea-change people started arriving. Rockne was a very different place back then. Your dad's job was . . . Well, it came with a lot more danger and risk than I was expecting. He returned at a very tumultuous time.'

Alex remembered the bit in her father's memoir about taking on the problems around drugs and fishing, and all the threats that came with.

'All I'm trying to explain is, you have nothing to feel guilty about. There was no way I was letting you stay there after all that had gone on, after all the hell that town—or certain elements of it, anyway—had put you through. I begged your father to take a transfer but he refused. He couldn't stand the thought of people thinking he let the Duncans drive him out of town. His own foolish pride caused our divorce.'

'Thanks, Mum. I'm sorry we haven't spoken more about all this before. It's just been hard.'

'I know.' Monica let out a deep breath. 'I think you're a little bit like him in that way—not to the same extent, thank goodness,' she added darkly. 'But I do worry that you tend to bottle things up instead of dealing with them sometimes.'

'I'll try to be better at it . . . but I'm not doing yoga,' Alex said, smiling wanly.

Her mother made an unimpressed sound.

Alex ended the call but didn't move from the couch. Those first few years afterwards had been a nightmare—literally. Every night, she'd woken covered in sweat, listening to the echoes of her screams. Every time she'd see someone who even slightly resembled Jamie, a cold shiver would break out along her back and her hands would tremble. It took a long time to work through the after-effects. However, after years of suffering in silence, Alex had eventually worked up the courage to find help. She wished she hadn't been too scared to do it earlier. As an adult, she knew if she'd told someone what had happened that night—her mother, Tanya, anyone really—they'd have urged her to get help a lot sooner. But she'd convinced herself she was to blame and her father's lack of trust in her afterwards seemed to justify her decision to keep it a secret. He hadn't believed her when she'd told him she had nothing to do with Jamie's death—not deep down. Not in the way her mother had believed her, or even Sully. She hadn't wanted anyone's sympathy and she certainly hadn't wanted to relive the whole thing publicly if she'd told the police about it. Besides, what would have been the point of accusing him of rape? Jamie was dead; he wasn't going to be charged over it.

But now, everything she'd done to come to terms with what had happened was threatening to dissolve. She didn't want to go back to that darkness—didn't want to experience that sick, empty feeling again.

'Morning,' Tanya said cheerfully when Alex arrived at the cafe for her coffee. 'Have you checked the Facebook page yet?'

'What Facebook page?'

'The Rocky Community page. Terri put up a post about the book club and how much fun it was and there's about twenty replies asking to join for the next one,' Tanya said. 'Seems like you started something.'

When Alex didn't instantly reply, Tanya tilted her head thoughtfully and studied her friend. 'What's going on?'

Alex opened her mouth to reassure her that everything was fine, only nothing came out. A surge of emotion rose up in her chest and, to her horror, Alex found herself blinking back tears.

'Hey,' Tanya said, coming around the counter to hug her, 'talk to me.'

'I spoke with Mum earlier . . . about Dad and what we were talking about. I found something he'd written and there was just so much stuff going on back then that I hadn't been aware of. Then Sully and I had a . . . not a fight, exactly, he just said something that caught me off guard. I thought I'd managed to put everything behind me—I've worked bloody *hard* to put it all behind me,' she said, looking up at her friend and seeing her nod in understanding. 'But ever since I came back here it's like it's all unravelling again.'

'I get it,' Tanya said softly. 'I mean, to an extent. When you walked in that door the other day, I felt like everything had gone back in time too. It's just been a shock because you haven't been back properly since it all happened. But that will wear off. Soon everything will be a memory again and we'll all just move on in the present and make new memories. Better ones,' Tanya said firmly. 'Everything will be okay. I promise.'

Alex desperately wanted to believe her friend. She wasn't a pessimistic person by nature, but it was more than just her own brain she needed to convince to let go of the past—it was other people, like the Duncans and Sully. How was she supposed to move on when they were all holding her back?

Tanya brought out two coffees and a couple of slices of mud cake, and Alex had to admit the food went a long way in helping her find her balance again.

'I noticed that Murna coincidentally posted a reminder for her book club about their next meeting. I think you might have rattled her cage a bit,' Tanya said, licking her spoon of the last of the mud cake.

'Oh for goodness' sake. This is like schoolyard drama.'

'Hey, you poked the bear.'

'I . . .' Okay, so that was a fair comment. She had no defence—she'd acted childishly by jumping in with the whole fake book club thing the other day—but, seriously, Murna was bloody annoying with her 'you can't join our book club' attitude. 'I probably shouldn't have done that,' she admitted.

'Actually, it was the best night. I really enjoyed it. I think you *should* do another one.'

'You do remember I haven't actually moved back to town, right?'

'Maybe you should.'

'My job with the embassy isn't exactly a work-from-home kind of thing.'

'Well, maybe you could find a different job that could be? Time for a change?'

Leave her job? The thought stopped Alex in her tracks. She loved her job. *You've loved all your jobs, though,* the little voice reminded her. Which was true. Change had never been something she shied away from in the past—she'd moved from place to place and job to job and had always looked forward to the adventure of it all, but it hadn't crossed her mind to do it again yet. An image of the little cottage in Chilham came up before her eyes and she focused on it, trying to see the intricate details she'd once had no trouble picturing. She was dismayed to realise she suddenly couldn't. She'd loved that little place. It was her dream. She was going through all the hoops in order to buy it, so was she seriously thinking about not buying it now? No, of course she wasn't. That was just crazy.

'Alex?' Tanya asked, looking at her with undisguised concern.

'Sorry?'

'Are you okay?'

'Oh, yeah. Of course. I was just— It doesn't matter. You should totally take over the book club. It'd be good for the town to have something fun to go to.'

'I don't have the time to organise a book club.'

'What's to organise? Make a time and a place and send out a message. Simple. You could even host it here. Charge everyone a fee for the food or get them to supply it. This would be a great place to have book club.'

'Just add it to the list of things to do,' Tanya said, rolling her eyes.

'Hey,' Alex said, suddenly recalling, 'do you remember Cassie Newton? From school?'

'Yeah. I see her around here sometimes. There's a sad story.'

'Oh? Why's that?'

'Don't you remember her in school? She was the popular kid, queen bee in her little gang. Gorgeous-looking girl. Then she got caught up with the Duncans. Got mixed up in drugs and went off the rails a bit.'

'The Duncans?' Alex echoed.

'She used to go out with Chris Duncan. Do you remember him? He was Jamie's younger cousin. He was in our year.'

'Yeah, I remember him,' Alex said. Chris had been with Tom that day in the car park.

'He was always a bit quieter. I thought if any of them were ever going to make anything of themselves it might be him, but he stayed around town and went into the family business, so there went that chance,' Tanya said.

'So is Cassie still with him?'

'Don't know—it's hard to tell. She's got a couple of kids to him, but they fight like cats and dogs, so I don't know if they're together or not this week.'

'That's probably why then.'

'Why what?' Tanya asked.

'Oh, she just said something strange—I got the impression she wasn't a fan of the Duncan family.'

'It's not exactly the kind of family you walk away from, if you know what I mean,' Tanya said seriously.

'I know they used to have a reputation—I mean with all the drug stuff and whatnot—but surely things aren't still that bad?'

Tanya shrugged. 'Let's just say the Duncans always look out for the Duncans. They've never been community spirited, and they keep to themselves and don't like to draw attention to their business. As long as everyone else does the same there's no issue, but the locals still give them a wide berth for good reason.'

It sounded feasible that there wouldn't be much love lost between Cassie and the Duncans if she and Chris were constantly fighting. Still, it was an odd thing for her to have brought up with Alex.

Alex decided it wasn't any of her business. The less she had to do with the Duncans the better.

Nineteen

Sully closed his eyes, listening to the gentle slap of waves against the hull and feeling the bob of the boat on the water. You couldn't beat it.

It was the second day of a three-day charter and he and his four guests had just finished a feed of fresh fish caught earlier in the day. This trip was made up of a family—a dad, his two boys and their grandfather. Sully always found it interesting to observe different family dynamics and how they worked. For him, father–son relationships were usually like watching something in a foreign language, without subtitles. He'd never had a relationship with his own father, largely because Theo had been in prison for most of his teenage years, but even before that his dad hadn't been into any bonding—except if you call grooming your kid to take over your illegal activities bonding.

Even though he'd come to terms with his relationship with his father as he'd gotten older, there was still the odd occasion when he felt a twinge of jealousy—like today. The genuine pride Trevor had for his son and grandsons when he spoke about them left Sully with a strange kind of longing in the pit of his stomach. He'd spent a lot of time with the older man during the trip; he found him interesting and easy-going. The younger three were more focused on their fishing, but Trevor seemed happy just to sit and soak in the salt air and ocean, throwing in the occasional line now and again. He was a retired air force squadron leader and had spent his life travelling the world. He'd been married to the same woman for sixty years, but had become a widower recently.

The others turned in for the night, leaving Sully and the old man alone on deck. Mellowed by a few wines and a full stomach, Trevor was reminiscing about his past. Sully didn't mind. He wasn't tired enough to sleep and Trevor was a great storyteller. Tonight, though, he seemed to be in a more melancholy mood and it kind of matched Sully's.

'You've got something on your mind, son?' Trevor asked.

'I was just thinking how you said earlier that you'd been married for sixty years. That's pretty impressive.'

'Are you married?'

'I was. For a while. We get on better apart now.'

The older man went quiet. His next words surprised Sully. 'My wife and I had a partnership. She wasn't the love of my life, but she was the love *in my life*, if you will. I had a woman I fell in love with years before I met my wife, and I lost her.

No matter how hard I tried to forget her, she always managed to be there, lurking in the back of my mind.

'I moved on—met Maureen, had children—and my life was as perfect as any man could ever hope for . . . But she was always there, my Elizabeth. Sometimes as hard as we try, we just can't replace certain love.'

Trevor paused. 'Is your Elizabeth still around?' he asked.

Sully stared at him. He'd been thinking about Alex most of the trip. He wondered how the man had known something so private. 'Yeah. She just came back to town actually.'

'You think you'll try again with her?'

'Nah,' Sully said. 'She's not planning on sticking around for long. Wouldn't be much point.'

For a long time, Trevor said nothing. Then he leaned forward to rest his arms along his thighs as he stared down at the deck. 'After my Maureen passed, I heard that Elizabeth was also a widow and still lived in my hometown. For two years I dithered about, trying to work up the courage to go and visit her . . . two years wasted.'

'What was stopping you?'

'I think I was worried that I'd built her memory up into something that wasn't real, that maybe when I met her again, I'd realise I'd been a fool my entire life, holding on to something that had all been in my head. But then I went to see her.'

Sully waited for him to continue, and when it didn't seem like he would, he asked, 'And? Was it the same?'

'It was. And more. The moment I laid eyes on her, it was like the years had melted away. For both of us. But only six months after finding her, I lost her again, this time to cancer. I guess the thing I'm trying to tell you is that I wasted two whole years I could have had with her, worrying over stupid reasons that didn't even matter in the end. Two years of loving her I didn't get to do. Don't ever take time for granted—no one can predict how much of it we have left.'

Sully nodded as Trevor got to his feet and said goodnight. The conversation unsettled him. Had he been thinking about trying again with Alex? Maybe the thought had crossed his mind briefly—he certainly enjoyed spending time with her and wanted to do more of it. Only, every time they were together, the past kept getting between them. Then there was her job and life on the other side of the bloody world.

He drew in a deep breath of ocean air. Out here, especially at night when you couldn't see a horizon, it was easy to think you could be the only human left on the planet. Some people found it lonely. He found it peaceful—usually. Right now, his mind was a jumble of stupid what ifs. What if he did want to try again? What if Alex did decide to stay . . . What if, instead of sleeping with Karla, he'd moved to Sydney with Alex? He'd tried many times over the years to imagine what that would have looked like and honestly couldn't. He certainly wouldn't have been able to build his business up there the way he had here. Maybe they just weren't destined to be the love story that Trevor and Elizabeth had been.

But what if you were? a little voice asked almost wistfully.

It was an idea he couldn't manage to shake for the rest of the trip.

The beach was quiet at this time of the afternoon. A few people were enjoying a late walk, but they were little specks in the distance when Alex set out. The sand was cool beneath her feet, so different from the the middle of the day when you could barely walk on the sand without burning the skin from underneath them. She realised how much she'd missed the beach. She'd been to plenty of other beaches over the years, but as nice as they were, they weren't . . . this one. There was definitely something unique about the beaches in Australia, though she couldn't really put her finger on what it was. Maybe it was simply that they weren't always crowded? There was just miles and miles of endless sand and ocean. There was a peacefulness here that you didn't get in many other places.

She hadn't seen Sully for the last few days. She had almost been expecting him to appear, and she wasn't sure if she was relieved or disappointed that he hadn't. Their last encounter had been playing on her mind a lot. It'd dredged up a bunch of old emotions she'd thought she'd managed to bury a long time ago. She knew Sully had been shocked when he'd realised Jamie's boasting hadn't been the lie he'd been telling himself it had been. And she wished she could have laughed the moment off and let him continue to believe nothing had happened that night. God, how she wished nothing *had* happened that night.

Alex stopped walking and allowed the waves to wash gently over her feet, the cold water helping to keep her grounded as the old memories tried to drag her back in time. She was stronger than she'd once been and they didn't pose as much of a threat now as they once had. Still, it was nice to have the chill of the cold water to focus on as it continued to lap at her feet. Jamie couldn't hurt her anymore. He'd taken something from her, something that she would never entirely get over, but he no longer haunted her. She'd wrestled back that power.

Her gaze moved to the headland in the distance. She felt only sadness for a life taken far too young. Had Jamie been destined, as her father had predicted, to follow in the family footsteps and get mixed up in a life of drugs and petty crime? Or might he have turned himself around? She knew what her dad would think: a leopard didn't change its spots. Once a crim, always a crim.

She'd like to think Jamie could have changed. Maybe if that night had never happened, his family wouldn't have become even more disillusioned and bitter and might have moved on with their own lives too.

Would her father have changed if that night had never happened? Would he have mellowed into a gentler version of himself once Alex had given him grandchildren to spoil?

She blinked rapidly—no, that particular daydream would never have happened. Sully and she would still have broken up that night and she would have left for Sydney like she'd been planning. She briefly imagined what life might have looked like if her parents had stayed married and she'd come home for holidays. She realised she was glad that particular future hadn't panned out. She wasn't sure she could have handled seeing Sully and Karla playing happy families on the beach with a toddler between them.

She turned away from the headland and continued her walk.

Out of nowhere, a large black dog came running towards her, barking loudly.

Alex froze, her eyes widening as the animal bared its teeth. She couldn't move—too terrified to drag her eyes away from those sharp teeth to check for its owner.

The dog gave a low, menacing growl and Alex could hear her heart pounding frantically in her ears. She forced her frozen feet to inch backwards but the dog, black eyes zeroing in on the movement, slowly lowered itself into a crouch, its muscular hind legs bunched and taut, ready to launch itself at her if she made another move.

Everything inside screamed at her to run—as fast as she could—but common sense told her she'd never outpace it. But how long could they continue this stand-off before it tired of the game and went for her throat? Almost as though sensing her indecision, the animal's growl became louder and all rational thought suddenly vanished—Alex ran. Terror propelled her, but as she turned she managed no more than two steps before she felt herself falling, hitting the hard, wet sand. With her eyes squeezed shut Alex braced for the impact of sharp teeth as they tore into her skin, but a loud, ear-piercing whistle cut through the air and the dog instantly stopped and turned to race up into the sand dunes.

As Alex battled to catch her breath, she spotted a lone figure standing with arms crossed and feet planted wide—the terrifying dog of moments before was now bounding play-fully around the man's legs. Tom Duncan stared at her for an unsettling amount of time before a smirk crossed his face and he turned and walked away.

Alex's heart thumped painfully against her rib cage and her hands shook. A shiver ran down her spine. Evil had driven her away from this place once before and it seemed it was hell bent on doing it again.

Twenty

Alex paused to take a calming breath before opening her front door.

'Hi,' Sully said, standing in the verandah, watching her about as warily as she was watching him. 'I took a chance that you might have a few minutes spare so we could talk?'

Part of her wanted to shut the door in his face, but instead she pushed it wider open and let him walk inside. She followed him to the end of the short hallway and stepped around him when he paused, leading him through the lounge room into the kitchen.

'Coffee?' she asked, already making her way to the sink.

'Sure. Thanks.'

'Have you been out on the boat?' she asked, hoping that, if they talked, she'd stop feeling so jittery.

'Yeah, just got back this afternoon.'

'Catch anything?'

'We always catch something,' he said with a crooked smile, 'but yeah, we had very happy guests with lots of photos to take home.'

'Do they keep many fish?'

'Yeah, most take their bag limit home with them. We clean and fillet it on the boat. But lots of people also prefer catch and release, which we encourage with the bigger fish.'

Alex nodded as she asked more questions about the types of fish he usually caught on his trips, letting him talk while she made their coffee. She used to like listening to Sully explain about fishing. Not that she particularly cared for it herself, but she loved the way his eyes and face would light up when he talked about it. He'd always had a passion for the industry. Coming from a long line of fishermen, it was in his DNA. It seemed his passion for the subject had only grown over time.

'I didn't actually come here to bore you to death about fish species,' he said, accepting the mug she passed him as they sat out on the deck outside the kitchen.

'You weren't boring me,' she said, blowing on the hot liquid before taking a sip. 'But why *did* you come here?'

'I owe you an apology. The way our last conversation ended . . . it hasn't sat well with me ever since. I'm sorry I said what I did.'

Alex placed the mug back on the table and nodded. 'That's okay. I started it by accusing you, so I'm sorry too.'

'I just want everything from back then dealt with, Al. I'm sick of it getting in the way every time we try and talk.'

'It's a bit hard to ignore.'

'We don't have to ignore it, but we do have to move on. There was more to our relationship than just that one night. We had something special.'

'We did. For a while,' Alex agreed, lowering her eyes from his.

'Then can't we try and remember the good bits?'

Alex got up and crossed to the verandah rail, needing to put some distance between them . . . or the old memories, she wasn't sure which. 'I haven't forgotten those,' she said quietly. 'It's just that the bad parts overshadowed all the good.'

'Only if we let them.'

'It doesn't matter now.'

'It does matter, Alex,' he said abruptly and stood up to join her. 'I've never forgotten you. You were one of the best parts of my life and I can't let all that just be swept away like it never happened. If it hadn't been for you making me feel like I was worth something, I don't think I'd be where I am today.'

'Of course you would.'

'No, I don't think so. I'm serious, Al. Before I met you, I was the no-good, no-hoper son of a man even people in the fishing industry didn't like. He was a mean, selfish arsehole and I didn't see any kind of future other than decking for some other trawler company for the rest of my life. Then you came along. I knew you were out of my league—way out of it—but I couldn't stop thinking about you. That day I asked you out, I didn't think I stood a chance, but from that moment on you changed my life. You saw something in me no one else saw. You made me feel like I was worth something and that I needed to make something of myself—for you. I wanted to be the kind of man you would be proud to take home to meet your parents one day.'

Alex felt her throat tighten. His voice had gone slightly husky with emotion and it wrapped around her heart, squeezing it tightly. 'You were always that person, Sully,' she said softly.

He shook his head. 'If I was, I didn't see it.'

'I did. And you would have found it without me, eventually. Look at everything you've done. That was without me. That was all you.'

'It came from what you saw and brought out in me. I get why you didn't want to be seen with me back then. I used to hate it, but I understand it. And it was probably the one thing that drove me: to make sure I became someone you were proud to be with.'

'I wasn't ashamed of you,' Alex said, now blinking at him. 'Sully, it was never that.' How could he think she'd been embarrassed by him? 'We were kids. I was ruled by my parents and their expectations. I wasn't ashamed of you, I was just afraid of my father stopping us from seeing each other. That's why I was so paranoid about keeping us quiet. You know that.' *Didn't he?*

'I know that was part of it.'

'That was the only reason,' she countered. Realising he'd thought she was ashamed of being seen with him upset her more than she'd thought possible. 'Sully, you had to know that?'

'You know, I've only been inside this house once before this.'

She remembered the time he was talking about. Her parents had been away for the day and she'd snuck him in. She'd often wished they could've had a normal teenage relationship where they'd been free to come and go from her house and he'd have experienced her mother's Sunday roasts. But that hadn't been their story. 'I'm sorry if I ever made you feel like I was ashamed of you. That wasn't how it was at all.'

'Yeah, I know. It's just the way it was back then.'

They became lost in their own memories until Sully broke the silence. 'I met a bloke on the fishing trip,' he said, staring out over the ocean thoughtfully. 'An old guy. He was telling me about how he let fear and doubts get in the way of reuniting with the woman he'd loved all his life but had let go,' he said, looking up and catching her startled gaze. 'From the moment I saw you again, I knew I'd never really stopped loving you, Alex.'

Alex blinked. Her heart felt like it was ready to launch from her chest. 'Sully.'

'I know, it sounds crazy. But it's true. Those feelings are still there, Al. That has to prove something. *Mean* something,' he added.

'How? I mean . . . It makes no sense that two people who've been apart for almost twenty years can still feel . . . like that.' She'd meant it to come out sounding far more forceful than it did. The thing was, as she tried to question it, she suddenly realised he was right. Standing here beside him now, it did feel as though all the years between had melted away and they were right back where they'd been before.

She didn't move as he leaned closer and when he tentatively touched her lips with his own, she found herself responding as though it had only been yesterday since they'd last shared a kiss, not a lifetime. It was completely overwhelming and she felt herself being swept up in the sensations and carried away.

She felt his heart pounding against his chest and the low moan he gave as she moved her hands slowly up and around his neck sent her own pulse racing in response. This was the same and yet so very different. Almost as though her body remembered the feel of him, only more filled out and defined compared to the muscular lankiness of the nineteen-year-old she'd known. God, she'd missed this.

She knew it was crazy and she shouldn't be reacting like this—they were supposed to be grown adults—yet there was no way she could drag herself out of his arms or away from his heady kisses. Sure, she'd been kissed before, but she'd never really let anyone kiss her quite like this. She'd always put boundaries up with men—it was never about allowing someone to get close, personal. It had only ever been about that instant relief, never about intimacy. Not until now.

His big hands held her waist, anchoring her to the ground when she felt as though she were floating away. Soon the need inside her reached boiling point and her impatient hands found their way to his waist to tug at the hem of his shirt and search for the heat of his skin beneath.

Clearly, Sully wasn't waiting around for any further encouragement and, with one swift movement, had whipped off his shirt and was helping Alex remove hers. 'Do you want to go inside?' he asked between deep kisses, running his lips along her neck.

She shook her head, uncaring how desperate that made her seem. Besides, out here was as private as anywhere inside the house. She removed her T-shirt and stepped out of her denim shorts, balancing awkwardly when neither of them were willing to break the kisses. There was a sense of urgency. It was almost as though their bodies had been waiting for this day for all those years even if their heads and hearts hadn't thought it ever likely.

Alex didn't want to think about her actions—all she wanted was to feel. Finally. God, she'd missed how good this was between them. She'd thought maybe she'd been romanticising how amazing the sex had been, after all— they'd been teenagers for goodness' sake—but apparently she hadn't been imagining it. Still, this had to be even better than back then? Otherwise, how on earth had they not been constantly doing this all day?

She felt herself being walked slowly towards the edge of the day bed, following Sully down as he pulled her to him.

The last of the afternoon light dipped below the mountains and they were left in a cocoon of pre-evening darkness. The air felt so good against her naked skin, Sully's fingertips creating a trail of goosebumps up her spine that made her gasp and arch into his touch.

'God, you're beautiful,' she heard him whisper as he smoothed back her hair and held her face between his hands. They stared at each other, taking their fill, searching the new and yet familiar face before them, before the urgency rose once more and took over.

Nothing else mattered except quenching the hunger.

Sully stared up at the dark sky above him as he fought to get his breathing back to normal. He didn't dare move a muscle in case he woke up and realised he'd just dreamed the whole thing—but the pain in his left thigh where the lounge was digging into it kind of put his mind at ease.

Alex was still draped across him, her soft skin under his fingertips smooth and warm. He thought he'd happily stay just like this forever, pain in his thigh be damned. It'd be worth it.

But almost as though sensing his discomfort, Alex wriggled off him, mumbling an apology that she was probably too heavy, and reached for her T-shirt, hastily pulling it on as she sat upright.

For a long time he didn't say anything—he was too scared of breaking whatever magical spell this was between them. Sure, he'd come up here this evening to lay his heart on the line, but never in his wildest imagination had he ever expected something like *this* to happen. Not this soon anyway. In all honesty, he hadn't even dared imagine what might happen after he told her how he felt, let alone anything further than that. He'd been preparing himself for her to slam the door in his face.

This . . . Well, he couldn't even begin to wrap his head around all this. It was more than he'd ever hoped for and it certainly proved that they still had chemistry. Bucketloads.

As Alex stood up to pull on the remainder of her clothes, Sully followed her lead, reaching for his own gear to get dressed. As much as he'd prefer they both stay naked and take this inside for round two, he figured it was probably wiser that they talked.

'I need a drink. Something strong. You want one?' Alex seemed fidgety and unsure.

'Sure. Whatever you're having is fine,' he said, running a hand through his hair quickly. 'Do you need help?' he asked.

He stayed seated when she shot out a hand almost in warning. 'No! You stay there. I'll get it.'

'Okay,' he said calmly, settling back, trying not to spook her any more than she already seemed to be. 'I'll wait right here.'

Was she regretting it? She must be, he decided, recalling the look on her face just now. Shit. He'd moved too fast. And yet she hadn't shied away from his kiss. In fact, she seemed to be into it as much as, if not more than, he had been, so he was fairly sure that wasn't the issue.

It was more likely she was already jumping ahead to what the bigger picture was going to look like. That was a justifiable reason to freak out, he supposed. She was certainly the one giving up more than he was if they wanted this to be anything more than a 'for old times' sake' thing. It was so much more than that—at least for him.

He didn't want to end up like Trevor. He wanted a second chance at a future with Alex. And not only because he felt robbed of the one they were supposed to have eighteen years ago.

Twenty-one

Alex stared into the kitchen sink as she braced her hands on the edge. What the actual hell had just happened?

This had not been part of her itinerary when she'd planned this trip home. She was supposed to get in and get out again without any delays. So far she'd stretched her initial four days, hosted a book club and caught up with more old friends than she'd expected. And now she'd just slept with her ex-boyfriend.

Oh dear God. What had she done?

She'd allowed herself to get caught up in Sully's nostalgic trip and completely lost her fricken mind in the process. Sure, the sex was great, but—Christ on a bike—why did she have to let Sully be the one to sneak in under her defences? He was not the kind of man you brushed off as a one-night stand.

There was something almost sacrilegious about messing with memories of your first love—you just didn't go back there and expect it not to be a huge deal. Dealing with that was the last thing she bloody needed right now.

She took down the bottle of whiskey she'd bought the other day and splashed a measure in the bottom of a glass. Winced as the burn ran down her throat. Crossing to the fridge, she took out ginger ale and mixed two drinks, testing hers before picking up both glasses and heading back out. Maybe if she got Sully drunk enough he might forget all about whatever insanity had driven him up here tonight.

'I know what you're going to say,' he said as she walked outside and placed his glass in front of him.

'You do?' Thank goodness one of them knew what to say.

'You think it was a mistake and we should forget it happened.'

She opened her mouth to agree but he rushed on.

'That's a perfectly reasonable response. It took us both by surprise. However, I don't think either of us can forget what just happened and we'd just be wasting time if we tried. Instead, I put it to you that we use whatever time you have left here to see what happens.'

'What exactly do you think is going to happen, Sully?'

'Best-case scenario: we realise there's still something special there and we give it a go.'

'Are you forgetting I live on the other side of the world? Don't you think that might be a bit of an obstacle?'

'People work relationships around distance all the time.'

221

'Not that much distance.'

'That's getting ahead of ourselves,' he said, shaking his head. 'Let's just see where it goes for the time we have left and then we can worry about the logistics.'

'It's crazy,' she said, throwing her hands up.

'So you agree that there's still something between us?'

'I didn't say that.'

'You're already stressing over the hows and whys. You think we have a shot at a future.'

'I'm simply pointing out the biggest fault in your plan. Even if things worked out, the distance would almost certainly be the one thing that made it impossible.'

'Nothing's impossible, Alex,' he said simply, taking a long sip of his drink. 'If you want something bad enough, there'll always be a way to make it happen.'

He *was* crazy.

'Come on, you have to see we're still good together. Do you really want to deny yourself that again when you don't have to? Even if only for the next few weeks?'

'Days,' she corrected. 'Not weeks. I'm not staying any longer than it takes to sort this out,' she said, nodding towards the house.

'Even more reason not to waste time.'

'I don't remember you being this . . . enterprising before.'

He shrugged. 'I'm a businessman now. I know how to hold on to a good thing when I see it.'

She flashed him a doubtful glance. 'I'm not promising anything. In fact, I'm going on the record right now to say there's no way this is going to go any further once I leave here.'

'So it's a deal then,' he said, standing up and draining the contents of his glass before placing it on the table. 'I'll pick you up tomorrow morning at six.'

'Six? In the morning?'

'Yep. We need an early start.'

'For what?'

'I'm taking you out on a charter.'

Alex opened her mouth and stared at him, but she struggled to find any words. She settled on, 'What?' sure she'd somehow missed part of the conversation.

'No heels.'

'Heels? Why the hell would I wear heels?'

'I don't know. You London types, who knows what you'd wear on a boat.'

'I've already been on your boat!' she said, then stamped her foot. Why the hell was he walking away from her while they were still having a discussion?

'Six! Be ready,' he threw over his shoulder.

'I bloody well won't be,' she said to the space where he'd just been. She stared after him. This was so stupid. She hadn't agreed to anything, and now he had them spending time she didn't have together just to prove . . . what? That they were good in bed?

For a moment she was distracted as she recalled what had happened earlier. Then she shook her head to clear her not-so-pure thoughts. This was just so . . . dumb.

The following morning, though, she was standing at her front door at six, dressed in a pair of denim cut-off shorts, a white T-shirt and a pair of white sandshoes, and she had no logical explanation for why.

In all honesty, Sully hadn't expected Alex to come with him. The whole way to her door, he'd been sweating. To his relief, she had been waiting. She wasn't wearing a beaming smile, but he could overlook the less-than-enthusiastic attitude since she was here on his boat and he had the whole day to prove to her that she'd made the right choice.

The sky had turned it on today, the clearest of baby blue skies against the deeper blue tones of the ocean filling him with the kind of peace he only found out here. This was his haven. The salty smell of the ocean, the breeze lightly caressing his face and the sun warm on his skin. He wanted to share all this with Alex, bring her into part of his world.

Up on the flybridge, on the top level of the boat, the views were spectacular—there wasn't another vessel in sight this far out and they could easily be the only two people left on the planet. His gaze shifted slightly to Alex where she sat quietly on the built-in seating. Her head was tilted back as the wind lifted her hair and a faint smile was etched on her face. He couldn't see her eyes behind her dark sunglasses, but he suspected they were closed. For the first time, he felt torn between what he wanted to watch the most: the scenery before him or the woman who had never let go of his heart.

Almost as though reading his mind, Alex straightened and turned her head towards him. Even through her dark glasses he could feel her gaze lock on to his face and his whole body stirred.

He throttled down, coming off the plane to slow the boat gently to a standstill, allowing it to drift, then headed down the staircase to the main deck. He went to the side where he'd set up the lines earlier to drag bait along as they headed out. Sure enough, one line was jerking and he lifted the rod out of the holder and began winding it in. Alex came to stand beside him.

'You want to reel it in?' he asked, already angling his body sideways for her to slip in and take the pole.

'I don't fish,' she stammered, but accepted the fishing rod he'd given her no real choice but to take.

He reached around her, guiding her hands and instructing her briefly on reeling it in. 'We've let it drag for a bit, so just let the rod do the work. Keep it up at about a forty-five degree angle to the water, aim it towards the fish. When you feel the fish slow down and it stops taking line, lift the tip of the rod up then reel in as you lower it back down to about forty-five degrees again and then just keep doing that. Lift, reel, lower. That's it,' he encouraged as she tentatively followed his instructions.

He caught the flash of crimson and silver as the fish came up and leaned over to pick up the net.

'Oh my God. It's a fish!' Alex said, causing him to chuckle, then quickly remind her to keep reeling and lifting when she stopped to try and get a better look at the fish.

Eventually, the fish broke through the surface and Sully scooped up the squirming, flapping body, bringing it over the side of the boat.

'A nice red. Good job.'

'A red? What kind of fish is that?'

'Snapper. It's a beauty,' he told her with a grin. 'How was that?'

'Pretty cool, actually. I had no idea fishing could be so invigorating.'

He gave another chuckle as he watched her wipe her hands on the sides of her shorts and screw her nose up slightly.

The water slapped at the side of the hull, as the boat rocked gently and for a moment he simply just took her all in.

'What's wrong?' she asked nervously, looking at him warily.

Realising he must have been staring, he cleared his throat and extracted the fish from the net. 'I better go clean this up for lunch.'

He hadn't been able to stop thinking about last night. He hadn't been able to stop thinking about *her* since she arrived back in town, but after the sex . . . It wasn't just sex, he swiftly corrected as he cleaned the fish at the rear of the boat, it'd been so much more than that. Something he'd never had with anyone else. That had to mean something, surely? After all this time, there was still something powerful, familiar yet new and exciting between them. It should have felt like being with someone new, since they'd been kids the last time they'd been together, but it hadn't. There hadn't been any hesitation. It was as if their bodies had instantly recognised each other, and that magnetism had sprung to life like it had only been yesterday, not almost two whole decades since they'd last been in each other's arms.

Twenty-two

'Maybe it's all the sea air or something, but this is the most delicious meal I think I've ever eaten,' Alex said between bites of the flaky white fish. Sully had cooked it on the large barbecue on the deck and brought out a salad and potato bake he seemed to have magically conjured up from the kitchen.

'It always tastes better when you've caught it yourself,' he told her, smiling.

A tingle of awareness ran through her. She'd forgotten how potent that smile of his was. She'd forgotten a lot of things.

Last night seemed to have changed everything. She wanted to be irritated—and to a certain degree, she was. After all, this had *not* been part of the plan. However, she'd be lying if she said she hadn't enjoyed it. But this was more than just enjoying a night of nice sex. Okay, it was so much more than nice. *Great* sex, she amended silently. *Mind-blowing sex, more like it,* the little voice scoffed as it offered her a selection of highlights from the evening. As if she needed reminding.

She cleared her throat and dragged her gaze away from the mouth that had driven her wild last night. 'I could get used to all this amazing cooking.'

'Glad you like it.'

'What would you have done if you hadn't caught a fish, though?'

'There's always steak in the freezer.'

They shared a smile but she found it difficult to hold his gaze without feeling that annoying tingling sensation. This really was getting ridiculous. She was a woman who'd lived overseas, dealt with huge customer accounts and worked with a government agency—where was her professionalism? Her worldly independence? It had somehow been replaced by this weird grown-up version of her seventeen-year-old self.

'Thank you,' she said when Sully stood to collect their plates. 'Can I help?'

'Nope, I just load them into the dishwasher.'

'It's all very sophisticated, this fishing thing.'

'This kind of fishing is,' he agreed. 'The trawling side of it isn't like this.'

'I remember. You used to come back from being out on the boat and sleep for a whole day.'

'It was pretty full-on back then—still is, to a certain degree, although the conditions have improved a bit. Still hard work, though.'

'I can imagine.'

'What about you? Are there parts of your job you don't enjoy?'

'I think every job must have its days but, yeah, there're certain people I work with who make life challenging. But the job itself is always interesting and I really love living over in the UK.'

'Don't you get homesick?'

'Not really. It helps having Mum there, even though I've been pretty slack at visiting lately. Typical, isn't it. Sometimes you can live in the same town as someone and see people from further away more often.'

'I know what you mean. For a place this size, it's surprising how often you bump into someone and realise it's been a year since you've caught up.'

Alex smiled. 'I guess occasionally I miss the weather and the sun—I could do with a mild winter like we have here instead of the bone-chilling cold. But I think I've gotten used to being over there, you know?'

'I can't imagine living anywhere else,' he said.

She understood far more than she felt comfortable admitting, even to herself. This was paradise. The crystal-clear water, the gorgeous shades of aqua, turquoise, emerald green and brilliant blues of the ocean. Some days, when she'd been walking on the beach, it was almost *too* beautiful—it didn't seem real. But it was, and she'd grown up with it on her doorstep and pretty much taken it for granted. It was like a different planet from London's busy streets and traffic, the biting cold and the dreary grey days she'd be going back to . . .

What if I didn't?

The thought startled her. She straightened her shoulders and frowned as she pushed away the unsettling idea. Why on earth wouldn't she want to return to London? Her life was at an all-time high: she had a job she loved, she'd found a house she adored and the idea of settling down after all these years of moving around was almost a reality. She was done with adventures, she wanted to be a real grown-up and own a house and put down roots.

You could do that anywhere, though . . . even here . . .

Why were these thoughts creeping into her head all of a sudden? No, she could not put down roots here. The last thing she wanted to do was end up back here. Like her father.

She felt the strangest flash of recognition race through her. Her father had returned to face his demons and clean up the place he loved. He'd gone out into the world and then come back. But her dad had tried to do something noble. She, on the other hand, had nothing really to offer by coming back here.

'Alex?'

She jumped as Sully dragged her back from her troubled thoughts. 'Sorry?'

'I asked if you wanted any more to eat?'

'Oh. No. Thank you,' she said quickly. 'I'm full. That was delicious.'

'Can't beat fresh-caught fish.'

Alex stood up and helped clear their dishes, ignoring his instructions to sit down and relax. 'I'm not a paying customer. The least I can do is clean up after you've cooked—again.'

He grinned. 'Hey, I'm open for an invitation to your place for dinner any time. Can you even cook?' he asked, eyeing her doubtfully.

'Of course I can cook,' she said, affronted by his assumption.

'Are you sure? I kind of had you pegged for the micro-wave heat-up.'

'I'll have you know I actually cook the best roast lamb dinner this side of the equator.'

'Maybe you should let me be the judge of that?' he teased as she packed the dishes he passed her.

'Fine. Tomorrow night.'

'You're on.'

'Did you seriously just orchestrate an opportunity to invite yourself to dinner?'

Sully's grin widened and he sent her a wink, which triggered a small thrill of something warm and a little bit tingly inside of her.

Once the kitchen had been restored to its usual pristine condition, Sully sent Alex out to the rear of the deck, joining her a few minutes later with a cocktail. 'Sit and relax,' he instructed, handing the glass to her.

'I've been relaxing all day,' she tried to protest, but even she had to admit it came out sounding rather weak. What was the point of fighting any longer? Deep down, she really didn't want to.

She sipped the delicious cocktail and watched Sully move around the deck as he checked fishing lines then sat down across from her, leaning back to close his eyes as the sun warmed his face.

How did the man manage to get even better looking with age? He pulled off the rugged, stubbly thing with casual ease. She had a feeling his look wasn't influenced by fashion. Today he was dressed in cargo shorts and a T-shirt and her eyes freely roamed over him, enjoying the way the soft fabric of his shirt lovingly hugged his torso. A memory of her fingers gently tracing the same path flashed through her mind and she swallowed hard. Enough of that. God, if she wasn't careful she'd end up—

Her mind suddenly paused in its perving to listen intently. *End up back in bed?* It supplied almost hopefully.

Of course she'd enjoyed their night, and more of that before she left wouldn't be the most terrible thing in the world to have to go through. But to what end? Sully was already hinting at wanting something a lot more permanent and Alex wasn't in a position to give him that kind of guarantee. Her life was in London.

She tried to still all the conflict going on inside her and just listen to a voice of reason. But while she waited for it, nothing came. Where was the logical, sane part of her that should be saying, *That's right! Your job, which you love, is on the other side of the world. You don't want to stay here. You want to go back to your real life.*

Instead, another part of her began listing all the reasons she didn't want to go back. She'd miss the beach, the long early morning walks and late afternoon strolls listening to the waves crashing on the shore. Technically, she could get those back in the UK. *But not in London*, the snippy little voice reminded her. The house she grew up in. *Nostalgia*, the voice continued. But the house she'd grown up in had been redecorated and her bedroom wasn't even the same. *As if a grown-arse woman would still be living in a candy-pink room with pop stars on the wall.*

Alex was beginning to think her inner conscience might actually be a smart-mouthed fifteen-year-old, which was a little disconcerting. But it had a point. Being back in her childhood home and the number of good memories that brought had surprised her, despite the bad ones threatening to ruin them. She did have an idyllic childhood; a family, security, space to explore and roam to her heart's content. Her childhood had been filled with laughter, sunshine, long days at the beach and plenty of fun—everything any kid could possibly want.

And let's not forget you have your best friend back in your life. There *was* that. Tanya. Over the years, Alex had made plenty of friends through her travels, including some she'd ended up travelling with before they went their separate ways. Some she'd made through work. A few she'd met in places like the gym or the supermarket. But none of them was Tanya. None of them was the kind of friend you could depend on. None of them knew her better than she knew herself. None of them knew all her secrets— *Well, most of them*, Alex thought, quickly squashing that train of thought. She *had* missed Tanya. She'd been an idiot to let that friendship go, but it was as though all the years they'd lost had faded away and they'd picked up almost where they'd left off. Tanya being able to forgive Alex for leaving without a goodbye only proved what an amazing person she was. Did Alex really want to lose that friendship again?

And then there was Sully.

It was ridiculous. People didn't fall back in love with their high-school sweethearts, did they? Okay, so she may have seen a headline or two in a magazine at a checkout counter about people finding love at school reunions and bumping into old flames at a retirement village, but her and Sully? After everything they'd gone through? *It was a long time ago*, the little voice pointed out and that was true. She didn't feel that sting of betrayal over him getting Karla pregnant anymore. They'd been kids, and life had other plans in store for both of them. Now, older and wiser, maybe there was a new plan on the table. What if this was one of those moments in life when the universe dropped a huge opportunity in front of you and you had a choice to either take it or ignore it?

She drained the remainder of her cocktail and set the glass on the nearby table. There were too many what ifs in her head right now. She closed her eyes and listened to the slap of the swell rhythmically hitting the side of the boat, feeling the gentle rock as the boat rode the rise and fall of the ocean beneath them.

Twenty-three

Sully tilted back his head and let out a long sigh. His plan had been to bring her out here, away from distractions and interruptions, and try to figure out if, somehow, they might have a shot at a second chance. He was the first to admit it was probably a crazy idea. On paper, there was little he and Alex had in common, yet that had always been the case and they'd fallen head over heels in love. Theirs had been a modern-day *Romeo and Juliet* love story. Separately they were opposites, but together, that was when the magic happened. Together they were perfect. Sure, back then they hadn't exactly been living in the real world, but now they were grown-ups. He had a thriving business and money of his own. There wasn't anything holding them back this time—except her job and the fact she lived on the other side of the world. But surely they could find a way around that?

He opened his eyes and let his gaze rest on Alex as she peacefully reclined on the sunlounge. Her shoulder-length hair, parted slightly off-centre, fell in a soft curtain around her face. The colour was a little darker than it used to be. Back then it had been blonde, a sandy beach blonde with the lightest hint of golden honey. She'd worn it long, sometimes pulled back in a ponytail but often left hanging down. He'd loved running his fingers through its length and could still feel the silky smoothness of the strands and smell the fragrance—green apples and sea salt from long days spent in the water. This older version of Alex had hair of a warmer shade like hot toffee. The shorter length suited her. She looked professional. Confident. This Alex had her life together.

Almost as though she sensed him looking at her, Alex opened her eyes.

He found himself unable to break the connection. 'Another drink?' he asked, clearing his throat hastily.

'No thanks. But would you mind if I made a coffee?'

'Sure.' He stood and she quickly sat up and swung her legs off the side of the lounge.

'No, seriously, let me. You've done nothing but cook and clean and catch fish. I'm sure I can figure out how to work the coffee machine.'

'You're my guest. Besides, it'll be easier for me to find everything than if I try and explain where everything is.'

'It's not that big a kitchen,' she said, following him inside. 'But fine, Mr Pedantic, you make the coffee.'

'I *am* rather fond of my coffee machine,' he said, giving the impressive stainless-steel beast a tender pat. 'It can be a little tricky to get the hang of.'

'Okay,' she said, but he noticed the grin that hovered on her lips.

His gaze stayed on her mouth until he forced himself to drag it away and concentrate on the coffee.

Alex swallowed hard. She'd held her breath as his eyes seemed to almost smoulder as he'd watched her. She wanted to scoff at the soap opera term but, for the life of her, she could not. Smouldering was the only way to describe the look he'd been giving her. She could feel body heat radiating off him in waves and her own sudden desire flared to life in response.

One minute she was leaning against the small counter watching him set up the coffee machine and the next she was moving.

Sully glanced up, his eyes widening slightly as she stopped in front of him.

'I changed my mind about the coffee,' she heard a sultry, vixen-like voice say. Holy crap, this felt like an out-of-body experience, yet she couldn't seem to stop it. Even while part of her was frantically scrambling to work out *why* she was doing this, another part she had no real control over had already decided she was going to get exactly what she wanted. She registered the sound of Sully dropping the coffee filter into the sink as his arms wrapped around her and he kissed her.

After an endless moment, she was lifted onto the counter. Her legs automatically wrapped around his hips as he slid her closer to his body, fitting perfectly together. *Like a freakin' glove*, she thought as their kisses grew deeper and more urgent.

When they eventually broke apart, they were breathing heavily.

'Wait,' Sully said, stopping her hands from removing her shirt.

'Seriously?'

'As much as I'd like to believe I'm still flexible enough to perform a miracle here, I'm not. Follow me. I've got a better idea.'

He helped her off the bench and led her down the stairs, through the first level and onto the lower deck.

'Is this the captain's room?' she asked curiously.

'It is today.' He grinned, stepping closer and wrapping an arm around her waist.

She breathed him in, the salty smell of the ocean mixed with sunscreen and something uniquely Sully. It was familiar yet different, somehow far more potent than her memories of him.

His teasing smile faded as they looked at each other, then he lowered his head and kissed her once more. From that moment on, everything else ceased to exist. There was only feeling. The warm skin of his chest after he pulled his shirt over his head. The hard calluses of hands that still managed to tenderly caress and rub against her. His mouth, which trailed hot kisses across her burning skin, driving her crazy with need. And she did need him. Desperately. If he didn't possess her right then, her body would be consumed by raging fire.

For the first time in her life, Alex took the lead. She didn't want anything that reminded her of the past, she didn't want slow and sensual, she just wanted him.

Pushing against Sully's chest, she followed him onto the bed, straddling his hips and wallowing in the sudden surge of sensual power the position gave her. Wordlessly, she edged her shirt up her midriff, watching as his gaze followed the movement like a hungry animal. When he went to reach for her, she shook her head and made him wait. There was something liberating about being the one who set the pace. For the first time, she was the one in control and it felt . . . good.

Sully watched, waiting patiently. Although his eyes were slightly hooded, he was anything but relaxed. She could feel his hard body—sculpted from a lifetime of hard work, not by hours in a gym with a trainer—beneath her and she let her fingers trace down his torso, touching every scar and mark on his tanned skin that a life spent out in the elements had branded him with. When she reached the band of his shorts, she smiled at his sharp intake of breath and watched his eyes darken with a renewed surge of desire. The intensity should have scared her—had she seen this in anyone else's face, it would have terrified her—but not here and now. Not with Sully.

Despite the hunger and need she saw on his face, she knew he would never do anything to hurt her. With Sully, she knew she'd always be safe. The realisation distracted her.

Any other time she'd had sex, it had always felt unnatural—as though she had to do it in order to prove to herself that what had happened to her all those years ago was not going to define her. But she'd never truly felt anything for her partners after the initial moment of release. It was always more a relief that it was over and she was fine. But not with Sully. She hadn't been ready for the avalanche of emotions that had threatened to explode after the last time. But now . . . she felt safe.

The knowledge gave her even more confidence. She reached behind her and removed her bra, letting it fall to the ground. She watched as Sully's eyes devoured her silently, reverently, and never before had she ever felt so beautiful. Had he said the words out loud, she'd have brushed them off and felt embarrassed and awkward, but *seeing* the words on his face—that was something far more powerful.

She leaned towards him, her hands touching his stomach and moving gradually upwards, pinning his arms over his head so he couldn't touch her, then touched his lips gently with her own. He tasted slightly salty, but there was a lingering hint of the malty hops from the beer he'd had earlier. She deepened the kiss and felt the reverberation of his low moan in response. Her body reacted instinctively, answering his call as their kisses deepened and became all consuming. She let go of his arms and felt them clamp around her, his hands roaming the length of her body before they both became frustrated at the remaining clothing and quickly dispensed of it with little regard to how it was removed.

They were yin and yang—hard and soft, smooth and rough, steel and velvet—and it all fit together exactly, like the perfect pieces of a puzzle.

Their bodies ignited and something else took over. The intensity should have frightened her, but it didn't. Sully moved her, flipping their positions, one big hand covering both of hers above her head, but he wasn't pinning her in position, simply anchoring her, holding her in place so she didn't spin completely out of control. Their eyes locked as he moved above her, her body wrapping around his and absorbing every part of him into her. He was her air and her lifeblood—at this very moment, she felt as though without him she would simply . . . stop being. There wasn't time to dwell on it, but it was impossible not to acknowledge the fact—but then she stopped thinking and simply surrendered to the moment.

He broke her into a million pieces, then instantly put her back together again as he held her tightly against him, their bodies breathing as one, their heartbeats perfectly in sync.

For the first time in forever, she was whole once again.

Sully lay with his arm over his face as he waited for his breathing to slow down. Alex was tucked against him, her smaller frame moulded to his side. Nothing had ever felt so good. It was like he'd suddenly had a missing limb grow back. The missing part of him he'd always needed.

The previous night he'd realised how much chemistry they both still had, but this . . . this went beyond that. It was more than just sex, it was like some kind of switch had been turned on, lighting up corners of his mind he hadn't even realised had been hiding in the dark.

He still loved Alex Kelly. Maybe even more than he had before. He wasn't sure how it was possible—they'd been virtual strangers for eighteen years—and yet, today, he knew he'd found his other half. He used to laugh at any conversation that involved soul mates. He'd learned all too well that love had a habit of blowing up in your face. He'd had an all-consuming love with Alex when they were teenagers, before he'd been stupid and thrown it away. Over the years, he'd written them off as a hormone-infused teenage romance. Believed he'd blown the memories of how electric they'd been together out of proportion. A trick of the imagination. He hadn't believed in soul mates . . . Till now.

He still wasn't sure what had been happening lately. Ever since Alex had come home, he'd been overcome by weird feelings. In the last few days in particular, the thought of her leaving again had almost crippled him with pain. He wanted her to stay, but until this very moment he hadn't realised just how deep this thing went.

He wasn't imagining how good the sex was between them. It always had been, but today something had changed. He'd felt—he gave a silent, slightly nervous chuckle; he was going to sound like an idiot—but he'd felt her down to an almost molecular level. She was *part* of him somehow.

243

Christ, he really was losing his mind. Maybe he had sun stroke or something.

He felt Alex move beside him and turned his head to look at her. His heart gave a kick. She was beautiful. Her hair was tousled and her eyes held a slumberous look that made him itch to reach over and kiss her. She seemed to be watching him as warily as he was watching her. Had she felt the same thing? He wanted to ask, but what if she hadn't? He'd sound like a lunatic.

'Are you okay?' she asked.

He cleared his throat before answering. 'Yeah. You? I wasn't too rough or . . . anything?' He cringed inwardly. He wanted to tell her how amazing what they'd just experienced had been, but he wasn't sure if it would scare her off, considering it was kind of freaking him out. This woman was important to him and he knew, somehow, they were meant to be . . . but how? Thinking about the day she would leave hurt more than he cared to admit. There *had* to be a way to make this thing work.

'I'm fine,' she said quietly, and his heart squeezed at the gentle smile she gave him.

'Is it just me, or is this thing—us—' he corrected quickly, 'what's happening, does it feel like it's somehow meant to be?'

He held his breath in the silence that followed and wished he could take his stupid stammering back. Why hadn't he just said something cool instead?

'It's not just you,' she finally said and he allowed himself to cautiously release his breath. 'This is . . . something.' She lowered her eyes to where she'd started tracing idle circles on his bare chest. 'Maybe it's just that we share a past and that's always going to feel different from being with someone you don't know.'

'Probably,' he said, hoping she wouldn't stop touching him. 'But it's more than just reliving the past. At the risk of scaring you off, I haven't felt like this in a long time. For the last few years I've just been going through the motions: work, raising Gabby, building my business; rinse, repeat,' he said with a weary smile. 'I'm not saying life was boring or bad, but ever since you came back it feels like everything is *different*.'

'Everything *is* different since I came back,' she murmured. 'My coming back has upset the status quo.'

He chuckled. 'Like a force of nature.'

'Unfortunately,' she agreed. 'But maybe not in a good way.'

'Where I'm concerned, it's in a good way,' he said, entwining his fingers through hers.

'Not where the past is concerned though. Or the Duncans,' she added, and he hated that her voice was so dull and empty.

'We need to let go of the past at some point, Al. So we can move on to something better.'

'I'm not deliberately holding on to it, it just keeps following me ever since I came back here. It's out of my control.'

'Then we should make a deal not to talk about it again when it's just you and me. We can control that much.'

He watched her consider his proposal.

She gave a small shrug. 'Okay. Deal. But I'm wondering if we'll actually have anything in common if we rule out everything in the past.'

'I can think of one thing we have in common,' he said with a slow grin.

She rolled her eyes. 'Trust you to think of sex.'

'What! I was thinking about fishing. Now that you've tried it, we have a hobby we can share. Jeez, woman, can you keep your mind out of the gutter for five minutes?'

'Yeah, right.'

'Sometimes I feel like all you think I am is a piece of meat,' he continued in a pathetic voice, watching her smile melt away the lingering sadness.

Twenty-four

Life almost felt like a dream for the next few days. Sully had come over for dinner the next night as promised and she'd made a roast dinner. The potatoes were a bit hard and the gravy had a few lumps in it, but overall it was better than she'd expected. Not that they wasted too much time critiquing the meal—they ended up in bed a short time after finishing it.

That was how the next few days went—Alex hung around the boat while Sully did whatever maintenance he had to do, then they'd go for a swim at the beach or pack a picnic lunch and go for a drive, heading down long, country roads and ending up in remote national parks, where they'd eventually find a quiet place to stop and eat. It had been years since she'd been to some of these places and she hadn't realised how beautiful the landscapes around here truly were.

'So tell me what makes London better than here?' Sully asked one day and Alex looked at him as though he was kidding.

'Ah, it's London? Hello? The culture, fashion and *epicentre* of the world.'

'And you're into fashion and culture?'

Fashion and culture? Well . . . yes. *No,* the voice inside said at the same time. What? Of course she was. She loved the excitement of the big city—all the history and hustle and bustle. *You used to,* the little voice reminded her. *But lately, you've wanted to move to the country like on one of those reality shows about escaping the big city for a quiet country life.* Okay, yes, she tentatively agreed, but it was still *near* London. She could still, technically, visit museums and head into the city any time she wanted to experience a bit of culture or glamour.

'I enjoy living and working over there.'

'But you could do the same kind of job over here? Right? If you wanted to?'

'Well, sure. I could work in the same field. But the point is, I like the job I have now over *there.*'

'You just seem . . . I don't know, more relaxed lately. Different from how you were when you first arrived. You were kind of uptight—tightly wound or something. Now you seem more like the old Alex.'

'I haven't been the old Alex in a long time.'

'Maybe you needed to remember what she was like again?'

'I don't think anyone is the same as they were when they were seventeen.'

'Maybe not in some ways, but I don't think a person's nature truly changes.'

'I admit, I wasn't expecting to feel quite so—' she paused, searching for the right word to explain how she was feeling, '—attached to this place.'

'Why wouldn't you be? This is your home.'

'It hasn't been that for a long time.'

'I know about you and your dad and what happened back then.' He stopped and frowned. 'Well, I guess it changed you in a lot of ways, but maybe it's just taken some time and distance for you to remember some of the good stuff you'd forgotten about.'

There was a lot of that going on. More than she'd antici-pated. She sometimes felt as though she was awakening from a very long hibernation. Small things like the touch of the warm morning sun on her face and the smell of salt heavy in the breeze as she walked along the beach of an evening made her close her eyes and breathe deeply. That in itself was something she hadn't done in far too long as well. As much as she hated to admit it, she *had* been feeling some-thing inside her healing—something she hadn't realised had been quite so broken.

'I haven't wanted to push it in case it was too soon, but I'd really like you to spend some time at my place, with Gabby and me . . . I mean, she's going to be moving away soon, but she's still part of my life and I'd like you to get to know her a bit better.'

So far they hadn't spent much time in anyone else's company, preferring to hide away in her house or on the boat. Neither of them had wanted the rest of the world to intrude on whatever this was, but Alex supposed they'd eventually have to venture out into public. And it wasn't like Sully's daughter was just anyone—she was his life. It was only natural that he'd want them to be comfortable and spend time with each other. But it did feel like a big step.

'Is it too soon?' he asked, sounding slightly deflated.

'No. I mean, it's just.' The intense look he was watching her with made her stop. She felt herself weaken a little. He really wanted this to work. It was all just . . . a lot. She was still trying to sort out her own feelings about this thing they'd somehow decided to fall back into. She couldn't even say she felt ambushed by it, because at any point she could have said no. But she hadn't. Try as she might, she couldn't deny there was still something very real between them.

'You're right. It's a good idea. I'd like to get to know her better.'

The relief that spread across his face helped to dissolve some of the uncertainty she'd been feeling and she actually felt a little calmer. A dose of reality might be a good thing, she thought, feeling a bit more confident about the development. Maybe having a third person around would help slow down the hectic pace they'd been caught up in and give them time to find out how a grown-up relationship would work when there was a kid involved. *It's not like I haven't already met her*, she told herself decisively. Gabby seemed quite friendly. How hard could winning over a teenager be?

Alex stopped in at the cafe and ordered a coffee from one of the waitresses, Lizzy, waving at Tanya as she looked up from the burger she was making, before finding a table to wait.

'Hey. You've been quiet lately. What's been happening?' Tanya asked, taking a seat between orders.

'Oh, nothing really,' Alex said, trying for a carefree tone. She swore under her breath when she saw Tanya's eyes narrow.

'You were a terrible liar as a kid, and you haven't improved. Spill. Now.'

Alex rolled her eyes but didn't protest. Maybe she'd even come here today just so she could talk to someone about what was going on—maybe have some sense talked into her.

'This is amazing!' Tanya gasped after Alex finished confessing. 'It's like one of those love stories—second-chance love!'

'I'm not so sure it was the smartest idea,' Alex admitted reluctantly.

'What? Why? Isn't it as good as you remembered?'

'It's not that.' Alex felt herself begin to blush and became flustered as her friend's eyes lit up delightedly.

'Oh my God, look at you! You're glowing!'

'Would you stop,' Alex said, lowering her voice and sending a glance around the room. 'It's just confusing. He caught me at a weak moment, and I agreed to give it a try and see if anything came of it, but . . .'

'But what?'

'I guess I thought maybe it would kind of fizzle out or something.'

'And it hasn't.'

'No,' Alex heard herself say almost mournfully. 'And now I don't know what to do. My holidays are going so fast and I'll have to leave soon and I just . . . I don't know what to do!' She looked at her friend almost desperately.

'You've fallen back in love with him,' Tanya said softly.

Alex nodded faintly. 'I think I have.' The idea had seemed so ridiculous only a short while ago.

'Wow.' Tanya sat back in her seat and eyed her friend compassionately. 'I guess you've got a really big decision to make.'

'Yeah,' Alex said miserably.

'I don't think anyone can really tell you what you should do,' Tanya said, 'but my suggestion would be to not ignore what your heart is telling you, even if your head is saying something different. Sometimes we can complicate things by overthinking them.'

'Right now *everything* seems overcomplicated.'

Lizzy called out from the kitchen and Tanya stood up to head back to work. Before she left, she put her hand over Alex's hand resting on the table and gave it a squeeze. 'You'll know what to do when the time comes,' she said gently.

❖

Alex waved goodbye to Tanya as she left the cafe with her takeaway coffee and crossed the road.

'Cassie!' she called, hurrying after the woman she'd spotted leaving the reserve. Something had been bothering her about their previous conversation and she'd been hoping she'd get a chance to bring it up somehow.

'It's Alex . . . Kelly,' she said, when Cassie seemed to stare blankly at her.

'Yeah. I know who you are,' Cassie said with a mixture of impatience and sarcasm.

'I've been hoping to bump into you again. I've been wondering about something you mentioned. Last time we spoke, you said something about Jamie.'

The other woman stared at her, her expression shuttered. 'I don't remember.'

'It's just that,' Alex started, then stopped, frustrated. Somehow she had a feeling Cassie knew something about Jamie, something about the night of the party, and she needed to know for sure. 'Was there anything about the night Jamie died that you might have been too scared to tell the police or anyone else about back then?'

'I don't know anythin',' Cassie said, shaking her head and taking a step back.

'I'm not trying to cause any trouble or bring all this up again. I just . . . I can't help but think—'

'What? That you want to shift the blame on to me? I don't think so. I ain't takin' the blame for what happened.'

'I wasn't suggesting you had anything to do with it,' Alex said quickly.

'Good, 'cause it wasn't me.'

'He fell off the headland,' Alex said calmly. 'No one was to blame.'

'Yeah, right,' the other woman scoffed, wiping a knuckle beneath her nose, her gaze jumping around, landing on anything but Alex.

'You still think I had something to do with it?'

'Well, didn't ya?'

'No. I didn't.'

'Seemed a bit suss, you leavin' town straight afterwards and not coming back.'

'I went away to university. It had nothing to do with—'

'Course it didn't,' Cassie said scathingly. 'Had nothin' to do with what happened between you and Jamie that night on the beach.'

On the beach, not the headland. Cassie wasn't referring to when he died. 'What do you know about Jamie and me that night?' Alex asked, almost against her own will.

'I know enough to guess that it wasn't what you were expectin'.'

For a minute, Alex couldn't respond. 'Why would you say that?'

'I know what Jamie was like. He had a mean streak, that one.' She lit up a cigarette and took a deep draw.

'How do you know that?'

The woman held her eyes as she blew the smoke out the side of her mouth. There was something so vulnerable yet defiant in her face that Alex felt herself crumble inside.

'Cassie, did Jamie . . . did he rape you?'

The almost hollow look in the woman's eyes sent a ripple of fear through Alex. 'You mean *too*?'

This time Alex felt her stomach drop to her toes. She knew. Somehow Cassie knew exactly what Jamie had done that night.

Alex sat beside Cassie on the rocks as they watched the tide retreat, leaving rock pools full of tiny seashells and fish behind. She tipped the bottle of alcohol to her mouth and let the strong spirit burn a track down her throat. Alex hadn't asked any more questions earlier, instead she'd headed into the bottle shop and returned, nodding at Cassie to follow her to the beach.

'When did it happen to you?' she asked Cassie.

'About a week before he did the same thing to you. I knew I was right,' she said softly, before taking a long swig of her drink. 'I could tell. I saw you when all that crap was goin' on at the police station. I saw the same look in your eyes, like you were dead inside somehow, and I knew. Only I thought you killed him and I was glad. Because if you hadn't done it, I was gonna.'

Cassie's words shocked Alex. Despite suspecting something had happened to the other girl, she hadn't expected her to have guessed she'd gone through the same thing. 'I honestly didn't do it.'

Alex watched Cassie's face drop as the truth of her words sank in.

'I'd kind of hoped it was you.'

'Why?'

'Doesn't matter—like I said, he's dead. It doesn't matter who did it.'

'You don't believe it was an accident?'

'It wasn't no accident.'

God, this was so frustrating! First her dad wouldn't give up on the idea and now Cassie. 'How can you be so sure? What is it that makes it so hard to believe?'

Cassie gave a shake of her head—just once—and her lips tightened.

'Because you know something? You suspect someone . . . other than me?'

'It doesn't matter no more. You said you weren't gonna drag up the past.'

'Jesus, Cassie!' Alex exploded, standing up and pacing. 'If you know something then you have to tell someone. The Duncans think I did it, even after all this time. If you think there's someone else who might have had something to do with it you need to speak up.'

'I don't know anythin'. And if you were smart, you'd stop askin' questions and stirrin' up trouble. Just let it be.'

'Just let it be? Are you kidding me? I'd love nothing better than for that whole horrible night to be put to bloody rest, but everyone else around here seems determined to keep digging it back up,' she snapped, turning away.

'If you say anythin', you'll have to tell them what he did to ya that night, ya know,' Cassie said, making Alex stop.

'Why didn't *you* tell anyone?' Alex asked quietly, some of the anger taken out of her sails.

'Same reason you didn't. There was no point. Even if he hadn't died that night, no one would have believed me. They might have believed you. You were a cop's daughter.' She lit up another cigarette and took a long draw on it. 'Yeah. They'd probably have believed you.'

'They would have believed you too,' Alex said.

The woman gave a chuckle and didn't bother hiding how condescending it sounded. 'Yeah. Right. His cousin's underage girlfriend. That woulda gone down a treat at the Duncan family Christmas picnic, wouldn't it?'

'Do you *want* to tell someone?'

'What would be the point now? He's dead. No one's gonna put him in jail, are they?'

'No,' Alex said, letting out a hollow sigh. 'But if it helped in some way.'

'It wouldn't. All it'd do is make more trouble.'

Alex saw real fear in the woman's eyes. She understood Cassie's dilemma—the Duncans wouldn't want to hear what Jamie did to her. Without a doubt, they'd say she'd probably led him on and the fallout with Chris wouldn't be worth the hurt of bringing up ancient history. Trouble was something

Alex didn't want either. Tom Duncan had been making his feelings perfectly clear ever since she'd arrived back in town.

'For everyone's sake, includin' yours, leave it alone,' Cassie said, taking the remaining drinks and walking away.

Twenty-five

Sully's house wasn't what she'd expected. For starters, it wasn't on the beach. His old family home—a weatherboard place with peeling paint and wonky front steps—had been one street back from the beach, but that had been knocked down years ago for a new house to be built. Instead, Alex drove through a gate set unobtrusively off the road out of town and followed a dirt track up through the bushland for a hundred metres or so until she came to a clearing where a new single-level brick home sat beside a couple of large sheds.

As she pulled up, Sully came out to greet her.

'Wow. This place is amazing,' she said, sliding her sunglasses to the top of her head. The circle of trees that surrounded the house were tall, easily twenty or thirty metres high. Their dark green foliage was in stark contrast to the deep blue sky above. It was so quiet she could hear the wind gently blowing the leaves between the riot of bird chatter that seemed to come and go in waves. In the distance she could hear the occasional call of a cow.

'I don't think I've ever pictured you as a farmer before,' she said after he'd kissed her hello.

'I'm not.'

'Then who owns the cattle?' she asked, pointing to a few brown and white animals happily grazing along the distant tree line.

'They're agisted. I bought this place so I could build some sheds and have room to store stuff and work on boats—that kind of thing. Come on, I'll take you for a tour.'

Alex followed him to the sheds. The first one had a massive set of roller doors up one end and a smaller entrance door at the other. They went inside. One section of the shed's interior was open plan, with a cluster of seating and a table, and off to the side of a kitchen area were a couple of rooms.

'I lived here while the house was being built,' he explained, showing her to the two doors concealing a bedroom and a bathroom.

The rest of the giant space was dedicated to storage for boats, jet skis, a car and an assortment of motor and quad bikes as well as netting and fishing paraphernalia.

Alex gaped. 'This is huge.'

'Yeah, I know. It seemed a bit like overkill at first, but then I somehow managed to fill it up . . . I'm thinking I might need to build another one soon.' He led her outside and they walked a short distance to the other shed, an open fronted–type farm shed but with a large, partially built boat taking up half of the space.

'You're building a boat?' she asked, once more surprised by Sully's hidden talents.

'Yeah, it's a bit of a side project.'

'How long ago did you start building it?' she asked, eyeing the timber-framed hull.

He rubbed a hand across the back of his neck and winced. 'About two years ago. It's what you call a work in progress. I haven't had time to get back to it since I started. One day I'll find some time, though,' he said, sounding almost wistful.

'Well, it's very impressive.'

'Be more impressive once it actually starts looking like a boat,' he said with a wry grin. He led the way back outside. 'I hope you're hungry, I've got lunch sorted. My specialty.' He indicated the massive stainless-steel barbecue set up on the back patio of the house.

The rear of the house had a tiled entertainment area that was separated by a glass stacker door that led into the open-plan living room and kitchen.

'Take a seat,' he said. 'I've got everything ready to go. Can I get you a wine?'

'Sure, but I can help, if you want to give me a job,' she protested as he walked away.

'Nope. It's all under control. Gabby!' he called, stepping inside.

The young girl Alex had met at the wharf appeared from a hallway, looking at her phone and listening to something on her earphones.

'Alex is here,' Sully said pointedly, and the teenager took the hint and withdrew the ear buds to glance at the table where Alex sat.

Alex waved, sensing this lunch idea hadn't exactly been on the top of Gabby's list of the most exciting things she wanted to do. Gabby put her phone on the kitchen bench and exchanged a silent look with her father. Alex was getting the distinct feeling this kid was not as enthusiastic about her invite to lunch as her father was. She wondered what Sully had told her. She hoped he'd listened when she'd asked him not to make it a big deal, that they were just seeing what happened for now, but she suspected Gabby had somehow already figured out that this was something more than just Dad inviting an old school friend over for lunch. She didn't seem overly thrilled by the idea. Great. Just what Alex didn't want to have to deal with.

'Hi Gabby. How are you?' Alex asked, plastering a smile on her face.

'Good. How's the packing going?'

'Sorry?' Alex replied, momentarily thrown.

'Isn't that what you came back here to do? Pack up a house or something?'

'Oh. Yeah. That,' she said, feeling stupid. 'It's almost done.' Only now she wasn't sure what the hell she was going to do with it all.

'I can't stay long,' Gabby said as Sully joined them, carrying glasses.

'Why? Where are you going?'

'A meeting at the reserve hall. We're painting more picket signs for when the news crew come out tomorrow.'

'News crew?' Alex asked.

'Yeah,' Gabby said, turning to look at her. 'They're doing a story on the Ermon Nicholades development. It's our last chance to get some real public support going.'

'Aren't they supposed to be releasing their updates on the community concerns from the meeting soon?'

'Next week. But we need to keep applying pressure to make them realise they won't get any support from the community and to show the council that we're not going to let them in without a fight.'

'You know, I'm not an expert at any of this,' Alex said, 'but I'm fairly sure they actually don't need the community's support. As long as they've done everything they need to do and have all the correct permits— '

'Murna said you weren't a team player,' Gabby interrupted rudely.

'Gabby,' her father snapped.

'Well, she did.'

'That's enough.'

'It's okay,' Alex said, trying for a calm smile. 'It's none of my business anyway.'

'No. It's a local matter. For locals,' Gabby said with a contemptuous sniff.

'Can we just not talk about the damn development for five minutes?' Sully asked, sounding weary.

'Sure, sweep it under the carpet. Just don't complain to me when this place turns into a smog-ridden metropolis.'

Sully shook his head briefly and reached for his beer.

'I noticed there's a horse over in the other paddock. Is that yours?' Alex asked, hoping to change the topic to something a little less confrontational.

Gabby smiled sweetly, but Alex's moment of hope took a nosedive as soon as the girl spoke.

'No. That's Mum's horse.'

Right. Karla. She and Sully hadn't really discussed Gabby's mother, other than that she'd remarried and moved away to the bigger regional city an hour or so north. There hadn't really been any need. It shouldn't be an awkward topic, but somehow, sitting across from the woman's daughter, Alex was feeling decidedly uncomfortable.

'Dad lets her keep him here,' Gabby added.

Alex smiled. 'Well, that's nice.'

'Just until she and Phil find their own property. They've recently sold the place they were in and had nowhere to put the horse. I'm really lucky that I have parents who still really care about each other.'

'Well . . . that's great. That you have that,' Alex said, in a somewhat stilted tone.

'Gabby, can you bring out the meat so I can start cooking?' Sully asked after the short, awkward silence that followed her statement. 'I'm sorry about that. I don't actually know what's gotten into her today,' he said, after his daughter grudgingly went to fetch the meat.

'Don't worry about it. It's probably just weird meeting your dad's . . .' She stopped and her gaze flew to his in alarm.

'His what?' Sully asked, a teasing smile playing on his lips.

'Friend?' she offered lamely.

'I kinda think she's picked up on a bit more than a friend vibe,' he said dryly, but mercifully let the moment pass. 'She's really a good kid, I'm not sure where this sudden smartarse thing has come from.'

'It's fine.' Alex waved a hand. 'Seriously.'

The plate of meat was plonked down on the timber bench next to the barbecue and Sully gave Alex an apologetic look then got to his feet.

'Your dad tells me you're going to uni soon. Are you excited?'

'Yeah,' Gabby said, lifting one shoulder slightly.

'What are you going to study?'

'Political science.'

'Oh. Interesting. So you have an interest in politics? Is that where you'd ideally like to work?'

'Maybe. I'm not sure yet.'

'Well, I guess there's no hurry to decide,' Alex said and idly traced the bottom of her wine glass with her finger as the sound of a sizzling hot plate filled the silence.

'So did you know my mother when you used to live here?' Gabby asked suddenly and Alex heard Sully drop the barbecue tongs and mutter a curse as he tried to catch them before they hit the ground.

'I knew her from school, yes . . . but not well.'

'You weren't friends then?'

'Not really . . . I mean, we weren't *not* friends, we just didn't have the *same* friends, I guess.'

'She said she remembers you.'

'Oh. Okay.' Fantastic. Alex took a hurried sip of her wine and wished the bloody steak was cooked already. 'I don't mind mine rare,' she called out to Sully, taking another sip.

'Almost done,' he said. 'Just getting a plate.'

'When do you leave?' Gabby asked and there was no mistaking that she wasn't overly saddened by the prospect.

'In a week or so.' It was going too fast all of a sudden.

Gabby's expression seemed somewhat annoyed.

'Here we are. Who's hungry?' Sully asked as he placed the food on the table. Not a moment too soon.

Alex hardly remembered tasting any of the meal and felt bad that all Sully's culinary skills had gone to waste, but the atmosphere, despite Sully's best attempts to revive conversation, remained chilly and uncomfortable.

'Well, that didn't go as badly as it could have, I guess,' Sully said as they listened to the engine of Gabby's car fade away, a small dust trail the only proof she'd ever been there.

Alex sighed. 'It did . . . she hates me.'

'No, she doesn't. She's just a bit out of sorts. I've never brought anyone home before.'

'Really?'

'Yep,' he said, folding his arms behind his head.

'How come?'

'Never been anyone I wanted my daughter to meet, I suppose. No one serious enough, at least.'

Well, no wonder the poor kid was acting so weird. 'Maybe we should have just left it . . . I mean, she's going away soon, she probably didn't need this to ruin her last couple of months with her dad.'

'I wanted you—and her—to realise how serious I am about us,' he said simply.

'I'm just not sure it was worth putting her through all that if this thing doesn't work out.'

'I'm still hoping we've got time to prove that it will.'

But time was the one thing they didn't have. Alex wished she had Sully's optimism but no matter which way she looked at it, staying here meant giving up everything she'd worked so hard for, with no guarantees that whatever this was would last. What if Gabby never came around and her opposition ended up driving a wedge between them? What if, once the honeymoon stage of this shiny new romance finally wore off, he realised she was just an older, less-than-perfect version of the girl he'd fallen in love with, and it all fell apart? Was she willing to risk all that she had in the UK?

Alex put her fingertips to her temple and massaged the throbbing area gingerly. There were an awful lot of what ifs floating around.

The sound of a ticking clock began echoing loudly in time with her unexpected headache.

Alex drove home later that evening, enjoying the summer twilight. Sully had a trip to prepare for and as much as she'd miss not seeing him for a few days, she knew she needed some space to try and work through everything she was feeling.

The lookout on the headland further up the beach from her house caught her eye as she drove, and impulsively she decided to pull in. From here she had a wide view of the small beach below and the rugged headland attached to it. Her eyes shied away from the rocks at the base of the hill. She hated that, after all this time, she still couldn't bring herself to look at it.

A sudden surge of defiance reared up inside her at the thought. She'd played in the rock pools at the base of that head-land her entire life. It wasn't fair that something that happened so long ago could still have this power over her.

No. The voice she heard inside her head was fierce. *No more.* She'd spent so long working through all her fears, dealing with what Jamie Duncan did to her. She'd honestly believed she'd dealt with it, but being back here, she realised there were still some ghosts that needed to be faced. If she couldn't look at this place, how on earth was she ever going to live here? She had to be able to know that she could face all of it and be okay.

Alex took the narrow track leading from the lookout to the beach below, noticing it had at some point been widened and made a lot more user friendly than the goat track it had been when she'd used it as a kid. She trudged her way across the sand towards the base of the rocky outcrop, passing abandoned sandcastles and sand drawings left by children who'd been here swimming earlier in the day. *It's just a beach.* There was nothing intimidating about it. She'd happily played here a million times herself as a kid. *There's nothing to be afraid of,* she told herself firmly. Sounds flitted through her mind: loud music and laughter. She caught the scent of camp-fire smoke and cigarettes. She pushed those memories from her thoughts and continued walking.

As she reached the rocks, her steps faltered and she took a deep, calming breath. As a child, these rocks had been an escape. They rose up high and had become the backdrop for whatever game she wanted to imagine. They formed a labyrinth of corridors the further back you went and provided the perfect location for hide and seek.

A shiver raced through her and she folded her arms across her chest and forced herself to bring up happy memories of this place. She heard giggling and childish whispers, felt the warm sun on her face on a hot summer day and held on to them tightly. *Breathe and release,* Alex heard her therapist remind her in that Mary Poppins accent she had that had always managed to soothe her. There was nothing here that could hurt her anymore.

Alex placed a hand on a nearby rock and let herself feel the cool, hard surface as she breathed in the salty, seaweed scent. Her hand slipped a little and she touched a sharp shell stuck to the rock's surface and she jerked away, instantly feeling the sting of pain along her back as old wounds reopened and began to tingle.

No! She staggered away from the rock as a light-headed sensation took over. Her breathing was shallow and loud in her ears. She forced her eyes open. *Look around you. Find five things you can see*, she told herself, placing her hand under her ribs and counting as she felt her chest move with each breath. She knew it was important to face the fear during a panic attack, to not run, as every instinct was telling her to do, in order to prove that nothing was going to happen, and that she was okay.

She felt the cold, wet sand beneath her feet and wiggled her toes, feeling her breathing begin to settle back into its normal rhythm. It had been years since she'd had an attack and the thought that she'd been back all this time and hadn't had one until now unsettled her considerably. *But you got through it*, the little voice spoke up proudly. And she had.

The cool air touching her bare arms reminded her that it was getting dark. Alex took one last look around. The glistening black of the rocks surrounded her. A fleeting memory of that night popped into her head. She remembered seeing movement in the shadows. The chill in the air grew colder and Alex turned away. She'd faced enough ghosts for one day.

Twenty-six

Alex couldn't sleep. There was too much to think about. How were she and Sully going to make it work? It had frustrated her when Sully had dismissed her question earlier. 'See how it goes' was not a plan in her mind. Could she give up her life in London to move back here?

She and Sully were better than ever. It was like the last two decades hadn't passed them by. But it wasn't all about how they were in bed, either—if it were only the physical attraction, things wouldn't be this complicated. After all, that kind of relationship burned hot in the early stages but the passion fizzled out if there wasn't anything else going for it once everyday life intruded. This was not the case with Sully.

Alex had always been able to talk to Sully, share her dreams. As teenagers, they'd made plans for the future with no real clue what life out in the real world was like. Now, as older, wiser adults, their conversations were based on life experience and were far more meaningful. They even talked on the phone—they'd been together in one form or another twenty-four hours a day and it was . . . nice. Okay, so it was better than nice. It was . . .

Alex sighed. They had all the things that made that new relationship experience so heady and exciting. Every time she saw his name appear on the screen of her phone, it felt like a burst of bubbles would launch themselves from the pit of her stomach to the top of her rib cage. She'd find herself smiling whenever she thought of a conversation they'd had or something he'd done and catch herself staring wistfully out the window like some eighteenth-century whaling boat captain's wife, waiting for her love to return home safely.

Love? *Was* it love? Sure, Alex had been in love with Sully before, but was it still that? Everything else had seemed to fall instantly back into place like they'd never been apart, but did love—the actual emotion—fall back into place the same way? Somehow, she didn't think so. The love they'd had when she was seventeen couldn't be the same as it was now. For one thing, they were very different people. They'd lived separate lives and grown in all sorts of ways through pain and heartaches and faced their own challenges, all without being part of each other's lives. Now, in many ways, they were strangers. Strangers who shared memories from a certain part of their childhood. Yet she could feel those old emotions beginning to stir once more. It had been a very long time, but she remembered how it had been with Sully and already she knew, deep down inside, that if this wasn't already love then it was only a matter of time before it was.

And if it was love, where did that leave her career? She already knew something had been changing about her London life, otherwise why would buying the cottage in Kent have seemed like such a good idea? But moving to Kent was one thing; moving back to Australia was something entirely different.

Changing jobs had never been a particularly huge problem for her in the past. She'd gained an enormous amount of experience by working in various industries and places and the embassy job was no different. Having that behind her would pretty much guarantee her a very decent job if she wanted to start looking elsewhere . . . But did she really want to uproot her life like that? It seemed crazy to even be thinking about it after barely a few weeks of meeting someone, but then again, this wasn't just any someone. This was the man she'd once thought she would be starting her life with when she left Rockne Heads.

No, it *was* crazy.

Even if she did decide to move back here, would being with Sully be enough? She'd been gone for eighteen years and the moment she returned, the town had dug up the past and thrown it in her face. And then there was the Duncans. They'd never forgive nor forget. The thought of constantly bumping into one of them and being abused was enough to turn Alex off the idea of returning completely.

And last but not least, there was Gabby.

Alex sat up in bed and placed her feet on the floor. There was no point even trying to pretend she was ever going to fall asleep.

Gabby was a great kid—smart and quick-witted—and she had her dad's loyal nature, which was a lovely thing, except that she somehow considered Alex a threat.

The only thing Alex thought she might have going for her to earn any kind of cred with Gabby—did kids even say cred anymore?—was the fact she lived and worked in London. However, that hadn't even seemed to gain her a glimmer of wide-eyed wonder. Gabby had just given her a bored kind of look and asked when she was going back there. So, the whole stepmum role she'd be taking on was yet another thing that wasn't looking even the remotest bit appealing.

There was not a lot going for Sully's big plan so far.

Alex swapped her PJ singlet for a bra and T-shirt, pulled on a pair of yoga pants that had never seen a day of yoga, slipped on her sandshoes and headed out the door.

The moon was full and bright, so much so she had no trouble seeing the path to the beach without having to use her phone torch. She'd never really been scared of going out at night here. Maybe it was naive of her to still have no fear—times had certainly changed—but she'd always felt safe.

Music caught her attention as she walked towards the reserve in town. It was coming from a house with a lot of cars parked outside. It sounded like a party was happening in the backyard.

Alex's steps faltered slightly when she spotted the car that had been parked outside her house the other week. Knowing Tom Duncan was somewhere inside that house was like a bucket of ice being dropped on her head. Suddenly a late-night walk on the beach seemed like the dumbest idea ever.

Frustration welled up inside her—how could she possibly think of coming back here to live when the mere thought of Tom Duncan could ruin everything?

She was about to turn away when movement from the side of the house caught her eye. She stilled, staying in the shadows of the trees. She could make out the shapes of three people, two definitely male and one, much smaller, female. As they moved into the glow of the streetlight, Alex felt her blood begin to chill. Gabby? What the hell was Gabby doing at a party someone like Tom Duncan would be attending? The two boys with her seemed a little older, but both were quite drunk. Immediately, Alex felt herself growing nauseous as unwanted memories forced themselves on her.

Stop it, she commanded firmly, but to little effect. Then she noticed Gabby was unsteady on her feet and leaning heavily on one of the boys and the fog in her brain cleared like someone had forced warm air onto a fogged-up windscreen in winter. Something was definitely not right about the whole situation.

Alex didn't have time to think her actions through, didn't wonder if this was really any of her business or not—she reacted instinctively. She crossed the road and headed straight for the trio, reaching between the two boys and grabbing hold of Gabby's arm.

'Hey!' one of the boys protested.

'Come on, Gabby. Time to go home,' Alex said, already sliding an arm around her waist and propelling her forward.

'Back off, lady,' the other boy growled and put his hand on Alex's wrist.

She grasped his arm with her other hand, twisting it and simultaneously landing a swift kick to his groin, which dropped him to the ground. She grabbed Gabby again and walked her away from the house as quickly as she could, mind racing and heart pounding. She'd always wondered if she'd actually remember any of the self-defence lessons she'd taken years ago. Apparently, all the endless drilling by her instructor over that eight-week course had cemented the moves in her head.

But Alex wasn't thinking about any of that as she half-carried, half-supported the young woman to her house. They stopped twice for Gabby to vomit, but Alex was too afraid they'd be followed from the party to offer any sympathy.

'Come on, Gabby, we have to keep moving,' she muttered the second time.

'I can't,' Gabby said, crying.

'We're almost home. Just a little further.'

Thankfully the house came into sight and Alex almost wept with relief as she opened the door then locked it behind them. So much for feeling safe. Admittedly, no one had bothered to follow them, so there appeared to be no real justification for any further fear, but she needed a moment to compose herself before completely letting her guard down.

Once she felt calmer, Alex took a final deep breath and let it out before turning her attention to Gabby, who was slumped against the hallway wall.

'Did they hurt you?' she asked. 'Gabby!' Alex raised her voice when she saw the young girl dozing off. 'You need to tell me.'

'No,' Gabby moaned.

'They didn't hurt you? You weren't—did they force you to do anything?'

Gabby shook her head and groaned once more and Alex was suddenly suspicious. She'd assumed Gabby had been drinking but this kind of reaction suggested something different. 'Did you take anything at that party, Gabby?'

'No,' she said, trying to keep her eyes open. 'I only had half a drink . . . but then I started feeling weird. I think my drink was spiked.'

'I'm calling the police,' Alex said immediately.

'No!' Gabby said, sounding a lot more alert. 'No police. My dad would kill me . . . and then everyone at that party. Please, Alex. Don't.'

'Gabby, spiking your drink is a criminal offence. They were planning to take advantage of you.'

'If you call the police, I swear I will never forgive you.' Gabby held Alex's eyes fiercely. 'Just leave it alone.'

'Gabby, I understand why you don't want the police involved—I get it. There was a time when I refused to tell the police about something because I was scared of what my dad would say, but I should have spoken up and I didn't. Trust me, dealing with it now is better than carrying a secret around with you for the rest of your life.'

'Nothing happened. You stopped it,' Gabby said almost grudgingly and Alex went limp as the remainder of the adrenaline that had kept her going left her system. What if she hadn't decided to go for a walk tonight? What if she'd been a few minutes too late?

'Nothing happened. They didn't touch me. I think I threw most of it up anyway. I feel a lot better.' Gabby must have read the uncertainty on Alex's face because she straightened. 'I will *never* forgive you if you call the cops or tell Dad about any of this.'

Perfect. Now she was supposed to keep this from Sully as well. Part of Alex related so well to Gabby's fears, but the grown-up version warned her that this was a bad idea.

'Go have a shower and clean up. I'll bring you some clothes to put on while I wash yours and get you something to eat,' she heard herself say.

Wordlessly, Gabby walked into the bathroom as Alex held open the door for her and handed her a towel.

'Call out if you need anything,' she said.

'I don't need anything,' Gabby said quietly, and Alex let out a long, deep, sigh. She was going to put the jug on, but she needed something stronger than tea right now. How had everything gone so wrong?

❖

'Where did you learn to do that, anyway?' Gabby asked when she came out of the shower dressed in another pair of yoga pants and a T-shirt. With no make-up, her hair still wet and hanging in ringlets around her face, she barely looked more than twelve years old.

'Do what?' Alex asked, sliding a toasted sandwich on a plate to her and pouring tea into a mug from a small teapot she'd found in the pantry.

'Whatever you did to Leroy back there.'

'Oh. I took some self-defence lessons once.'

'After whatever you didn't tell the police about happened?'

Alex glanced over at Gabby in surprise. She hadn't been aware she'd been really listening or that she'd recall it. 'A fair while after. Yes.'

'I think I might like to do something like that too,' Gabby said with an off-hand shrug. 'I never thought I'd be in a situation like that. I never thought it would happen to me.'

'I don't think anyone ever does,' Alex said gently.

'Did someone spike your drink?'

'No. I just made some bad choices. I was angry and drinking . . .'

'And no one was there to stop it,' Gabby said, making Alex's throat close with emotion.

'No.'

'If Dad ever found out—he's been warning me about going to parties and hanging out with some of the people I

279

know from school. He'd be devastated if he ever found out I went to one and something almost happened. But it's more than that,' she said earnestly. 'I actually think Dad would go over there and hurt someone. He'd go to prison, Alex.'

'I know he'd be upset, but I'm sure it wouldn't come to that. He's a pretty smart guy.'

'Not if he finds out it was a Duncan that did it,' Gabby said solemnly.

Alex felt her eyes widen in alarm. 'A Duncan? Tom Duncan spiked your drink?'

'What?' Gabby stared at her in horror. 'No, not him. Leroy is his son.'

Tom Duncan's son? Alex felt the blood drain from her face. Dear God. Was something like that genetic? She supposed it didn't have to go that deep, it could just be how you were raised. The cruel streak that ran through that family was passed down from father to son—they copied what they saw.

Knowing a Duncan was involved did, in fact, change things, though. Now she understood why Gabby was concerned about Sully finding out. The feud between the McCoys and the Duncans went way back and history repeating itself would not bode well for any of them.

'Did what happen to you happen when you were still living here?' Gabby asked.

'Why would you think that?'

For a moment the girl didn't say anything, just stared into her cup. 'Dad has always been super overprotective, and he's never given me a reason why I couldn't go to parties when I started getting older, just that I was never allowed. One time he did say it was because when he was a kid something bad happened at a beach party. He also said that he was young once and knew how teenage boys' minds worked.' Gabby gave a soft snort, then sobered a bit. 'Now I'm wondering if maybe he was talking about you.'

'No. It wasn't me,' Alex said quickly.

Gabby just held her gaze silently until Alex felt the urge to shuffle in her chair. 'I think he was talking about the party when Jamie Duncan was killed,' Gabby said.

'Your clothes are going to take a while to dry,' Alex said quickly, 'so how about you just stay here tonight.' She really didn't feel comfortable knowing Gabby was going home to an empty house, but also wasn't sure how she would make her stay if she didn't want to. 'Did you drive to the party?'

'No. I got a lift into town. Staying would be good, if it's not too much trouble.'

'Okay, come on, I'll make a bed up for you.'

'Thanks, Alex,' Gabby said quietly after Alex handed her a pillow in a fresh pillow case. 'For everything.'

'You're welcome. I'm just glad you're okay.'

Alex climbed back into her own bed but, despite her body crying for rest, her mind replayed tonight's scene over and over on a loop, until eventually she fell asleep, only to dream about another party a long time ago.

Twenty-seven

After the party, Alex jumped every time she heard a car door close outside, expecting Tom Duncan to arrive sooner or later. When two days had passed without a visit, she surmised that Leroy had probably been too embarrassed to tell his father he'd been beaten up by a woman. Heaven forbid there be any kind of repercussions for a boy attempting to drug and rape a young girl. It infuriated her that those little shits weren't being held accountable for what they did, but without Gabby agreeing, there was little Alex could do. She hadn't seen them drug Gabby's drink and the boys could simply say Gabby had taken the drugs willingly. And since they hadn't gotten far enough to do anything physically, Alex couldn't accuse them of rape either.

She still hoped she might be able to bring the incident up with Gabby later. After all, if they got away with it this time, what was stopping them from trying with someone else?

Sully's arrival home from the charter was severely dampened due to the fact Alex was so torn about keeping her silence and Gabby was noticeably morose. It didn't take long for Sully to pick up on the strange vibe that hung around his homecoming dinner as the three of them sat at the table.

'So what's being going on while I was away?' he asked, trying to spark some conversation that involved more than the few yes and no answers he'd managed to wrangle from his daughter.

'Not a lot,' Alex said, shaking her head and shoving another forkful of salad into her mouth.

'Dinner was great, I've got to go,' Gabby said, abruptly standing and pushing her chair back.

'Wait on. I just got home,' Sully protested.

'Yeah, sorry. I've got something on with Clarissa and the girls.'

'Hey!' Sully snapped, making Gabby stop in her tracks and turn slowly. 'Since when has it been okay to not say goodbye to everyone?'

'Oh. Yeah. See ya,' she said, lifting her eyes to Alex and holding the gaze briefly, almost as though she was daring Alex to confess.

'Have a nice time,' Alex said, calmly.

'I don't know what's gotten into her lately. Did you two have a fight or something?' he asked.

'Why would you say that?' Alex asked, wishing she'd pleaded a headache or something and stayed home.

'I don't know, something just feels off.'

Alex shrugged. 'Who knows? Teenagers,' she muttered, hoping she sounded genuine. She asked him about his trip, knowing the subject would distract him from asking more questions she'd rather not answer.

After the meal they worked together amicably, cleaning the kitchen and making coffee, and Alex found herself imagining how this would feel if it were an everyday situation. The truth was, it wasn't altogether terrible. She was realising just how easy it would be to picture them as a couple.

'You're very quiet tonight. Are you sure everything's okay between you and Gabby? I get that it's probably a big adjustment for you, having a kid around when you're not used to it.'

'She's not really a kid, though, is she?' Alex replied. 'She's pretty much an adult. And having her around isn't an issue for me. I think she's great.'

'I thought maybe the whole stepmother thing might be freaking you out a bit,' he said as she settled into the seat beside him with her coffee. 'We haven't really spoken about it in any kind of detail yet.'

'Maybe because it hasn't really been a thing.'

'But it would be,' he said, 'if this becomes permanent.'

Alex's heart dropped as it always did whenever he brought up their future. She knew he wasn't trying to pressure her into anything, but they were running out of time and she *was* feeling pressured, like she needed to give him some kind of answer to something she still wasn't completely sure she wanted.

No, it wasn't that. She *did* want Sully. They'd fallen back into a relationship as easily as though pulling on a pair comfy old slippers—there was nothing to force, everything just . . . fitted. Perfectly. Well, almost perfectly. If only there hadn't been this pendulum swinging over her head, ticking loudly as it counted down the days till she had to leave.

'I can't give you an answer right now,' Alex said finally, as her jitters reached breaking point. The words came out far more sharply than she'd intended and she wished she could call them back as she caught a flicker of hurt crossing his face.

'I wasn't trying to push you for an answer. I was just pointing out that I understand you're taking on a lot of stuff and it's probably freaking you out a little bit.'

'To be honest, I do get freaked out when I think too much about it,' she said softly. 'I've only ever had myself to think about and you've got Gabby.'

'I do. As well as the business, which is why I can't really pick up and move to you. So I get it—you're the one who's being asked to do a lot of the giving up if this thing between us is going to work, and I feel really bad about that. But I don't want to lose you again, Al.'

The roughness of his voice made her breath catch. The decision should be simple—she didn't want to lose him either. And it was simple when she was here with him. Everything just felt so right. But then once she was alone, reality came knocking until she reluctantly let it in and listened to it rattle off a list of objections. What about her job? What about her little cottage? Hadn't *that* been the dream only a few weeks ago? What if this was just going to be replaced by something else in another couple of weeks?

Alex inwardly screamed in frustration. What was happening to her? She'd always been able to make good decisions—even when they were seemingly spur of the moment. Never once in her adult life had she ever doubted a decision she'd made. Until now. Now, it seemed like everything she started to plan was crippled by indecision and uncertainty. What if it was the wrong choice? What if it didn't work out? Her uncertainty had started when her friend Holly had voiced her concerns about the cottage and then when she came back here, everyone was questioning the wisdom of selling the beach house. She just wanted it to stop!

'I don't know what to do, Sully,' Alex said, wiping angrily at her eyes as they filled with frustrated tears. 'I just don't. I'm due back at work in less than a week, and I just can't give you an answer right now. I'm sorry. I know you want me to just give it all up and tell you I'm staying, but it doesn't work like that. I can't throw away ten years of my life after a few weeks here. I need more time to figure out what I want. I don't even know if I *can* stay here.'

'What do you mean?' he asked, a frown etching between his eyebrows.

'I don't know if I can handle living in a town as small as this when every day I run the risk of bumping into a Duncan, who'll think nothing of yelling derogatory names as they go by. Do you seriously think I want to live like that?'

'It's only because you came back and everything got stirred up again. It'll die down. They'll get over it.'

'They'll never *get over it*. No matter how many times their appeals are denied, they'll never stop thinking I had something to do with Jamie's death. I still look out my window when I hear a car, expecting to see Tom or one of Russell's relations sitting outside watching my house, Sully. I haven't felt a hundred per cent safe since getting back here. I can't live like that.'

'I didn't know it was that bad. I thought it was only those two times.'

'I don't even know anymore if it's real or if I'm just imagining they're still following me,' she said. 'All I know is it's no way to live.'

'I'll go and see Russell. Make him bring his boys to heel,' Sully almost snarled.

'I don't want you to get involved, Sully. I never wanted to stir up all this trouble in the first place. That's my whole point. I don't know if I can ever live here again. Nothing's the same as it used to be. It'll never be home again.'

'You don't know that for certain. It'll just take time.'

Alex shook her head and closed her eyes.

'I'm not going to let this town ruin the only chance we might have to be together again,' Sully said, sitting beside her.

'You can't stop it, Sully. It's bigger than you and me.'

'Watch me,' he whispered softly. But there was a steel edge to his words. He lowered his head and kissed her.

She knew she should argue, but she also knew Sully was stubborn and would only argue back until they were just going around in circles, so she gave into the need to be close to him and let him kiss her. She knew, though, that it was only a matter of time before they'd have to face the reality that a future together might never actually happen.

Twenty-eight

Sully straightened, his gaze narrowing on the man and boy heading towards where he stood on the dock, talking to his trawler skipper as they unloaded their catch. What the fuck was Russell Duncan doing here? A Duncan didn't just casually drop by a McCoy boat.

'McCoy.' Russell's gravelly voice rumbled out of the man's chest. Russell Duncan was not a small man and could easily be mistaken for an old bikie. Which wasn't too far of a stretch to make, considering the dubious ties the Duncan family had always had to certain outlaw motorcycle gangs.

Sully nodded, remaining silent but alert, waiting to see which way this surprise visit might go. Judging from Russell's grave expression, whatever he'd come here to say wasn't going to be good.

'McCoy,' the man said gruffly again. 'I wanted to come and face you man to man. This treaty between us wasn't made lightly. There's been a lot of bad blood between our families in the past, but you know I stand behind the handshake we made.

'This here's me grandson, Leroy. He's here to learn about consequences and what happens when he does stupid shit that puts his whole family and livelihood at risk. He's got something he wants to say. Tell him,' Russell growled, sending a glare at the kid beside him.

Sully briefly let his eyes move from the old man to the younger boy, curiously.

When Leroy remained sullenly silent, Russell clipped him over the ear, almost sending him stumbling over the edge of the pier. 'Tell. Him,' Russell repeated coldly.

'I'm sorry about your daughter,' Leroy managed to mumble through tight lips.

Immediately Sully's attention picked up. 'What about my daughter?'

'At the party on the weekend. I'm sorry about what happened to her.'

'What happened to her?' Sully demanded, getting into the kid's face.

'She— Me and a mate,' he corrected quickly as his grandfather made a low noise in his throat, 'put somethin' in her drink.'

'You what!' Sully's hands clenched the kid's shirt front, not caring how terrified the boy now looked.

'Nothin' happened!' Leroy squealed. 'That bitch Kelly woman jumped us and took her home.'

Kelly woman? Sully paused. 'Alex?'

'Yeah,' the kid mumbled.

'Tell me what happened—all of it,' Sully demanded coldly. His mind was racing and nothing was making sense. He'd been with both Alex and Gabby since the weekend and neither of them had said anything about this.

As the story came out in the kid's belligerent voice, Sully felt his simmering temper rise to boiling point. What. The. Actual. Hell.

Alex was finishing up in the front garden, just spreading the last of the sugar cane mulch on top of the garden beds, when the sound of a car pulling up made her spin around. Her relief at discovering it was only Sully was short-lived, however.

She watched him slam the door and head towards her with a less than welcoming expression. 'What's wrong?' she asked.

'When were you planning on telling me my daughter was almost raped on Friday night?'

Oh. Shit.

'I can't believe this, Alex! What the hell were you thinking?'

'What was I thinking?' she repeated, snapping out of the stunned stupor his unexpected anger had produced.

'By not telling me. I'm her father! You didn't think to call me?'

'I wanted to.'

'Oh, okay. But what? You didn't get a chance? We spent the whole weekend together and there wasn't one moment when you couldn't have brought it up?'

'Gabby was upset.'

'You think? She was drugged and almost raped, for Christ's sake, Alex. Of course she would have been upset. But you're supposed to be an adult and step up, not keep your mouth shut. Do you have any idea what you've done?'

'What *I've* done?'

'You've ruined any chance of the cops being able to charge them with anything. They could have found the drugs in her system and used it as evidence—now they've got nothing.'

'I tried to talk her into going to the police—'

'Tried?' he asked. 'Well, that's comforting. You should have tried harder—or called me.'

'I couldn't force her to go, Sully. I'm not her parent. And you were out at sea. What the hell were you going to do from out there?'

'More than you did here, I can guarantee.'

Alex bit back the hurt his words caused and took a moment to breathe before trying to speak calmly. 'I understand this is a big shock and that you're upset.'

'Too bloody right I'm upset. I'm pissed off that the one person I trusted would keep something like this a secret. How could you be so . . . so . . . irresponsible?'

She'd been trying not to take his remarks personally, giving him the benefit of the doubt, but it was getting really hard.

292

'I'm sorry I didn't tell you,' she said softly. He had every right to be furious. She'd give him that.

But his next words hit her like a slap to the face.

'I know you're inexperienced with teenagers, but this was just common bloody sense, Alex. It's not rocket science.' He turned to head back down the path to his car. 'I thought you were smarter than this. Apparently I was wrong,' he shot over his shoulder.

Although she was reeling from his dismissal, part of her felt she deserved it. She should have found a way to get Gabby to tell the police. Even though Gabby's reasons against it had resonated deep within her.

Sully was just upset, Alex told herself over and over, but she still felt empty and slightly sick. He was right. She'd let him down. She should have called him if she couldn't get Gabby to report the boys. She should have trusted that Sully wouldn't do anything stupid and end up in prison himself. She'd failed. She wasn't stepmother material—she was barely adult material. How stupid to have even thought she could be part of Sully's life here.

At least this made one thing easier.

She packed up her gardening gear and went inside to open her laptop.

Twenty-nine

'You miss her, don't you?' Gabby said softly as they sat around the fire pit.

There was no point denying it—he was honestly too tired to care about hiding his emotions right now. 'Yeah.'

Sully had known he'd overstepped a boundary as soon as he'd left Alex's house. He shouldn't have taken his anger out on her. After Russell and Leroy's visit, he'd gone straight from the wharf to her place, still too worked up and furious to think straight. He should have taken some time out to try and calm down before he saw her.

The one person he should have been furious at—Gabby—had been staying at a friend's house overnight and by the time he'd tracked her down and told her to come home, he'd managed to calm down enough to talk about it.

'Dad,' Gabby said after a few moments. 'Do you love her?'

Sully's heart lurched at the words. 'Yeah. I do. I don't think I ever really stopped.'

He gazed at his daughter's face and let out a small sigh. He knew how confusing this had been for her. He'd momentarily forgotten that, despite how grown up and mature she always seemed for her age, Gabby was still a kid who had a mother and a father and who owed her loyalty to her mum first and foremost.

'Gab, I know that must be hard to hear.'

He saw her chew her lip as though mulling over her thoughts. 'I know you and Mum are divorced and you've been living separately for a long time . . . I guess I just wish that I had memories of you looking at her the way you look at Alex.'

He felt like a jerk. He knew he had nothing to really feel guilty about. He and Karla hadn't been married for years, but for his daughter's sake, he really wished he could have loved Karla the way she'd deserved. 'I cared about your mum, Gab. We really tried to make our marriage work for your sake, but sometimes people just . . . We both had good intentions but they weren't enough in the end.'

'I know you tried. But I also know Mum's happier now than she's ever been. I don't even know why I feel weird about you and Alex. It's not as though you two were cheating on Mum or anything. I just . . . I've never seen you the way you were when Alex was here.'

Sully clenched his hands around the can he held as he fought off another wave of longing. Christ, he missed her. He couldn't believe she was really gone. She'd only been here a few weeks but it felt like so much longer. How the hell was he supposed to go back to life the way it was before?

'I feel bad that I was part of the reason she left.'

'You had nothing to do with it, Gab.'

'I overheard you two talking the other night. About her not being ready to be a step-parent. It wasn't Alex's idea to not tell you about the party,' Gabby said softly. 'I made her swear not to say anything. I felt so stupid that you'd been right. I should have known better than to go to it on my own. It was my dumb pride that forced her to stay quiet.'

'You didn't force her to do anything. Alex is an adult. She should have told me.' He watched Gabby chew on her bottom lip as she seemed to be gathering up her courage to admit something.

'I knew she wanted me to like her. I played on that. I made her think if she told you, I'd make life even harder for you both. I'm sorry, Dad, I don't know *why* I was acting so terrible. I feel really bad.'

His heart dropped as he imagined Alex's dilemma. He'd known Gabby was being difficult and that Alex had felt out of her depth at the thought of becoming a stepmother. He was still angry that she'd kept it from him, but he could understand why she'd maybe think doing so might help bring her and Gabby closer.

'She didn't leave because of our fight,' he told his daughter gently. 'There was a lot more to it. It wasn't because of you.'

Alex would be back there by now. Back in the middle of all the chaos and excitement of the big city where she'd decided she wanted to be more than here—with him.

'Dad . . . I need to tell you something. Something really big.'

The cold air that hit Alex's face as she exited the airport took her breath away. Bloody hell, it was freezing.

Her mother linked her arm through Alex's and gave her a squeeze. 'Bit of a shock to go from summer to winter. We'll be home soon and we'll be warm as toast.'

Alex smiled. She had missed her mum while she'd been away. In front of them, Bart was manoeuvring her large suitcase and heading for a taxi. They'd both been standing in the arrivals lounge waiting for her and the sight had somehow managed to crack the stoic front Alex had been holding on to ever since leaving Rockne Heads.

'A nice cup of tea will see you right after that big flight,' Bart said as they made their way through the traffic towards home.

'Or would you prefer to go straight to your place, darling?' her mother asked.

'Oh, no,' Bart said, sounding alarmed, before he managed a smile. 'Misery loves company and all that,' he added. 'I mean, we've missed you and we want to hear all about your trip.'

'She might not be feeling up to it, sweetheart,' her mother said, eyeing her husband pointedly.

'It's fine, Mum. I'm okay.' Alex wanted nothing more than to go home, get straight into bed and sleep for a week, but clearly her parents wanted to spend some time with her, so she really ought to at least try and be polite. Her parents? The thought made her pause. She didn't often think of Bart as her parent—at least, not before she'd gone back to Rocky. She gave a tired chuckle as his cheerful face beamed at her. A lot of things seemed to have changed since she'd been away.

They pulled up outside the lovely old Georgian house and Alex admired the pretty picture the house made, tucked away in a private square with lots of deciduous trees and a large parkland across the road. It was an impressive house with four floors and a number of reception rooms and bedrooms.

Bart opened the glossy black front door and they stepped into the entrance hall.

'Let's see about that cup of tea then, shall we?' he said, clapping his hands before heading towards the rear of the house.

The kitchen was sleek and modern. In fact, the whole house had been tastefully renovated into a very contemporary home. *The exact opposite of Four Winds*, Alex's little voice pointed out. The fact she was comparing this place to the house in Rocky instead of the house in Kent momentarily confused her, but there wasn't time to dwell on it before Bart and her mother began excitedly filling her in on the latest family news.

'Maisy and Nigel announced they're having a baby last night at dinner,' her mother said, her smile widening.

'Another one?' Alex replied, before quickly saying, 'Oh. That's fantastic.'

'We're very excited,' Bart said from where he was pottering around making the tea.

'It was nice that you and Tanya managed to reconnect again,' her mother said as she placed a plate of delicious-looking cakes and sandwiches on the table and took a seat across from Alex.

'It was.' Alex felt a small pang of sadness. That goodbye had been one of the hardest. But at least this time she'd said goodbye and knew that they would never lose contact again. They would always be able to FaceTime and talk on the phone regularly, which would be almost the same as being there.

Another wave of longing washed through her. It was almost like homesickness, only that would be stupid, because she was home and that had just been a holiday.

The phone rang and Bart stepped out of the kitchen to answer it, leaving Alex and her mother alone.

'I think this trip changed a lot of things for you, didn't it?' her mother said, her head tilting slightly.

'What do you mean?' Alex asked slowly.

'The last few times we spoke while you were over there, you seemed different. Lighter, somehow. Happier. Very different from how you've been here for the last little while.'

'I didn't feel unhappy here before,' Alex said carefully.

'Maybe because you didn't realise how much happier you could be? I think this trip might have reminded you of the difference.'

Well, that was just great. She didn't want to be reminded of what she didn't have back here.

'What happened with Sully? I heard you were seeing quite a bit of each other while you were there.'

'Wow, gossip even travels across the globe nowadays?'

'I've been speaking with Gloria. She mentioned you and he seemed quite close. She seemed happy about it, though, so don't worry,' she added, seeing wariness cross Alex's face. 'I know you were heartbroken about breaking up with him before we left—even if you did keep it from your father and me. It was a long time ago.'

'Yes, he and I tried to pick up where we left off. It didn't work out. Again.'

'Why not?'

'For a lot of reasons,' Alex said. She really didn't want to go over it all again. She'd had a twenty-seven-hour trip to dissect it, without gaining anything other than a headache.

'Seems to me, if two people can pick up where they left off after being apart for as long as you both were, then there's something special there. Maybe it's worth trying to figure it out?'

'Mum, he lives in Rocky. I live here. How do we figure that out?'

'You don't have to live here, though, do you?' her mother pointed out lightly.

Alex stared at her silently. 'You want me to leave?'

'I *want* you to be happy. You haven't been for a long time.'

'Yes, I have. I have my dream job, I live in a great city—'

'And that may have been enough at one point. But I think you know there's something missing.'

'You're saying that's Sully?'

Her mother shrugged.

'I can't just move back there. I mean, for starters, I'd always be "that Kelly girl",' she said, making quotation marks in the air. 'No one back there would let me forget my past. And besides all that, what about you? I can't just move to the other side of the world and leave you here.'

'Why not? You did it before,' Monica said, then chuckled at Alex's look of dismay. 'Oh, stop it. You know what I mean. Your dream was to come over here and work for a few years. It was my fault that a few years turned into ten because I followed you, married Bart and made a life here. I think, deep down, you gave up any plans of ever going back because of me.'

Alex opened her mouth to protest but then the words sank in and she actually considered them. It was sort of true. Once her mum was here and settled, it just made sense that London became home.

'I don't think it was your *fault*,' she finally said. 'I mean, I've never really thought about it like that before.'

'Exactly. Then you had a trip back to Rockne and things changed. Going back was always your original plan. Maybe not to Rockne Heads, exactly, but that was before you reconnected with Sullivan. By all accounts, he's really made something of himself. Gloria was singing his praises over the phone. Everyone changes over time. Which is why the decisions we make also need to change from time to time. Look,' her mum said gently, placing her hand on top of Alex's, 'I would miss you terribly if you moved away, but you can't put your life on hold if that's one of the reasons you're staying here. I will always be your mum first and foremost, but I've got a family around me here too who will keep me busy. You won't be leaving me alone. I have my life and you have yours. You need to do whatever it is that makes you happy. I'd rather have a happy daughter living her best life on the other side of the world than have a sad one merely existing just up the road.'

Monica's words stayed with Alex long after she'd gotten back to her flat and started to unpack, her heart heavy and her head full of unanswered questions.

Thirty

Sully sat in the Duncans' office across from two of the men he'd grown up hating. Russell Duncan rocked back and forth in his padded chair, the springs squeaking with each push of his foot against the ground. The sound grated on Sully's nerves like someone running their fingernails down a chalkboard. Tom Duncan, older by a few years than Sully, perched on the corner of the enormous desk, arms folded and resting on a beer belly that had developed after he left crewing onboard the boats for an office job in his father's business.

Sully knew the fishing industry hadn't supplied the Duncans with the amount of infrastructure they had, but, going by the state of wear and tear he'd noticed, nothing had been upgraded in a very long time—probably since their drug business had started to dry up significantly. There didn't seem to be much extra income coming in.

Two more men leaned against the wall behind him: Chris, a Duncan cousin, and some other guy Sully didn't know— no doubt another recruit from the family business that they brought out when they needed a show of power. Like today.

'Your message got me curious, McCoy,' Russell finally said. 'What exactly do you think you can do for us?'

'You want closure on Jamie's case. I can give it to you.'

The tension in the air rose noticeably. 'And how can you do that?' Russell asked softly, his tone at odds with his expression, which was about as relaxed as a snake about to strike.

'I recently came across some information that I think you'll find interesting. It might even be enough to convince the police to reopen the case.'

'Word is you've shacked back up with that Kelly bitch. Why would you be giving us anything that would put her away?' Tom snarled.

'Because she didn't do anything. But I know who did.'

'He's got to be lying to save his girlfriend,' Tom said with a harsh laugh as he looked over at his father.

'Why don't you tell us what you know and then we'll be the ones to judge if we take it to the cops or not,' Russell suggested.

'Nope. I want a guarantee first.'

'Of what exactly?'

'That you'll back off where Alex is concerned. There'll be no more intimidation, no more abuse in public—no more anything where she's concerned.'

'That depends on what you tell us,' Russell said.

'I want the guarantee or I keep my mouth shut and the case stays closed.'

'How do you know the cops aren't already going to reopen it?' Russell asked.

'Because we both know you have no new evidence, or they would have done it by now. Besides, I think you bloody well owe me after the shit your grandson tried to pull. I didn't go to the cops when I had every reason to.'

The closed anger that replaced the cool mask on the older man's face was not a comforting sign. 'It was dealt with privately and I gave you my word he won't be bothering your daughter again.' There was a noticeable chill in the air as Russell sent a glare at Tom, who shifted on his feet like a pent-up boxer in the corner of the ring, waiting to hit someone. 'Fine. No one looks sideways at the Kelly woman,' Russell said in a booming voice.

'Okay.' Sully stood up.

'What are you trying to pull here, McCoy?' Tom demanded. 'What's this info you reckon you have? Dad agreed to your terms.'

'I know. And I'll uphold my end of the bargain. I'm heading into the cop station right now to give them a statement.'

'That wasn't the deal.'

'I never said I'd give the information directly to you. I'll give it to the cops. This gets dealt with officially—not by Duncan law.'

'I reckon you better reconsider your answer, mate,' Tom said, stepping over so he was only an inch away from Sully's face. They were of similar height, but Tom outweighed Sully considerably—although the majority of it wasn't muscle anymore.

'I reckon you should get outta my face before you regret it. And I am *not* your mate, *mate*,' Sully shot back.

'Tom. Get back,' Russell instructed. 'If you're bullshitting us, kid, I can promise you, there's going to be consequences.'

'Dad! For fuck's sake! We have a right to know what he thinks he knows.'

'I just want this shit dealt with once and for all!' Russell yelled, banging his hand on the top of the desk.

Sully almost felt sorry for the man—he'd aged a lot in the last two decades and, as a father himself, Sully had an idea what losing a kid would have done to the bloke. 'I wouldn't have gotten involved unless I had something I knew was going to make a difference. I'm just not risking it by letting you deal with it instead of the cops. Alex's reputation needs to be officially cleared and that won't happen if you make this go away illegally.'

'You really know who murdered my son?' Russell asked.

'I do. And they'll be dealt with by the law and by the book or you go the rest of your life not knowing the truth. I don't think you're willing to do that. Are you?'

The big man let out a sigh. 'No. It's been dragging on too long.'

Tom gave a disgusted snort but stepped away and let Sully pass. 'You better hope you know something, McCoy, otherwise your little girlfriend will find out just how scary I can be.'

'I know what's at stake,' Sully growled back. 'I've given my word.' He looked the older Duncan in the eye steadily and reminded himself that Alex was safe. They obviously didn't know she'd left. But he couldn't let himself dwell on her leaving right now—it was too dangerous to let his guard down around these people. She was safe, and now all Sully cared about was finally clearing her name in association with Jamie bloody Duncan once and for all. It was the least he could do for her.

The gravel beneath his boots sounded loud in the evening stillness and Sully was busy processing what had just happened, so he jumped slightly when the voice came out of nowhere.

'Why would you want to bring all that back up again?' Chris demanded, breaking away from the shadows.

Sully stopped. 'What do you mean?' He hadn't even noticed that Chris had left the office.

'You of all people shouldn't want people reopenin' that case.'

'Why?'

'You weren't as squeaky clean as you made out back then. It'd be a bit tricky if the cops reopened the case and discovered you'd lied about that night.'

'I didn't lie,' Sully said.

'You sure about that? Sure enough to risk becomin' the number one suspect?'

'How do you figure that?'

'You were up on the headland that night with Jamie.'

Sully went quiet. Then he said, 'I wasn't anywhere near the headland.'

'I reckon you're lyin'.'

'I reckon if you're going to start throwing around accusations like that, you wanna make sure you have some kind of evidence to back it up.'

'Oh, I do.'

'What are you saying, Duncan?'

'I'm sayin', if you go to the cops and keep stirrin' up trouble, a video of you and Jamie fightin' on the headland that night might just make its way to the police.'

'Are you threatening me?'

Chris shrugged. 'Just givin' you a friendly piece of advice.'

'Maybe I'm willing to call your bluff, 'cause I know for a fact that whatever video you think you have isn't going to show me killing Jamie . . . 'cause he was alive when I left him.'

The other man's eyes flashed with venom. One minute he was just being a smartarse Duncan, the next he looked . . . unhinged.

'You'd be surprised what a bit of editin' can achieve— anyway, it won't matter, the cops won't be lookin' that hard at it since it's compellin' and pretty bloody damnin' and gives them a new suspect with the perfect motive.'

'What if I give them someone else with an even bigger motive?' Sully asked in a quiet, even tone. He watched the man's face tighten.

'Now *you're* bluffin',' Chris snorted, his face relaxing into a smirk. 'I don't know what game you're playin' with the old man in there, but I know for a fact you don't have any evidence.'

'You sure you want to call my bluff? If you saw the fight between Jamie and me, then you had to be hiding up there for a reason. You must have thought it was your lucky day when I turned up.'

Chris had lost his smirk and was looking confused once again.

'What was the plan, record me, kill Jamie and then frame me for his murder?'

'Why would I kill him? He was my cousin.'

'Must have been a pretty good reason,' Sully continued. 'But if you had a video, why didn't you hand it in to the police?' He stopped, his mind racing ahead to fit all the pieces together. 'You didn't have to use it since they had Alex as the main suspect. You just sat on the evidence waiting to see if you needed to use it or not? Was that it?'

'Good thing I held on to it, hey. Keep your mouth shut or I'll use it this time.'

Sully noticed Chris's eyes were darting about and his hands had begun shaking. *Fucking drugs*, he thought with disgust. Chris had been a half-decent kid back when they'd been growing up—well, decent for a Duncan, anyway. But he'd succumbed to using just like the majority of his cousins and brothers had. And the drugs made them unpredictable. Which is why Sully really didn't want to push the bloke any further . . . but he had no choice.

'I know about Cassie, Chris. I know what Jamie did to her. And I know you went to the headland to confront him—but before you could, I turned up and you had to go and hide in the bushes, and that's when you decided to record our argument. Tell me I'm wrong, I dare you,' Sully said, taking a step closer. He was sick of all this pussyfooting around. He just wanted to get to the truth.

'You don't know anythin' about Cassie!' Chris yelled, his mouth twisting and his eyes burning furiously. 'Shut your damn mouth!'

'Jamie always treated you like shit, didn't he. I saw it back then—everyone saw it. He made you feel like crap. But then he found an even better way to torment you—he decided to sleep with your girlfriend.'

'He didn't sleep with her. Cassie didn't even like him. He forced himself on her,' Chris screamed. The veins in the side of his neck bulged as his face contorted angrily. 'That bastard raped her! In front of me. He made me watch.'

Jesus. Sully's guts clenched in disgust. He knew Jamie was a sadistic bastard, but he hadn't realised he'd been that sick.

'She was cryin' and beggin' me to stop him . . . and I—' Chris was sobbing now, snot and tears running down his face. 'I couldn't do nothin'. I shoulda stopped him. I shoulda killed him then, but I . . . couldn't.'

'So you waited till you got the chance at the party instead,' Sully prompted carefully. He felt like a jerk, pumping the guy for information when he was more than a little mentally fragile.

'Yeah, I went to the party to kill him that night,' Chris said, glaring defiantly as he wiped a forearm across his nose. 'I tried to do it on the beach, then I followed him up to the headland, but you interrupted and I had to wait. I thought maybe you were there to do it, but you hit him and then left him there. I knew I couldn't let him leave that headland. If you were too weak to do it then I had to do it. I told him he had to pay for what he did to Cassie and he just laughed at me. He turned his back on me like I was just . . . nothin', so I picked up a rock and I ran up behind him and I hit him with it. When he fell, I hit him again and again, until he didn't get up . . . Then I dragged him over to the cliff and I watched him smash onto the rocks below. He looked like a rag doll,' Chris said, almost to himself. 'He didn't look so tough anymore.'

'Why didn't you just tell the police about Cassie's rape?'

'Because he had to die. He wasn't goin' to stop. He proved it that night with Alex, didn't he? Only this time, I knew he wouldn't get away with it.' Chris gave a disgusted snort. 'I always thought you were a hardarse, just like Jamie and Tom. But you let him get back up. You had the chance to kill him and you didn't.'

The way he was staring at Sully made Sully's skin crawl more than he cared to admit. 'Why would I want to kill him? I was pissed off at him for making out with Alex at the party but I wasn't planning on ruining the rest of my life by killing him over that.'

Chris's eyes narrowed before he threw his head back and cackled in a deranged way. 'Holy shit! You don't even know, do you?'

Sully frowned. 'Know what?'

'About Alex.'

'What about her?' As soon as the question left his lips he wanted to pull it back in. Somehow he knew whatever this idiot was about to say wasn't something he wanted to hear.

'Why do you think I didn't kill him on the beach?'

Sully stared at him silently, too confused and, quite frankly, too scared to hazard a guess.

'Because he was there with Alex. I saw them, Sully.'

Sully's jaw clenched tightly. Yeah, he knew he hadn't wanted to hear any of this. But it wasn't something he didn't already know. Alex had as good as admitted what had happened that night.

'He forced her—like he forced Cassie. I was there in the dark, watchin'.'

What the fu— Sully felt his extremities begin to tingle as his head went fuzzy.

'Forced? What are you saying?'

'He raped Alex that night. I thought you found out and that's why you followed him up onto the headland.'

Raped? The word seemed to echo inside his head. But before he could say anything else, red and blue lights were flashing all around them, glowing like disco lights against the buildings of the marina as police sirens split the air.

In the chaos and noise of people yelling and Chris screaming abuse as the police handcuffed him, Sully stood like a cold, lifeless statue.

Alex hadn't willingly slept with Jamie that night—she'd been raped. And he'd turned his back on her to start a life with Karla.

He'd just let her walk out of his life.

Thirty-one

'Dad . . . I need to tell you something. Something really big.'

'That night, before all the other stuff happened,' Gabby said, 'I walked in on an argument. At first I didn't know who it was then I got a good look at the guy and realised it was one of the Duncans—Chris. I've seen him around but I don't really know him or anything. He and this woman were fighting. She was screaming at him that she knew he'd done it and that he should have told her. She was hysterical,' Gabby said, shaking her head. 'They didn't know I was there, and I was going to leave, but then she mentioned Alex. She said she thought Alex was close to having it figured out—that it wasn't going to take her long to make the connection about

314

who killed Jamie and that he had to leave town before the others found out or they'd kill him.'

'She said *what?*'

'I know. I wasn't sure at first if it was the same Jamie, but she kept crying and went on and on about how Chris shouldn't have gotten involved, that she loved him, and she kept saying it wasn't his fault. Then he started crying and saying it *was* his fault—that if he hadn't been such a coward, he'd have killed Jamie the night he raped her. It went on for ages, and I was too shocked to leave . . . But, Dad, he confessed to killing Jamie *for her.* He said that was the only decent thing he'd ever done and he was glad that Jamie was dead. That's when she started on again about him having to leave town and she'd follow with the kids, because she was worried that Alex was going to tell the police what she suspected, once she figured it out.'

Holy shit. Sully couldn't believe what he was hearing. *Chris* had killed Jamie that night? Why hadn't Alex said anything to the police if she knew? Maybe she hadn't figured it out after all?

Sully muttered something about fetching more firewood for the fire pit and then moments later found himself sitting in the darkness of his shed. Thinking.

Maybe he and Alex were over. He couldn't really blame her for leaving—he hadn't given her much to hang around for after their fight, but he could do something to make at least one thing better. He could clear her name by revealing the real killer.

He couldn't sit still a moment longer. Two hours later he'd given his statement to a detective at Moreville police station and immediately offered to help get a confession from Chris Duncan. Finally they could close this whole damn chapter once and for all.

Thirty-two

Alex's phone rang as she walked out of her boss's office. She glanced at the screen and was surprised by the name of the caller.

'Hi,' she said, twisting her watch around on her wrist to check the time.

Tanya barely let her get out a greeting before she said, 'I'm sending you a link right now. Watch it.'

'What?' Alex asked, but Tanya had already disconnected. A few moments later an email notification popped up and Alex gave a confused huff before walking into her office and taking a seat. She opened the link.

'The case of the death of a young man eighteen years ago in the small seaside village of Rockne Heads has just had a surprising twist. Detectives for the North Coast Area

Command have announced that, after the revelation of new evidence, they have arrested a man for James Duncan's murder.

'The thirty-six-year-old man has pleaded guilty to the charges and will be sentenced in the coming weeks.'

The vision swapped from the newsreader to footage outside a courtroom. Alex instantly recognised Russell Duncan and his family swarming around a police paddy wagon as it delivered a man to the courthouse. Alex felt her breath catch in her chest as the man got out and looked at the camera, and she locked eyes with a pale-faced Chris Duncan.

'It is believed Christopher Duncan is the cousin of murder victim James Duncan. We will reveal more about this story as events unfold,' the reporter outside the courthouse said, and the screen returned to the studio and the solemn-faced anchor.

Alex slumped in her seat, feeling as though all the air inside her lungs had been released, leaving her limp and deflated. Then she straightened and called Tanya back.

'Did you watch it?'

'I did . . . But how? What happened?'

'It was Sully. Apparently there was some big undercover operation and he got Chris's confession. He's like a real-life Jason Bourne or something.'

Alex tried to imagine how Sully would be taking that particular nickname and smiled to herself. 'Wow. That's . . . amazing.'

'The broadcast only went to air about an hour ago and already there's reporters in town interviewing people about it.'

Alex was grateful she'd left when she had. She wasn't sure she wanted to go through the whole press mob again.

'It's all over,' Tanya said.

'Yeah. I guess it is. That's really good. I'm glad.'

'I just thought you should know.'

'Thank you. Look, I'm at work, I better go. I'll call you tomorrow, okay?'

It really was over. The Duncans would no longer have any reason to terrorise her. She had her life back.

And Sully had given it back to her.

She smiled tentatively. This was definitely a sign that the gamble she'd just made might be worth the risk after all.

Three weeks later, Alex stood on the verandah at Four Winds and watched the sun slowly rise, the horizon leaking yellow, orange and red in a brilliant display, making her wish—not for the first time—that she could paint.

The air was cool, not the blistering cold of England, which she'd left thirty-odd hours earlier, and the fog settling in the valley behind her promised a hot day on its way. January in Australia. If anyone had told her, this time last year, what would happen by the end of that year, she'd have never believed them, and yet, here she was. Back in Rockne Heads.

She'd received a text from Gabby a few days before Christmas. She had said she hoped Alex would forgive her for how rude she'd been and went on to say how much her dad missed Alex and that he'd probably kill his daughter if he found out she'd told her, which had made Alex smile reluctantly as she remembered the tone Gabby would have used if the conversation had been in person. Gabby had also wanted Alex to know that she was sorry if she played any part in the break-up with her dad.

Alex had hesitated before replying. She wasn't mad at all with Gabby, it was just so unexpected to hear from her. She found herself wiping at the tears that began to well up— she'd only recently stopped the unpredictable crying that had begun on her return to England. When she'd gotten herself under control, she'd written a heartfelt text back, assuring Gabby that she in no way blamed her for anything and she was happy Gabby had messaged her.

They'd stayed in touch, and Alex looked forward to getting brief updates on what was going on in Rocky. Each message, though, pulled on her heartstrings, as thoughts of Gabby always turned to thoughts of Sully, from whom Alex hadn't heard and didn't expect to. After all, she'd been the one who'd left. She'd started a number of text messages to him, only to erase them before working up the courage to hit send.

Christmas arrived and she'd celebrated with her family. For the first time ever, she'd felt . . . lonely. As she'd looked around the room on Christmas morning and watched everyone surrounded by their partners and children, her mother and Bart wrapped in each other's arms, looking on proudly at their little brood, she realised she wanted this. She wanted to have someone to bring home to celebrate all the good times with her family. She wanted her own little family to bring home. She wanted Sully and Gabby to be part of this. The knowledge had hit Alex like a bolt of lightning and her entire world had turned upside down.

All those years of trying to figure out how to make herself whole again and the answer had been staring her in the face. Sully was her cure. He had been all along. He was the only man who could put together all the chipped and broken pieces she'd been trying to stick back in place for the last eighteen years.

She'd spoken to her parents and they had all cried a lot, but they'd given their unconditional blessing, with the proviso that she bring Sully home to meet the family as soon as possible. Then it was a matter of packing up her apartment, arranging for everything to be shipped to Rockne and saying goodbye to the last ten years of her life.

She'd expected it to be a lot harder. But she knew in her heart that it was time to move on with her life.

Alex had deliberately planned to arrive under the cover of darkness, like some covert operation, simply to avoid the local gossip mill from announcing she was back. She'd found out from Gabby that Sully was due home from a charter the morning after she arrived, so she planned on surprising him. She wasn't a hundred per cent certain that an ambush was the best way to approach the situation, but it was the only plan she had. She had no idea how Sully would react and part of her wanted to turn tail and run back to London. If what Gabby said was true, he missed her, which was a good start, but there was no guarantee that he'd be open to risking his heart on her again. She just had to hope that he would. She'd taken a huge leap of faith, she just had to hope it was the right one.

Thirty-three

Sully had been operating on autopilot for the last few days. He wasn't sure why he couldn't shake this stupid unsettled feeling that had been lurking since Christmas. He'd tried to put his heartache aside, not only for the sake of his business, but for Gabby too, and for the most part he thought he'd succeeded. But where he'd once found peace and solitude in the quiet times out at sea in those precious few moments before his clients were up and about, or late at night when everyone was sleeping and he had the ocean to himself, all he felt was loneliness and a gaping emptiness. His mind kept bringing up memories of Alex—their time on his boat had imprinted her image everywhere. Sometimes, he even swore he could smell her, like some ghost hovering on the edge of his senses.

Which was why, when he looked up after securing the boat and jumping onto the dock, he almost brushed off the appearance of Alex as just another apparition. But when she didn't fade away as she usually did, he stiffened in shock.

She was nervously chewing her bottom lip and attempting to hold a smile, until it too seemed to waver and he realised he'd been staring at her for what seemed like an eternity. He forced himself to snap out of it.

'Hello, Sully,' she said cautiously.

'Alex. What are you doing here?' He winced at the harshness of his tone. He hadn't meant it to come out like that.

'I . . .' she started, before pausing. Then she squared her shoulders and took a breath. Part of him felt better now he realised she was feeling as unsure about things as he was. 'I wanted to thank you for your part in bringing Chris Duncan to justice,' she said as she twisted her fingers together in front of her. 'I thought about calling to say thank you, but I wasn't sure you'd want to hear from me, to be honest.'

'I would have,' he said. 'Wanted to hear from you, that is.'

Her hands stilled at that and she held his gaze steadily. 'I missed you so much.'

That was the only answer he needed. He stepped forward and she put her arms around him, holding him tightly as he pulled her against him. Try as he might, he couldn't stop the well of tears that sprang to his eyes, and he blinked them away fiercely. He honestly never thought he'd get to feel Alex in his arms like this ever again and the pain of that had been paralysing whenever he'd allowed himself to think about it.

Yet here she was. In his arms. He swore she would never leave them again.

'I thought I'd lost you,' he said, burying his face in her hair at her neck.

'I'm sorry I left like that.'

'I'm sorry I took my fear for Gabby out on you. That's what it was—I didn't blame you for any of it, I was just . . . If you hadn't been there . . .'

'It's okay. I get it. And I should have told you.'

He pulled away slightly to look down at her. 'I know what happened with Jamie that night. When you were with him.' He felt her body tense in his arms but he ducked his head to hold her eyes. 'I will never forgive myself for turning my back on you when you needed me the most. I'm so sorry.'

She shook her head and a sad smile touched her lips, but it didn't reach the grief in her eyes. 'I didn't tell anyone. I was too ashamed. It wasn't your fault.'

'I shouldn't have let you go with him.'

'You couldn't have stopped me.'

'It was my fault you did, though. I hurt you. I drove you into the arms of a fucking rapist!' he said, raising his voice, the emotion he'd managed to keep under control for so long finally breaching the surface. He'd wanted the opportunity to kill Jamie again once he'd realised what had happened, and the fact he couldn't had been eating him alive ever since.

He felt Alex tighten her arms around him.

'I made the choice. It doesn't matter, now, why or how any of it happened. The fact is, it did. But I've dealt with it. I've put it to rest. Everything turned out the way it was supposed to for us. As much as I loved you back then, Sully, neither of us would have been where we are today if we'd stayed together. We had to go on our own journey so we'd find our way back to each other—whole again, instead of broken.'

Her words touched something deep inside of him. The truth of them hit him like a punch to his gut. It didn't make any of it easier to think about, but it did help it make sense. 'I love you, Alex. More than I ever thought I could love someone. When you left, it was like I was only half a person. I need you in my life, and I don't care if that means I have to make some sacrifices and move to the other side of the world with you. Just promise me you'll never leave me behind again.'

'I promise. But there won't be any sacrifices. I'm back for good. I realised after I left that I belonged here. With you.'

'For good?' It was too much to hope for and it was going to kill him if he'd heard it wrong.

'For good. I'm not selling Four Winds.'

'But your job . . . I can't let you give up your career. I was a dickhead to think you should do that.'

'I'm not giving up my career. Well, not exactly. I'm not working for the Australian Embassy in London anymore, but I'm still in the same field—luckily I'm good at my job and they didn't want to lose me completely, so I got a transfer. I can work remotely from here, but I'll be doing a bit of commuting to and from Canberra and Sydney for a while. It'll be a bit of a compromise. Think you can handle that?' she asked, raising an eyebrow at him.

'We'll make it work. As long as I have you in my life again, that's all that matters.'

'I was hoping you'd say that,' she said, her own damp eyes smiling. 'I love you,' she said before touching his lips with hers.

'I've never *stopped* loving you,' Sully told her, his voice husky with emotion. He felt like his heart was going to burst through his chest at any moment. 'Welcome home, Al.'

Thirty-four

'Before we open tonight's book club,' Tanya said as she finished pouring herself a glass of wine, 'I would like to propose a toast.' She eyed the room of women who'd gathered in the surf club. Their group had outgrown Alex's house about six months ago and they'd had to find a bigger venue.

'Tonight marks the one-year anniversary of the Books, Booze and Bitches Book Club,' Tanya started.

'I thought we decided on cheese?' Michelle interrupted.

'Books, Booze and Cheese just doesn't have the same feel,' Amanda said.

'I thought it was Broads?' Terri added, sounding confused.

'I think Books, Wine and Friends sounds a lot nicer,' Gloria said.

'Guys, you're killing my vibe here.' Tanya pouted then cleared her throat. 'As I was saying, our humble book club is one year old today!'

A round of applause came from the floor and Tanya continued, 'I think I speak on behalf of everyone here when I say our little town has been through a very tumultuous time, with lots of changes and quite a few ups and downs, but I think we're coming out the other side now. Rockne Shores has dragged this place into the future and despite the resistance of some, it's proven to be the best thing that's ever happened. We've got access to a new medical centre and nature walks and bike tracks that have given tourists a place to ride away from the main street. Personally, as a business owner, it's been life-changing. We've had a number of new shops open in town and I see so much more potential with our growing population bringing new ideas and new people to town.

'Yes, our little town is expanding, and yes, a lot of us remember how it used to be when we were growing up, but nowhere stays the same forever—not unless it also stops being productive and loses its younger and older generations. We had to grow or we'd simply have withered away. I say we raise our glasses to the future of Rockne Heads. Long may it continue to be the best place in the world to live!'

Alex drank from her glass and looked around the room. It seemed hard to imagine she'd been back almost a year. She'd moved in with Sully after Gabby left for university and had continued to rent out Four Winds as holiday accommodation. Each morning when she woke up beside Sully, Alex lovingly traced his features with her gaze—grateful that they'd finally managed to end up together. Life had certainly thrown them enough curveballs, so it was about time they got to savour the good times and bask in some happiness for a while.

She noticed Murna was still absent from their book club. Alex had extended an olive branch more than once, inviting her to come along and join them, but so far she'd declined.

After the announcement that Rockne Shores was going ahead, Murna and her team hadn't stood down as expected, but had continued attempting to stop development despite being overruled at every turn. Alex had to admit the woman was not easily deterred. Even as building commenced, Murna had arranged an around-the-clock presence of protesters outside the gates, until the numbers began to dwindle. Eventually, only a few signs remained on the gates, which faded and disintegrated in the rain.

But new and pressing matters soon arose and Murna and her team were once again worked up into a frenzy of outrage about something else. Alex wondered how they managed to harness so much rage over so many issues, so consistently. It sounded like an exhausting way to live when there was so many good things to be embracing and celebrating instead. Still, it seemed like this was what Murna considered her calling in life, and who was she to get in the way of someone's calling?

Frequent flying back and forth to meetings in the city meant Alex had enough on her own plate to keep her busy.

In between work trips, though, there was Sully and the life they'd made together, which was everything she could ever hope for and more.

They'd made the trip to her parents' place so Sully could meet her family and, as expected, he had won everyone over instantly. For the first time, Alex sat at the large dining table surrounded by her stepsiblings and their families and felt like she truly belonged. How could she ever have thought that she'd been fulfilled? She hadn't even realised how lonely she'd really been. Now her life and her heart were full of love and happiness.

As she walked through the front door and dropped her handbag on the hall table after book club, she went to where Sully was lying on the lounge, watching TV. She climbed over him, settling against his side before kissing him deeply.

'Wow, you should go to book club more often,' he murmured. 'What was that for?'

'Nothing. I just really missed you.'

His chuckle echoed against her chest, and she sighed as he ran his hands slowly along her hip. 'Not that I'm complaining.'

'Sully,' she said and waited till he looked at her. 'I think we should get married.'

She felt his hand pause as he searched her eyes for some kind of sign that she might be joking.

'Unless you'd rather we just kept things the way they are,' she said when the silence went on, giving her a moment of uncertainty.

'No.' He rolled off the lounge. 'Give me a minute,' he said, leaving the room.

Alex watched him walk away and dread rose inside of her. Why the hell had she gone and opened her big mouth? When would she learn just to leave things be?

She was so busy working herself into a tizzy that when he came back and kneeled down next to where she was scrunched on the lounge, she could only look on in surprise.

'You got in before me,' he said.

'What are you talking about?' she asked, as her gaze went to the hand he lifted, revealing a small box. He placed it on her lap.

'I was going to take you out on the boat for a romantic sunset dinner on the weekend and ask you to marry me, but you had to go and be all spontaneous.'

Alex felt her eyes widen in horror as she gasped loudly. 'Oh, no . . . I'm such an idiot,' she managed through the hands she held across her mouth. 'You could have just . . .'

He chuckled. 'Just what? When your woman suddenly asks you to marry you, you can't exactly say no, can you?'

No, she supposed he really didn't have much choice.

Alex groaned and dropped her head forward to rest against his chest. 'I'm so sorry!'

'Don't leave me hangin' here, Al. You still haven't given me an answer. Will you marry me or not?'

'Somehow that's not quite the way I envisioned you asking the question,' she said weakly, overcome by unexpected emotion.

'I'll re-enact the whole thing properly over dinner on the weekend, I promise,' he said gently.

'Okay. In that case, yes, I'll marry you, Sully.'

'Thank Christ for that,' he murmured, and leaned in to kiss her.

Epilogue

The wind blew her hair around her face and Alex fought to keep it tucked behind her ear. Summer was almost over and the afternoon light was beginning to get shorter and the air cooler.

From the top of the headland the ocean stretched out forever in front of her. She lowered her gaze back to the head-stone and let her fingers trace the top of the rough granite.

'Hey, Dad,' she said softly. 'Sorry it's taken me this long to visit.'

As a kid, she'd liked coming to the cemetery. It hadn't felt morbid or creepy. This was where people were buried, but they were people who'd been loved. There wasn't anything scary about that. Her ancestors were among them and she always felt a connection to her past every time she came here. But when her dad died, it changed things. She hadn't been able to bring herself to come here until today. But now it was time to put the pain she'd been carrying around for so long to rest.

'I brought you something,' she said, looking at the book she held in her hands. 'I had your manuscript printed. I thought it belonged in the library on the shelf with all the other books at Four Winds.' In the end she hadn't been able to give away or throw out any of the things in the beach-house library. It all belonged to the house, and so did her father's memoir.

'I hope you don't mind, but I added the findings of the trial in at the end, just so the whole thing had closure.'

Chris had decided it was in his best interests to make his confession and let the law deal with it as opposed to having Duncan justice dealt out. It seemed prison was safer for him than Rockne Heads.

'I just wanted you to believe me that I was telling you the truth about what happened, even if I was keeping some of it to myself. I wanted you to be my dad, not a cop, just that once.' Alex wiped a tear that fell and breathed in deeply as she looked at her father's name carved in the headstone. 'I'm supposed to forgive you in order to allow myself to be free . . . But the truth is, Dad. I'd already forgiven you. I think I was holding on to all that pain because I blamed myself for not reaching out to you and making peace with everything while I had the chance. I hope we can both find peace now.'

The wind dropped and Alex felt the sun warm her shoulders briefly before the cold breeze picked up again. She swallowed past a lump in her throat and turned away from the headstone. As she did so, she caught a movement at the far side of the cemetery. She recognised the huge shape of a man and a smaller woman who stood next to a head-stone. The woman bent over, picking the odd weed from around the grave. The man looked up and Alex held Russell Duncan's gaze.

Her breath caught in shock and more than a little trepi-dation, but then the man, his bushy grey beard blowing in the wind, lowered his head slightly in a nod of acknowledgement, or as some kind of recognition—she couldn't quite tell. Alex gave a small nod in return before walking back through the gate of the white picket fence that bordered the cemetery to head home.

Home. That's what it was now.

Finally, she was home.

Acknowledgements

Big thanks to Cory, Darren and Terry for fishing and boating related info.

Gemma Pritchard, for your help, and Jo Lane for just being such an awesome person! Also to Kaitt Blakemore for the usual roughing out of an idea, which always follows 'that should be in a book!'

To my awesome friend Lyn, who always gets the job of reading through and trying to decipher all my notes as my first reader in very rough form—I don't know how you manage to do it.

And to all my amazing readers who continue to support me every time you buy one of my books—I wouldn't be able to do this without you.